Cover by by Ana Grigoriu-Voicu, books-design.com.
Edited by Stephanie Parent
www.oliviahayle.com

saved by the boss

OLIVIA HAYLE

1

SUMMER

"A boss a day keeps bankruptcy away," my aunt says. She's perched on the edge of my desk with a wide smile on her face. "Isn't that what we've always said? And Anthony Winter is the biggest boss of them all!"

"Yes, but he's not signing on as a high-paying client. He's our new owner."

"No," Vivienne corrects me. *"Co-owner."*

"With a fifty-one percent stake."

"Still an important distinction." She walks to the gilded mirror in the corner of my office, one of two at Opate Match. We're small, but we deliver love to New York's elite. Started by Vivienne Davis twenty-five years ago.

Now sold by Vivienne Davis, two days ago.

And she doesn't seem the least bit concerned the venture capitalists she's sold it to will dismantle us.

I try a different route. "It's your life's work."

"Yes," she agrees, fixing her lipstick in the mirror. Rearranging her honey-wheat hair, styled into shoulder-length curls. "But we've been close to bankruptcy for years. I hate that word. After today, let's never use it again."

"We have plenty of clients."

"Not enough, Summer. You're worrying, darling, and it'll give you wrinkles if you're not careful."

I sigh. Ace lifts his golden head from the floor at the sound and flicks his ears, attuned to my moods. "I wish I could be as happy about this as you are. I know it's a good thing, it's just... well, there will be changes."

"Dear, I'm the one who should worry, not you!"

"I know, I know."

"They're not allowed to fire any employees in the first three years, I made them put that into the contract. You'll meet Mr. Winter when he drops by the office tomorrow. He's the serious, grumpy type. Definitely committed to turning our numbers around." She gives a small laugh. "In truth, I think our ability to turn a profit is the only reason he's willing to stand me."

I meet her smile with one of my own. My aunt is an excellent judge of character. "He's too good for a matchmaking company?"

"He thinks he is," she says. "We'll see about that. But I don't doubt his commitment to turning this ship right side up. We need some business savvy, Summer, and we need their capital."

I sigh. "Yeah, you're right. I look forward to meeting him tomorrow."

"Good." She puts her vintage handbag over her shoulder and gives me a winning smile. "I have to head out for lunch, or risk keeping the Walters waiting even longer. Did you hear they're celebrating their twentieth wedding anniversary this summer?"

"I did, yes. That's fantastic."

"One of my triumphs. Suzy is out of the office too, had to run some errands. You'll take a break, won't you, darling?"

"Yes, I will. Ace and I will hit the park for lunch."

"That's a good dog," she says, patting Ace's head on the way out. "How about we have lunch at Olive next week? It's been a while."

"I'd love that," I say.

"Then it's a date," she says, smiling. There's the sound of

heels on hardwood and then the decisive snap of our front door closing.

I lean back in my office chair and look down at Ace. My golden retriever looks back at me.

"Opate Match," I tell him. "Sold, like a piece of furniture. To a venture capitalist."

He cocks his head like only a dog can, as if he's trying to solve a puzzle. But this is one I don't have the answer to. Opate is Vivienne's pride and joy. She's poured her sweat, blood and tears into making it work for decades.

I know the decision to take in outside investors hadn't been easy, even if we needed it. But her optimism seems unfailing.

Ace trails me as I head to the coffeemaker in the reception. Suzy's desk is abandoned and the door to my aunt's office left ajar. The three of us have tried to save this sinking ship for over a year, but competing with free dating apps, well… it hasn't been easy.

I look out the window at the sun-drenched New York street and take a sip of my freshly brewed espresso. Selling out feels like the end of an era.

The buzzer rings on our front door. I frown, heading to Suzy's desk. None of us have clients scheduled for the rest of the day.

I press down the answer button. "Opate Match, how can I help you?"

The voice is masculine and clipped. "I'm here for a meeting."

A meeting? We don't have anyone scheduled, but Suzy's made mistakes before.

"Of course," I say. "Come on in."

I hide the coffee cup behind a steel statue of Cupid and brush away some biscuit crumbs from my skirt before opening the door.

I don't recognize the man who enters. He's also tall enough that I have to tilt my head back to meet his gaze. Dark-haired and suit-clad, but so are most of the men who come seeking our matchmaking services. No hints at his profession there.

3

Early thirties, I'm guessing.

I extend a hand and give him my warm, professional smile. "I'm Summer Davis. It's a pleasure to meet you."

He looks at my hand a second too long before clasping it in his for a brief shake. "I'm here for a meeting with Vivienne Davis."

There's a frown on his lips, as if the prospect tastes sour on his tongue. He's one of the more reluctant clients, then.

"Yes, that's right," I say. "She delegated the meeting to me, but I'm sure we'll get off to a great start. I take it this is your first time here?"

His scowl deepens. "It is."

"Excellent. Let's get you sorted. You're welcome to step into my office, just through here... would you like a cup of coffee?"

"No."

"All righty. Just let me know if you change your mind." I close the door behind me and motion for him to have a seat. Despite the scowl, he has a good look. Not classically handsome, I'll admit. There's something too rough-hewn about his facial features for that. But he's tall and broad-shouldered, with an old-world masculine look. Not to mention he has the dark, scowling thing down pat, and there are tons of women who like that.

Yes, I think. I can work with this.

I take a seat opposite him and fold my hands together on the oak desk. "First and foremost, I'd like to thank you for coming in today. It's the first step, after all."

The stare he levels at me is unnerving. "Right."

"I'm aware of how difficult it can be to try something like this, especially if you haven't used any form of matchmaking services before. But we're complete professionals, and I promise you that our service is always first-class. We'll never pair you with someone we don't believe will be a good fit."

He leans back in his chair, hands curving around the armrests. Something flashes in his eyes. Is it amusement? This man is impossible to read, but I'll figure out his language.

"Good to know," he says.

"Not to mention we have complete client confidentiality."

"Right." His gaze travels from me to the framed images on the wall beside me. They're wedding photographs.

A real chatty Cathy, this guy.

"All successes," I tell him. Couples who meet through Opate often send their wedding photos to us, together with handwritten thank-you notes. I'd saved every one. "What made you approach Opate Match?"

He looks down at the sleeves of his suit jacket, re-adjusting them. Is he smiling? Offended? He's giving me nothing to work with, and it's not like I have access to his initial emails with Vivienne. No, I'm flying blind, but I'll have to pretend I'm not. Is he a stockbroker or an oil tycoon? Interested in men or women?

I'm walking a tightrope over here.

"What made me approach Opate Match..." he repeats, his deep voice filling my office. "Truthfully, I've never had much respect for agencies such as yours. I've long been somewhat of a... skeptic, you might say."

I nod. This is not unusual. "That's understandable when you've never been a client of one before."

"Most dating services and websites seem to be quick ways for people to find sexual partners," he says, looking straight at me, a glint in his eyes. It's clear he thinks he's offending me.

I lean back in my chair. If he thinks he'll unnerve me, he has no idea of the matches I've brokered. Three times divorced? I'll find someone perfect for them. Can't date in public for fear of the press? Bring it on.

"There are certainly some who use dating services for that end," I agree. "But Opate is not one of those services."

"Oh?"

"No. We pride ourselves on making lasting matches, ones our clients are pleased with long-term. Naturally, what people do with their free time is outside of our hands, but once we know what a client wants, we'll never set them up with someone looking for a different level of commitment."

He gives a slow nod. "And the couples on the wall there?

They all wanted the same level of commitment from the beginning?"

"For the most part, yes."

"Hmm."

"You don't seem convinced," I say, adding my widest smile. "I understand that blind dating can be unusual, intimidating even, when you're not used to it."

He drums his fingers along the armrest. "You believe in this company. In what you offer."

"Of course I do," I say. "I wouldn't work here if I didn't."

"Many people work with things they dislike."

"Not me."

He gives another quiet hum and glances from me to the room around us. The hardwood floors and white walls, polished tables and expensive armchairs, filled with the elegant minimalism so common in high-end decor. "Opate Match profiles itself as a company for elite matchmaking. Matches for the rich and famous, I believe, is one of the tag lines."

"Our clientele is well-heeled, yes." I tip my head in his direction. "Like you."

When in doubt, flatter a client.

The look on his face makes me think he's fighting against rolling his eyes. "Right. Well, I understand the merits of that... but it doesn't convince me the company deals in true love."

I've had clients in my office who have cried, screamed, cursed the person they were just on a date with for not wanting to continue. This man might be obstinate, but he's far from the most difficult case I've had. Has he been burned in the past?

"How so?"

"It's prestige dating," he says. "Trophy wives and rich men, or Upper-East-Siders who didn't have the good fortune of meeting their future spouse at an Ivy League college. They're not here for love, Ms. Davis. They're here for an arranged marriage."

My hands fall flat on the desk in front of me.

It's one thing to be accused of being a service setting up

people for the sole purpose of sex. It's something else to be told I don't deal in love.

"Our clients, due to their status, have a very unique set of challenges when it comes to dating. Not all of them can walk into a bar and talk to a stranger," I say.

He inclines his head. "That can be difficult, yes. But for more people than just the so-called elite."

"You're right. A difficulty with dating isn't unique to the people who hire us," I say, smiling wide again. Whatever he might say, I'll crack him. I'll just have to work a bit harder. "But we always pre-vet clients before accepting them. The level of personal interaction between myself or Vivienne with each client means that the matchmaking is a far smoother process. There's no need to spend three weeks dating someone to later learn you're incompatible on some fundamental level."

"You've turned a messy, human process into something logical?"

"In some ways, yes. But we don't control it. We're just facilitators. The real magic happens when our clients leave this office, ready to meet with someone who's just as ready as they are to find a life partner."

He gazes back at me. "I see."

"Is it all right if I begin with some introductory questions? Just to get to know you better and round out your client profile."

"Go ahead," he says. Still with that half-scowl, half-amused look on his face. Like he can't believe he's actually here, sitting in this chair, about to do this.

I pick up a notepad and lean back in my chair, crossing my legs. Always better to have the first meeting face-to-face, to connect with a client. The computer comes later.

"Remind me," I say, "how old are you?"

"Thirty-three."

"Terrific." I note it down. "Now, I understand your reticence about us as a company, but I assure you, you're in good hands. We'll be transparent about the entire process."

"I appreciate that."

"Are you looking for a male or female partner?"

There's a smile on his face. "I'm interested in women."

"Excellent."

"Will you praise me after each answer?"

"Only if you'd like me to." I lower the notepad. "Actually, how do you feel about praise? Is it a vital part of a relationship, or just good to have?"

"Knowing that," he says, skepticism lacing every word, "will help me find a life partner?"

"Well, it will help me learn more about what kind of person you are. How you see relationships in general. Let me ask you this instead: what's your ideal long-term relationship?"

"I'm not sure I believe in long-term relationships."

I put the notepad back on my desk. This one has been burned indeed. He should have walked in stamped with a giant red caution sticker. "And why is that?"

"True love is a fairy tale," he says. "Nothing lasts in life, and certainly not love."

There's a quick succession of knocks on my office door. I don't have the time to reply before it's opened, my elegant aunt on the other side. Her face turns into a serviceable smile as soon as she sees the two of us.

"I'm sorry to have kept you waiting," she says, breathing fast. "I'll be happy to meet with you in my office now. Summer, would you mind getting Mr. Winter and myself a cup of coffee?"

My heart stops as I look from her to the man in front of me, the one who never gave me his name. The one who didn't say a word when I made my assumptions.

He rises from his seat and buttons his suit jacket in one smooth gesture. "A pleasure meeting you, Miss Davis," he says. "It was very enlightening."

2

SUMMER

Ace trots by my side to work the next day, close at heel, one of the few things he's kept from his guide dog training.

"Look at that," I tell him as we pass a *for sale* sign on the door to Charlotte's Coffee Corner. For years, it's been one of my New York staples, a familiar part of the route I take to and from work.

I should have bought more coffee there. If only I did, she might not have had to sell. To go out of business. To surrender to someone else's demands.

Anthony Winter and Acture Capital can do whatever they want with Opate now, the clientele, the staff. Vivienne spent weeks pouring over the contract, but even so... I don't trust it.

I don't trust him. He'd said not a word to correct my false assumptions yesterday. Vivienne had sent me an apologetic email after he left, the subject line in all caps. I MISTOOK THE DAY!

Ace's tail wags as we step into the lobby of our office building and I smooth my hand over his silky ears. He's beautiful, my loyal dog, the one I can always count on. Good thing my aunt agrees with me. She likes to say having an animal in the office gives it soul, and I'm grateful for that, because I can't imagine leaving him with my parents.

"Ready to meet the others?"

Ace looks up at me with alert, chocolate eyes. *Yes,* they say.

"There'll be someone else here today. Someone we have to be nice to, even if we don't want to. No biting." I'm smiling even as I say it, and his tail wags harder. So fearsome.

I open the door to Opate and he makes a beeline for Suzy at reception. She grins when she sees him and puts down her lip gloss. "Hi, buddy," she says, burying her hands in his fur in greeting.

The door to Vivienne's office is open and voices emanate from within. I step closer and my aunt looks up from her desk, golden reading glasses perched on the edge of her nose.

"Ah, Summer! Come in, come in. I was just talking to Mr. Winter here and his associate, Ryan…"

"Walker," a young man supplies.

"Walker, yes. They will be here often in the coming weeks to pick our brains on the company and to learn how it works."

Ah, I think. They're scouting it out before they make any changes, which means we have to be on our best behavior during this time.

And I'm already off to a bad start with Mr. Winter.

He's sitting in one of Vivi's chairs, arms draped along the armrests. The gaze he shoots me is as dark and inscrutable as yesterday. No hint he even remembers our exchange.

I give him a bright smile. "We'll do our best to make you feel at home then, gentlemen," I say. "When I don't have client meetings, my door is always open to answer questions about the business and our practices."

Both men's gazes drop to my knees and a second later I feel the solid weight of a golden retriever pushing past me in the doorway.

"Our favorite employee," Vivienne says. "This is Ace, my niece's dog."

The dog in question is busy scouting out the two men. He receives a pat on the head from Ryan, but he's ignored entirely by Anthony, who only looks from the dog to me. I'll have to apologize when I get the chance. Try to smooth things over from yesterday.

Oh, the things I'd said to him. Asking our new *owner* if he had a partner, or if he preferred women or men. Heat rises to my cheeks.

"Miss Davis was helpful yesterday," Mr. Winter says. "I know she'll continue to be so in the future."

I give them both my sunniest, brightest smile. "Whatever you need," I say and pat my leg. Ace returns to my side and we head into my office.

I've survived the first, shameful encounter. Whether I survive the second remains to be seen.

I'm sorting through our ever-shrinking pile of client applications when a single knock on my door sounds. Anthony Winter, hands by his sides, suit jacket unbuttoned. He's nearly tall enough to graze his head on the doorway.

I turn away from my computer screen. "Mr Winter. Come on in."

He stops a solid few feet away from my desk. Says nothing.

I clear my throat. "I'd like to apologize about yesterday. About mistaking you for a client. I realize that wasn't what you'd expected, and well… I'm sorry."

He pulls out the chair opposite my desk and sits down. Stretches out long legs in front of him. "I'm not," he says.

"You're not?"

"Like I said, it was enlightening," he says and lets his gaze travel from mine to the pictures on the walls. My triumphs, my successes.

I open my mouth. Close it again. And then: "I'm sorry to ask, but why did you buy Opate Match?"

He raises an eyebrow. "Why did I buy your aunt's company?"

"Yes. Judging from yesterday… you don't believe in our services."

"No. But I believe in your ability to generate profit."

"Well, that's something, I suppose."

His gaze returns to mine. "Tell me more about your business structure, Miss Davis. I'd like to hear it from you."

From me?

But I clear my throat and dive into an explanation of Opate Match, detailing clauses and structures he's doubtlessly already aware of. Things he knows, or he wouldn't have bought the business.

But Anthony just listens, occasionally tapping his fingers along the edge of his armrest. "At the moment, Opate is limited to the East Coast. New York specifically, even if you get a fair amount of clients who are just traveling through. Correct?"

"Yes."

"How do you feel about expanding internationally?"

My eyebrows rise. "Internationally?"

"People paying this amount of money for prestige match-making services like the idea of exclusivity. Traveling around the world for a date with a similarly-minded person... well, that might only add to the appeal."

"Yes, well, it might not make for lasting relationships."

The look in his eyes tells me he doesn't see that as a problem. "Ryan is a coder and programmer."

"Oh."

"He'll start working on a prototype app."

My hands drop into my lap. He sees it, another eyebrow rising. Almost as if he's intrigued against his best wishes. "You don't approve?"

"I can't say I do, no."

"Why not?"

"Our strength is our personal service," I say. "We provide something you can't get anywhere else. We *know* the people who come to us, so we can actually set them up with people they have a chance of succeeding with. If we let people decide that themselves on the basis of self-generated profiles, all that swiping... Our success rates would plummet."

"It would allow you to expand."

"But at what cost?" I shake my head, but soften the gesture

with a sunny smile. "If you're asking for my opinion, that's it. The personal touch makes Opate Match."

He taps his fingers against the armrest again. "Right."

"'I know you don't believe in it. Our services, I mean, or that people come here with good intentions." I shrug. "Judging from our conversation yesterday, I mean. You're very cynical, Mr. Winter."

Both of his eyebrows rise at that. If there's a hint of amusement in his eyes, it's there and gone so fast I can't register it. "Cynical, Miss Davis?"

"I know the majority of our clients believe in love. They're here filled with hope, and nerves, ready to try something new. The ones who open themselves up to the process are usually the ones most likely to succeed."

"Right." There's a world of skepticism in that single word. It fills my office, multiplying and expanding.

A determined dog shoves the half-closed door open. Ace trots in and sits down on his haunches next to Anthony, his gaze fixed on the man's face.

Anthony looks from me to the dog. "You have pets here."

"That's Ace. He's great at getting clients to relax, actually. More than one nervous person has sat in here with their hand in his fur as they tell me about themselves."

Anthony's gaze turns from me to my dog, as if he's doubting this. Ace keeps looking at him.

I can't help but smile. "He's waiting for a hello."

"Hello," Anthony says. But then he relents, reaching out and resting a large hand on the top of Ace's head. His fingers sink into the golden fur and the telltale sound of Ace's tail against the floor picks up. *You brilliant traitor,* I think. He has always had a knack for figuring out when someone needs a bit of canine distraction or comfort, another of the skills he'd kept from his guide dog training days.

Anthony's gaze holds resignation. "You really are a hopeless romantic, then."

"I'm sorry?"

"A hopeless romantic," he repeats. "You believe in the core values of this business. You believe in love." He says the last word like it has sharp edges.

"Yes," I say, leaning forward. He might be our new owner, but isn't it in the best interest of the business if he learns what we're truly about? If he understands what makes us successful?

"If only you could *see* how well this process really works," I say, "you'd become a hopeless romantic too."

"I doubt that, Miss. Davis."

It's a crazy idea. One of my wilder ones. And perhaps I'm overstepping my boundaries, but... I already did that yesterday.

"Well," I say. "Let us set you up on a date."

His eyes settle on mine with an intensity that makes my mouth dry. "Pardon me?"

"If you want to see how this business truly works, I'm happy to show you. Three dates," I say, improvising. "I'll make the arrangements for you. If you still think there's no merit after you've been on all three, and if none of the women are people you'd consider having a second date with... I'll admit defeat."

"Defeat?" he asks.

"Yes. I'll admit I was wrong, and Opate Match isn't for everyone." It's a gamble, and my heart pounds in my chest with the audacity of what I'm proposing. Vivienne would have my head if she knew. Or she'd laugh at the sheer nerve.

There's never any knowing with her.

Anthony narrows his eyes. "And if I deem one of the dates good enough to warrant another?"

"Then you'll admit you were wrong about this company. *Your* company, in fact. Either way, you'll have gained some experience about how our business works."

His jaw tightens, eyebrows drawing together over dark eyes. He's coldness itself, and I'm about to freeze.

But then he gives a single nod. "You have yourself a deal."

My smile is entirely genuine. "Oh, that's great. You're really going to enjoy this, I promise."

"I'd be careful about making that promise."

A few taps on my keyboard and my computer sings back to life. "That means I'll create a quick client profile for you. Nothing fancy, but just enough so I can set you up with women I think will be good matches."

He shifts in the chair. "Ah. Okay."

I glance over. "It'll be quick."

"Take your time, Miss Davis. As I have no intention of losing this bet, I don't mind it being done thoroughly."

I have to hide a smile as I open up a new client profile. Perhaps this is the way to crack him, then. Friendly competition and bets. He can't help but be drawn in by them, intrigued despite himself.

"What age span are you interested in?"

He gives a faint sigh, like he can't believe he's sitting here, answering this. "I've never considered one before."

"Well, you're thirty-three," I say. "How about we put you down for twenty-five to thirty-five, give or take a few years on either end?"

"Sure."

"How would you describe your ideal relationship?"

There's complete silence on the other side of the desk. I look over to see him wearing an expression somewhere between masculine exasperation and pain. It's clear he's rethinking this bet.

"We can skip that one," I say. "Moving on, moving on... I just need enough to set you up with women I think you'd enjoy spending time with."

"I'm not picky," he responds. "They need to be able to hold up their side of a conversation. Some humor."

I've never met a single person who said they weren't picky and actually meant it. People who claim to have no demands inevitably have the most.

But I can't tell him that.

So I smile and make a note of it in his application. "Humor's important for you, then. How about I ask you a few easy questions? These are some fun prompts we use to get a sense of a client's personality."

He sighs again, like I'm imposing on him. "Sure."

"What's your favorite holiday?"

"My favorite holiday?"

"Yes."

"Michaelmas."

"Really?"

His lips twitch. "No," he says. "I shouldn't mock you."

"Not if we're going to do this bet properly."

"Christmas, then. Put me down for Christmas."

I write down a great deal more than simply "Christmas." *Sarcastic, dry sense of humor. Dislikes pretense. Needs a patient hand.*

"That's a great choice," I say.

"Is this the part where you praise me for my responses again?"

I tilt my head in acknowledgement. "Right, you didn't enjoy that. I'll refrain. Now, here's another prompt... What's the best part of your day?"

He taps his hands along the armrest, gaze turning to Ace. My dog has sprawled out beside Anthony's chair like he's never been more relaxed in his life.

"My morning cup of coffee," he replies.

I note it down, and I know I shouldn't comment, but... "Yet you didn't want a coffee when you came here yesterday."

"I doubt your machine is very good."

I glance up at him, but there's a wryness to his features. He knows he's being provocative.

I give a one-shouldered shrug. "Compared to whatever fancy one you have at home, it's likely not, no."

He nods. Looks past me again.

I clear my throat and return to my prompts. They're fun, easy ways to establish rapport with a client. To tease out things about their personality you'd never get from asking people to describe themselves.

I'll establish rapport with Anthony Winter, even if I have to be the one doing eighty percent of the work.

16

"Have you ever broken any bones?"

His eyebrows rise, but he responds. "A collarbone. Left wrist."

"You're not left-handed?"

"No, right."

"How did it happen?"

"I used to climb." He turns his head back to the pictures of the wall, breaking eye contact. "It doesn't always go as planned."

An accident, then. Not that getting information out of him is easy.

"That sounds thrilling, climbing," I comment, noting *adventurous* on his client profile. "I've only tried on one of those indoor gyms once. God, that was difficult."

"Hmm," he says.

"I didn't plan on going, but it was with a boyfriend, and he insisted. It didn't last. My interest in climbing, I mean. Well, he didn't last, either."

I never ramble on like this with a client. But here I am, filling up the silence. Perhaps he'll feel more comfortable if I make a fool of myself.

Anthony's gaze shifts back to me. "Indoor climbing gyms aren't fun. He should have taken you somewhere outdoors."

I clear my throat. "Yes. Well, perhaps one day. Let's see here... oh, this is a fun one. Give me two truths and a lie about yourself."

"Two truths and a lie?"

"Yes. I'll see if I can parcel out the lie."

He crosses his arms over his chest and glances back at the half-open door to my office. "I'm born in January, my social security number ends in thirty-seven, and this suit is new."

Oh, this man is frustrating.

I don't let it show, giving him a smile. "One of them is a lie?"

"Yes." There's challenge in his eyes. Clearly, he thinks he's outsmarted my prompt. His three things are about as personal as asking someone about the weather.

"You're not born in January," I guess.

"Wrong. My social security number does not end in thirty-seven."

I smile, like he's won a point, and return to the client profile. *Enjoys being difficult,* I write. *Could be devastating if he decides to flirt with a woman in earnest. Doubtful he'll ever do something he doesn't want to.*

"You learned a lot about me from that response," he says. "What did you just write?"

I ignore his question. "What are your thoughts on marriage?"

He drums his fingers against the armrest again. A cue that he's uncomfortable? Or just bored?

"Good for some, bad for others," he replies.

"And where do you land?"

"I doubt it's something for me."

My stomach sinks at that. He really is going into this with a cynical mindset, not just to the matchmaking service, but at the idea of love and relationships in general. I might lose this bet.

But I refuse to admit that until it's time. And who knows, by then he might have found one of our fellow clients far too attractive to remember this little sparring match.

"Not what you wanted to hear?" he asks.

I shake my head. "The thing that makes Opate Match work is that we don't set people up based on what they project to the world. We set them up based on who they actually are. So I won't suggest you to one of our clients who are looking for marriage within the coming years."

"Good," he says.

"How about kids? Something you'd like in your future?" It's a standard question, but it feels invasive asking my new boss this. The man who holds the fate of Opate in one of those large, constantly-armrest-drumming hands of his.

But if I can win him over to respecting our business model... maybe I can protect Opate.

"No kids," Anthony says.

I note it down, even if it's a shame. With a comforting

strength to him, it's easy to picture a child riding on his shoulders. I bet he'd soften then, in a way these silly prompts could never accomplish.

"That's all right," I tell him. "We have plenty of clients who share your sentiment."

"Plenty?" he asks.

"Plenty," I echo. It's not, strictly speaking, a lie. We have a lot of female clients who are unsure about kids, and a few who have a strict no-kids-ever policy.

"Dogs or cats?"

Anthony looks up at the ceiling, the picture of a man tortured. "Knowing if I have a preference for cats or dogs will help me find everlasting love?"

"Ah, we don't promise everlasting love, Mr. Winter. We promise healthy relationships with well-adjusted people."

"How romantic," he mutters. "Dogs, then. Put me down as a dog person."

Ace shifts at his feet, letting out a soft canine sigh. Almost like he's agreeing. I smile as I make a note of it in Anthony's client profile. He might huff and puff as much as he likes, but my little house won't blow over. It's getting sturdier with every thing he says, the contours of his personality emerging little by little.

It wouldn't be enough with a paying client, but it'll have to be enough with him, because I doubt he's going to endure a lot more of this.

"One last question," I say. "Where do you see yourself in five years?"

Anthony's gaze shutters. "Not that one."

"No?"

"No."

I nod and smile. "Okay, no problem. We'll go silly instead, for the last one… What would the title of your autobiography be?"

Anthony's jaw tenses as he thinks. Looks away from me. "Hindsight is twenty-twenty," he says.

I think that might be the saddest thing I've ever heard. He

turns back to me, like he's remembering who I am. He clears his throat. "Is that all you need, Miss Davis?"

"Yes." It's not, not by a long shot. "Would you be free for a date a few days from now? I'll email you with the details. It won't be a long encounter, likely an hour or two at a café."

"That's good," he says and rises. Ace lifts his head and we both watch Anthony stop by my office door.

"Yes?" I say.

"What we've spoken about, it stays between us."

"It does," I say. "Anything we discuss as a client to match-maker is bound by confidentiality."

He nods in response and steps out of my office, shutting the door behind him. I stare at it for far too long, one question and one only in my head. Who the hell am I going to set this man up with?

3

SUMMER

Suzy leans against her desk, arms moving as she describes her weekend. It was filled to the brim with excitement, just as usual, and a complete contrast to mine.

"Ivory wasn't packed at all this time," she says. "Are you sure you don't want to come along this weekend? There are a ton of great guys there."

"I'm sure," I say. "Last time was enough."

She shakes her head. "It's a great place to meet guys. That's where Chase and I met."

"The DJ, right?"

She brightens. "The very one!"

Truthfully, Suzy dates more than I can keep track of. She moved here two years ago and threw herself into crafting her dream New York life with enviable enthusiasm. Her social media is full of cocktails on rooftops.

She looks down at Ace, his head in her lap. "Can I be honest with you?"

"Of course you can."

"I'm not sure I'm going to stay with Chase much longer."

That's not a surprise. "Oh? Why not?"

"I thought dating a musician was amazing at first. But...

well, he's thirty-two and doesn't have a place of his own. I don't know if that's really for me."

I smile at her. Beneath her veneer, Suzy's good stock. "I think you might be right."

"That doesn't mean, however," she says, holding up a hand, "that Ivory doesn't have great quality guys. Before Chase I met the banker there, remember?"

"I remember."

"So you should come along. You've been single for too long, Summer."

I give her a confident hair toss, playing it off with drama. "What do you mean? I'm thriving on my own."

"But wouldn't it be *fun*? You're so good at matchmaking, it should be easy for you to find someone yourself!"

I shrug, turning toward the coffee machine. My best friend Posie often says the same thing, but it doesn't seem like there's a correlation between the two.

"I go on dates," I say. "Plenty of them."

Suzy makes a sound of disbelief. "Yeah, right. Do you know what? You should go out with the delivery guy!"

"With Dave? Where did that come from?"

She gives me a triumphant look. "He always lingers when you're around. I've caught him stealing glances toward your office every time he's here delivering our packages. Remember the time he played with Ace for ten minutes?"

"Everyone loves dogs."

"Yes, but he did it after I told him Ace was *your* dog. Before then he'd always rushed off."

I take a sip of my coffee, my cheeks heating up. Suzy, despite her kind nature, mostly swims in the shallow end of the pool of life. She is, however, a great reader of men's interest. "You think so?"

"Oh yes. Try talking to him the next time he's here and you'll see just how responsive he is. You're gorgeous, Summer, and he's average. He won't know what's hit him."

I shake my head at her. If there's one thing I've learned in my matchmaking days, it's that beauty and appearance matters little when two people don't have chemistry. And when they do, it doesn't matter at all.

She holds up her hands. "Sorry, sorry. I know you don't like ranking people on their looks."

"No, I don't."

"Well, it's the truth."

I take a sip of my coffee and decide to deflect. It's a tried and true method with Suzy. "Where's Vivi? She's been out of the office for a long while."

"Oh, she said she might not come back after lunch."

"She did?"

Suzy looks sheepish. "Yeah. I mean, she sometimes does that. She has no more meetings this afternoon."

"Right, that's true." Still, I look at Suzy and she looks back at me. There'd been a time when my aunt had lived and breathed Opate Match, using her charisma and connections to turn this place into a small but powerful company.

Now she's checking out more and more often.

"She didn't say what she was going to do," Suzy adds.

I shrug. "Well, maybe she had another hairdresser appointment."

We both know that isn't true. She always goes to the blow-dry bar on Thursdays, but Suzy nods. "Yeah. Maybe."

My phone rings and I give her a smile, heading into my office. The name on my phone brings me right back to professional-land. I set down my cup of coffee and hit reply.

"Hi, Isabelle."

"Summer!" Her voice is excited—a good sign. "I know we talk *after* the dates, but this time I had to call you before. I'm on my way to the café now."

"Oh, that's terrific. I'm happy you're excited."

"That has to be a good sign, right? Yes, it is. I read the information you sent me about him three times last night. He's really quite impressive, isn't he?"

I think of Anthony Winter opposite me in my office, the

rough-hewn features, the unrelenting gaze. The uncooperative silences.

"Yes, he is. A man with a presence."

Isabelle gives a small *oooh* of appreciation. This will be the sixteenth man I've set her up with. A small, unhelpful part of me suspects Isabelle enjoys dating too much to commit, and has no problem paying our matchmaking fees with her inherited fortune.

"He's charmingly grumpy," I tell her. "A man you need to draw out of his shell."

The sigh on the other end tells me I've phrased it just right. "I can do that," Isabelle says. "I'll lure him right out. Can you imagine, a Winter? He can be as grumpy as he wants."

That gives me pause. Vivienne knows all the families in New York, and yet she hadn't told me anything about Anthony's.

"Good," I say, not sure if I want to encourage her way of speaking about him. "Best of luck with the date, Isabelle. And remember what we spoke about last time?"

"Oh, yes, Summer. Thanks for reminding me," she says. "I'm so excited! And now I'm almost here! I'll talk to you afterwards."

I lower my phone and release the breath I'd been holding in. Anthony Winter and Isabelle Ashford. Not a bad set-up, even if she's a serial dater. She's a great example of the clients we have. Someone who'll love to go on this date whether or not it actually ends up in… you know. Anything.

Petite, redheaded, an art gallery owner. Someone to match Anthony.

I hope.

He's coming here for a debrief tomorrow, and I know I'll be given a scathing review if I've misjudged this.

———

Isabelle calls again not fifty minutes later.

"Oh no…" I murmur, looking from my phone to Ace. Good first dates last a lot longer than this. "Hi, Isabelle."

24

"It's me," she says.

"I wasn't expecting to hear back quite so soon. Is the date over?"

"Yes, we cut it short. Although it didn't feel short."

I ask the next question with dread. "How did it go? First impressions?"

There's a delicate pause, and Isabelle doesn't do delicate. I grit my teeth.

"Well, he's not very talkative, is he?"

"He's definitely more of the strong, silent type," I agree. "Which can be good, at times. It means he gives others more space to express themselves."

"That's true, Summer. I'm sure there are women who'd like that." Another pause, and her words don't need to be spoken to be heard. *A woman who isn't me.* "He certainly has a lot of… well. He's memorable, you know?"

"Sure is," I say. No white lie there.

"I was willing to overlook the silent thing, the fact that I had to drag responses out of him. And oh, he had magnificent hands. Men sometimes do, and you know I like men's hands. But even so…"

"Yes?"

"The thing is, Summer, I just can't see myself dating a guy who collects dolls. I'm sorry. I know you're so good at what you do and I always enjoy my dates, but this is a hard no for me. I didn't know it was before I met him, so I suppose I learned that about myself tonight?" She laughs, once more the Isabelle I'd spoken to an hour ago. "So you can add that to my profile. Won't date a guy who collects dolls."

It takes me several moments to form words. "Anthony Winter… collects dolls?"

"Oh yes. It was the only subject he seemed passionate about. Porcelain ones, too." Her voice drops an octave. "He said he has them all on display in his apartment. He'd just ordered a rare one from Russia. Had it flown here with its own attendant."

"Christ," I mumble.

"That's what I thought too. You know, I've heard this before about some of the old New York families. Not about the Winters specifically, of course. But about others. They have their little quirks. Perhaps that's what comes with too much time on your hands." Isabelle laughs again.

"Yes, well, I suppose we all have to have hobbies. I'm sorry this date wasn't a hit for you. I'd hoped it might be."

"Oh, Summer, I don't mind. Anthony's older brother was in school with my brother, but I'd never spoken to him before. This was nice. Unexpected... but nice."

"I'm glad you see it that way."

"Absolutely. And you know what?" she says, voice turning optimistic. "Collecting dolls might be a wonderful pastime, for some. We shouldn't pass judgement. Who knows? Without it he might have turned to hard drugs or liquor, or something."

"Yes," I say. "Quite."

"I'll talk to you later, Summer. Thanks for tonight."

She hangs up with a cheery goodbye. Good to know nothing rocks Isabelle Ashford, not even being set up on a date with an adult man who apparently collects porcelain dolls.

When Anthony strolls in through Opate Match's doors the next day, I'm ready for him. My professional smile has a knife's edge to it.

His dark eyes meet mine. "Miss Davis."

"Mr. Winter."

"Is your aunt out of the office?"

I speak before Suzy can. "She is indeed, but she'll be back shortly. Why don't we head into my office? I can give you another overview of our clientele. You were so interested in it last time."

His lips tug, a slight shift in the muscles. "All right."

Ace makes it into my office before the door shuts. He sprawls on the carpet beneath my desk, his tail on one of my shoes and his head next to Anthony's.

"I'm interested in the clientele?" Anthony asks. His gaze is fixed on me, penetrating in a way I refuse to let make me uncomfortable.

I knot my hands in front of me on the desk instead. I'd worn a blazer today and put my blonde hair into a high ponytail, all to feel more in control of this conversation.

"You're sabotaging the bet," I say. *J'accuse, Winter.*

Anthony raises an eyebrow. "Sabotaging the bet?"

"You collect porcelain dolls?"

"They have a separate room in my apartment," he deadpans.

"You lied."

He leans back in the chair. "Yes, I did."

"That goes against the bet. If you're to get the true Opate experience, you can't deliberately undermine yourself on dates."

"I have to be on my best behavior?"

"Yes. Don't be anything other than what you are. If you keep sabotaging, well..."

"You won't admit I won the bet fairly," he says. "Is that it?"

"Yes."

"Fine. I won't sabotage any more of the dates."

"Thank you."

He leans forward, bracing his hands on the edge of my desk. They're good hands, I admit. Perhaps I'm not Isabelle with a hand fetish, but... yes. Strong, broad across the back, with wide knuckles and long fingers. They'd probably feel amazing gripping your skin.

"Miss Davis," he says.

I look up. "Yes."

"For the record, I told her about my imaginary doll collection to end the date. It was clear to me that we wanted different things, and I didn't want to lead her on."

"Oh."

"I won't sabotage going forward, but once I've determined that the date won't work out, I won't waste these women's time."

"No, that's good." I nod. "I approve."

Another ghost of a smile on his lips, even if it looks dusty, a seasonal item he rarely takes down from the attic. "I'm glad to hear it."

"Just so I understand you better... what made it clear you two wouldn't be a good fit?"

He glances from me to the pictures on the wall. The wedding pictures. I still can't figure out why they intrigue him so much. "I could tell."

"Right. Well, if you were to elaborate just a smidge?"

He sighs. "She was too serious."

I just stare at him.

"What?" he asks, a bit testily.

"Nothing. No, that... makes sense," I say. Isabelle was too serious? Anthony is the most serious person I've ever met.

"I'm available when you have decided on a second candidate," he says.

I can't help but smile at the phrasing. *Candidate.*

Here I'd thought Isabelle was a good attempt. She was from his own social circle, similar backgrounds, similar in age. But perhaps... Ciara. She's a new client, young, who said she was looking for someone older and with a distinguished career.

While I might not approve, I can't judge others' motives. I'm just here to make connections.

"I think I have someone for you," I tell him.

4

ANTHONY

I blink up at the indistinct crown molding on my bedroom ceiling, as if it will clear my sight. As if all I need to do is squint and I'll see as clearly as I once did. Funny how the impulse hasn't disappeared.

Is it worse than it was yesterday? Is it better?

Every day, I do the same fucking dance of monitoring my own deterioration, as if I'm a weatherman predicting a storm. But does it matter *when* it strikes? In a week or five years, the hurricane will hit, and the results will be the same. One day I'll be trapped in darkness with no way out, and when that's a reality, squinting won't do a goddamn thing. The darkness will be the only color I'll see. Or will I lose that, too? Blindness is the absence of sight, after all, and black is a color.

I close my eyes as the familiar wave of panic sweeps through me. Is this what it'll be like? A prisoner in my own head, forever reliant on others. Led around or helped by paid assistants. Entirely dependent on their mercy, while they could do whatever they wanted, with me helpless to stop them. I press the heels of my hands over my failing eyes.

Any other body part, I think. *Any other.*

No one is listening to make the trade, of course. No roadside devil I can bargain away years of my life with to stave off the decline. Just me and my failing vision, the claustrophobia and panic rising with every second spent in blackness. I breathe through it until the pressure inside my chest grows unbearable, until needles scream beneath my skin.

Then I pull my hands away and blink at the faint sunlight streaming in through my bedroom windows.

Not yet, at least. Not yet.

Is it faint sunlight? Or does it just look that way to me? It shouldn't still bother me that I'll never know the answer to that, but even two years after the diagnosis, the knowledge burns.

I push out of bed, the heap of blankets a testament to my restless night. The diagnosis had taken sleep away from me, too, that day in the doctor's office. Together with my girlfriend and my future. *I'd like to report a robbery...*

But this kind of theft is legal.

The hot water from the shower scalds, but I welcome the sensation. Let it sweep the clamminess from my skin. A cup of black coffee from freshly ground beans settles some of the darkness. Relegates it back to manageable levels.

There's nothing coffee doesn't make better.

Remnants of take-away boxes litter the kitchen table as I walk past it to my home office. Turn on all the lights, including the new spotlights I'd had to install just a few months ago.

My office is flooded by light.

Even so, the headache that hovered behind my eyes yesterday evening is still here, my sleep be damned. Reading the print on my computer is bound to bring it out in full force.

Time to dance with my demons.

I give myself ten minutes to scan the headlines of the news before moving on to my emails. Acture Capital employs several assistants, two top-tier accountants, a lawyer on retainer as well as a wealth manager. We regularly acquired companies, using our human and financial capital to turn them from struggling to successful. Just now, one of our four partners was CEO of one of America's largest consulting firms. Another was negotiating the purchase of a multi-media company.

And I'd been put in charge of a fucking matchmaking company. The sheer humiliation of it makes my skin crawl. No doubt Tristan, Victor and Carter assumed I had other business projects ongoing at the same time. Save Tristan, all of them also assume I'm still involved in the family's hotel business.

None of them know I spend most of my days holed up in this New York townhouse.

Or that I haven't spoken to anyone in my family for two months.

I scan through an email from my financial advisor, recommending a few investment opportunities. Save them to read more thoroughly later. Pass over the one from my older brother before looking at it adds guilt to the cocktail of negative emotions pulsing through me.

My gaze snags on an email thread from my business partners. The email chain has devolved, as it so often has since I'd lost the fateful poker game that put me in charge of Opate Match. In one email, Carter asked if he could be taken on as a client at a discount. Tristan replied that I was the one who had to test out the wares. Victor ended the email thread by telling all of us he had better things to do than talk about this. *Clutter up your own inboxes*, he'd said.

But he'd always been an asshole.

I'm not about to tell them that somehow I'd already been roped into testing out Opate's service by Summer Davis, because I still can't quite believe it myself.

Dates? I'm going on *dates?*

It won't amount to anything, but I can't tell her that, not when she'd looked at me like I'm a puzzle she wants nothing more than to solve. She'd bet on the wrong man when she'd dared me to it.

I shouldn't have gone along with it.

But her naive optimism and belief in love galled something inside of me, itched at the bitterness that sometimes threatened to choke me.

Summer Davis. Blonde, cutesy, with a matching golden retriever sidekick to complete an image fit for an advertisement.

I frown at the text on my computer. Had it been this difficult to read only moments before? No, I'm sure it had been clearer. It's been months since I had to increase the size of the on-screen text. I enlarge it a few sizes more, and the text becomes clearer. Even if doing so makes me want to punch the screen, shattering the damn thing as well as my hand in the process.

At least my hand would heal.

I'd stopped working in the office soon after my diagnosis, preferring to sit here, where I can control the light source and the computer. Where I can shut it all down on bad days.

My phone rings, but there's no one I'm in the mood to talk to right now. Right after the diagnosis, I'd interacted with the world regularly, but I'd learned soon enough that things just got worse when I did. I couldn't conceal my rancor.

Call it black curiosity or restlessness, but I answer my phone. The number is unknown to me.

The voice on the other end is feminine, professional and familiar. "I have another date for you, Mr. Winter," she announces, without preamble or hello.

I lean back in my chair and close my eyes. Her voice is interesting. Deep and soft, but with a distinct bubbliness to it.

"I hope you've found someone better this time," I tell her.

"I won't respond to that," she says primly. "Isabelle is terrific, as are all of our clients. Some people simply don't work together."

And some people don't work together with anyone. "Right."

"Are you free Thursday for lunch?" she asks. "I think this one will be good."

Why am I putting myself through this charade? I should say no, but the sound of her voice and this inane scheme is something, *anything*, to soothe my restlessness.

"Yes, I'll meet your candidate."

"Her name is Ciara," she says. "Do you want to go into this blind, or with a bit of information?"

I grit my teeth. "Not blind, if I can help it."

"All righty. She's twenty-three and a model. Originally from Georgia, but has been in New York for the past few years."

"Twenty-three?"

"Yes. Is that a problem?"

"No, I suppose it's not."

"She suggested a Japanese place for lunch. Is that acceptable?"

It had been a long time since I'd rotated Japanese food into my takeout schedule. "Yes."

She breathes a sigh of relief, as if she'd expected me to be prickly about that. "Okay, good."

"I suppose you'll want me to come to the office afterwards," I say. "For the debrief?"

Summer's voice is pleased. "That's right. It's such an important part of the process for us."

Meeting with this model would be... well. It'd be quick. And then I'd get to see Summer flustered again, her hopeless romantic idea of this job fighting against the facts she saw sitting right in front of her.

Me.

"I'll see you then," she says. "I'll email you the restaurant details. And Anthony?"

My eyes drift closed at the sound of my name. "Yes?"

"I don't want you to self-sabotage again."

Here, where she can't see me, I smile at her pointless optimism. "I won't."

As if anything I do could make my life worse.

———

I keep my promise not to self-sabotage.

I can't, however, say the same for Ciara. She sits in front of me like she considers herself a piece of art to be worshipped, a woman who measures her worth in gold. Where Isabelle had been interested in having a conversation, Ciara's focus is on seduction.

She rests her head in her hands and blinks in slow, deliberate movements that sweeps dark lashes over pale cheeks. It has to be a good day for my vision, then, if I can make out these details. And I'm wasting it by looking at her.

"Anthony Winter," she says, like she's testing the flavor of my name. It's the third time she's said it. "Why does that sound familiar?"

I put down my chopsticks. The food is good, and the restaurant is well-lit. It's a shame the company is so poor. "It shouldn't."

"And yet it does." Another slow blink, before her face shifts into a teasing, charming smile. "I'll figure you out."

"I doubt it."

Her smile falters only for a second. In a top that shows off her midriff and a designer bag she insists on keeping on her lap as we eat, she returns to her sashimi. "I love Japanese food."

"It's great, yes."

"I was in Tokyo recently, for Fashion Week. Pretty stressful, but... you know. Comes with the job. I work as a model." The look in her eye makes it clear this is when I'm to be impressed. That I'm to make an overture of some sort. Fawn, perhaps. Or let my gaze rake down her body like she'd done twice to me already, the second more brazen than the first.

I do neither.

She asks me where I live less than halfway through the date. While she just nods and comments *nice* when I tell her, there's a glint in her eyes at the words Upper East Side. Makes several comments about looking for stability, for a man who provides.

I pay the check and leave her without more than a polite *take care of yourself,* but despite my lukewarm interest, she insists on hugging me. My distaste notches up another level. At her. At myself, too, for putting myself in this position.

I'm not particularly gentle in extricating myself from her arms. Ciara has confirmed every single one of my suspicions about Opate Match and their clientele. Like so often when you market something for the elite, this is what you get. Shallowness and superficiality. Certainly not true love.

This was who Summer Davis thought I'd want?

I'm not set to return to Opate Match until tomorrow, but my feet carry me there regardless, and I open the office door with more force than needed. The lights in the reception are dimmed. Once you start noticing how rarely places are well-lit, it's all you see. Or in my case, it means you can see even less.

The receptionist looks up at me with wide eyes. "Mr. Winter. If you're here to see Vivienne, you just missed her. She's at a client meeting uptown, I'm afraid."

"Miss Davis?"

"She's here, and she just finished with a client. Do you want me to... oh." Her voice trails off as I reach the closed door to Summer's office. Knock twice.

"Come in!" she calls.

I push the door open. Her drapes are completely pulled back and with that amount of natural light, it's easy to make out the surprise on her face. The sunshine gilds her blonde hair, falling in waves over her shoulders. Yes, I think. Today really is good day, because I can even make out the shade of blue in her eyes.

"Mr. Winter. Back from your date?"

"Yes."

"I see," she says. "Judging from your expression, I'm guessing it didn't go well?"

I pull the chair out opposite her and sit down, crossing my arms over my chest. "Oh, I think it went as well as could be expected."

Her eyes narrow, as if she's expecting a trap. "How well was that?"

I'm as unable to stop taunting her as I had been on the first day we'd met. "I'm offended, actually."

"Offended?"

"Yes. You analyzed my personality and made the conclusion that Ciara is the kind of woman I'd be interested in?"

She meets my gaze for a few long moments before her shoulders slump. "It was a gamble," she admits. "I knew it could go either way. And for the record, I'm not one to speak ill of other clients. I won't."

"I'm allowed to, am I not?"

"Yes," she acknowledges. "Was it that bad?"

"Let's just say she'd made her intentions clear before we'd ordered the food. A rich man who could keep her."

"Oh," Summer breathes. "Well, you said your last date was too serious, so I made sure this one wouldn't be."

The irony tugs at my lips. "Perhaps an overcorrection."

"I gave you someone bubbly."

"You gave me someone who still chews pink bubblegum."

"So you're saying I've drawn the wrong conclusions about you," Summer murmurs, hands flying over her keyboard as she fires up her computer. There's a look of excited calculation I recognize from my first visit to this room.

When she'd thought I was a client.

"Are we going back to me answering ridiculous prompts?" I ask, drumming my fingers along the armrest. Looking away from the bright lightness that is her. "How long would I last in a zombie apocalypse? What was the name of my first pet?"

She laughs, like I've made a good joke. "They were very informative last time."

"I doubt that."

"People say a lot when they think they're being shallow. Now… this means I only have one more try."

"Yes."

She turns those sky-blue eyes on me. "And you didn't like Isabelle or Ciara."

"I did not." If anything, they'd only strengthened my preconceived notions. I find myself holding my tongue on that score, though, as she looks at me with playful challenge.

"It might take me a bit longer to think this through," she says. "As you're not only a client but the co-owner of Opate Match, you'll get the absolute best service I can provide."

The emphasis on co-owner makes me snort. Acture Capital has a fifty-one percent stake in the company, negotiated at painstaking lengths.

"Good. Because you remember what you have to admit if it doesn't?"

"Yes, I do. Matchmaking isn't for everyone. But that won't happen. I'm determined." The smile she shoots me is one of triumph, even if she hasn't won yet. She's surprising. Naive, perhaps... but funny. Unexpected.

I doubt anyone else would have led me down this path, or gotten me to agree to the outrageous idea of three dates. Not when I hadn't been on a date in over a year before this.

I bite the inside of my cheek and look away from the expectancy in her eyes. Toward the half-blurry images of couples on the wall. Smiling with false happiness in stylized poses.

I surprise even myself with my response. "How about I give you two weeks? There's an event I'm attending on Friday the fourteenth. I could use a date to that."

Summer's eyebrows rise. "You'd be okay with that? Having a first date at an event?"

"Why not?" I shrug. It had been a foolish suggestion, but here I am, committed to it.

"No, no, that's great. If the female client is amenable to that, it'll work great." She gives me another sunny smile. "Two weeks, then, to find your soul mate."

"Good luck," I say. "You'll need it more than me."

5

SUMMER

The summer rain is a torrent outside my office window, stronger than New York has experienced in weeks. It's needed, but I still don't like it. Not when I know what it'll mean for the windows in my apartment.

No matter how many rolled-up towels I stuff against the window frames, water still finds ways to seep through. I might applaud its ingenuity, if I wasn't living with the consequences.

I sigh. Ace looks up at me from his sprawl at my feet, eyebrows raised the way only a dog can.

"Nothing's up," I tell him. "Excited to go to my parents this weekend?"

He gives a huff and settles his head back on the floor. Manhattan's not the place for a dog, and my parents would be more than happy to add him to their little pack upstate, but...

I want him here with me.

"You're the real matchmaker, aren't you?" I tell him. My door is closed, with neither Suzy nor my aunt here to witness just how often I talk to my dog. "Clients take one look at you and they melt."

Ace turns on his side and pushes his snout against my ankle, his nose cold.

"That's right. Now, if only you could charm Anthony Winter too."

Ace doesn't reply. Smart move, too, because the man seems utterly resistant to charm of all sorts. And utterly dismissive of the women I've set him up with.

How do you win a bet against someone who is determined to play unfairly? He might say otherwise, but I doubt he gave Isabelle a proper shot. Ciara, well… that's a different story.

Which reminds me.

I reach for my phone and put on a wide smile as I dial Ciara's number. She'd asked me to call her back.

"Summer," she says. "I'm so glad you called."

"I'm here to help."

"I just want to touch base about the date last week."

I grit my teeth. We've already spoken about it. "Absolutely. What about it do you want to discuss?"

"Like I said right after, I'd really like to go on another date with Anthony. The date ended so quickly, he didn't have a chance to grab my phone number." She laughs, like that had been a silly mistake on Anthony's part.

"I see," I say. "Well, it's always up to both parties if they'd like to schedule another date."

"You're right, and I think in this situation, it is certainly mutual," she says, voice lowering. "Honestly, I'm a bit impressed, Summer. I'd heard great things about Opate but I couldn't imagine my first date would be with Anthony Winter!"

I frown. "Were you aware of him before you went on a date with him?"

"Okay, I admit I wasn't. But I Googled him before, of course. Did you know his family owns Winter Hotels? You know, the giant chain?"

I didn't. I clear my throat. "Well, we do pretty extensive interviews with clients when they join."

"Oh, that's right. Of course you know." She sighs, a tad dreamily. "He wasn't very talkative, but that's okay. There are more important things. Would you be so kind as to give Anthony my number and let him know I'm available? That'd be lovely. Oh, I have to go."

I open my mouth. "I'm not sure if—"

"Thank you! Ciao!" Ciara hangs up before I can let her down. It's always a tricky thing to do, but I've learned to do it with tact, reminding clients that not every connection is a hit on both sides.

Now I'll have to write her an email.

But first, I type Winter Hotels into the search bar of my computer. Contrary to our normal clients, I have nearly no information on Anthony Winter.

Pictures of a familiar sky-rise emerges. It's one I've walked past multiple times in New York, a proud staple of Park Avenue. With over a century of history, the hotel is a veritable New York landmark. An institution.

He's not just any old season. He's a Winter.

Which means Anthony is as old money elite as they come. He hadn't spoken out of ignorance or dislike when he derided our clients for being elitist or status-seeking.

He'd been speaking from experience.

I lean back in my chair and stare at the imposing image of the Winter Hotel, a pre-war building on Manhattan's most expensive address. So I have to set him up with someone… well. He'd want someone *not* of that world, judging by his comments.

But I've learned a thing or two about what people *think* they want, and what they actually do.

They're rarely the same thing.

Anthony needs someone he can take home to that old money family of his, but not someone who takes it too seriously. Someone with one foot in and one foot out. A woman who appreciates his sarcastic sense of humor and can draw him out of his shell. A woman comfortable with money and prestige without placing undo value on it.

In short, he needs a female client we don't currently have at Opate. How am I going to pull this off?

Ace rises from his sprawl half an hour later and heads to my closed office door. Three sharp knocks sound a few seconds later.

"Come in!"

Ace's tail wags softly as Anthony Winter takes a step inside. He looks down at my dog, a frown on his face.

"He's always here, isn't he?"

I turn away from my computer. "He's good for business."

Anthony doesn't comment, but he runs a hand over Ace's head, his fingers smoothing over one of the floppy ears. "A matchmaking company with a mascot," he mutters.

I straighten in my chair. "Can I help you with something?"

"Yes," he says. "I came by to speak with your aunt and wanted to ask you about the bet. Do you have someone ready to accompany me on Friday evening?

I meet the solid, dark gaze across the room. What did I agree to? Finding a woman this man will approve of is impossible.

"Soon," I lie. "I think I've found the perfect woman for you."

His lips tug. "Right."

"I'd also like to apologize for Ciara. I admit that you were right about her not being a good fit for you. I've noted it down as another data point, and your next date will be much better."

This time, he has to look away to hide a smirk. "Well, I'm glad you acknowledge that I can make my own decisions about partners."

Damn. I make my smile wide and serviceable. "You certainly can, Mr. Winter. All I ask is that you keep an open mind."

"I will," he says. "You'll send me details regarding whoever you choose?"

"Yes."

"Excellent." Anthony returns to my office door, his gaze on Ace. "I'm looking forward to seeing how this bet ends, Miss Davis."

"So am I, Mr. Winter."

His eyes flash, as if I've made a joke only he understands, and then he closes the office door behind him. I stare at the empty space and regret every decision I've made that's brought me to this point.

I do not have the perfect woman for him.

I'm starting to doubt she exists.

6

ANTHONY

"Looks good," I say.

Tristan gives an approving hum, glancing down at his phone. "Imagine it filled to the brim with people, too. We'll be packed in here."

The giant ballroom is a bit gaudy, perhaps, but it's just what the clientele will expect. People who attend charity auctions in mid-Manhattan on a Friday evening aren't going because they expect Louvre-level class. "It'll do."

Tristan snorts. "So enthusiastic."

I glance down at my watch. It's nearly ten in the morning, the day of the function, and Miss Davis hasn't gotten back to me with my date for the evening.

I don't know what I'm hoping for most—that she does, or that she doesn't.

The idea of walking around here in the dim lighting, with all these people, having to make idle chitchat... I'd rather suffer through one of my migraines.

"I'm not sure why Victor needs us here at all," I say.

Tristan slides his phone into his suit pocket. "Of course you are," he says dryly. "He wants the pizzazz we add."

I raise an eyebrow at him. "The pizzazz?"

"Yes. We'll bid highly and it'll give us a chance to mingle.

Carter has some executive at a multi-media company he wants us to meet." Tristan waves a hand. "We're here to see and be seen."

"And you'll stay for exactly fifteen minutes," I accuse, "before escaping back to your beautiful girlfriend and your son."

Tristan's smile is shameless. "Yes, but I'll bring as much pizzazz as I can for those fifteen minutes."

"I can't believe I was happy for you in the beginning. I wish I could take it all back," I say, shaking my head. "You smug bastard."

Tristan's smile just widens further, and despite my words, we both know I'm still thrilled for him. He'd found happiness in a way that had been denied him for years. Doesn't mean it isn't still insufferable to watch, sometimes.

He doesn't ask me why I hadn't responded to his text about coming around for dinner yesterday, and I'm grateful for that. He doesn't push.

Victor strolls toward us, weaving around tables covered in white linen. His hands are in the pockets of his slacks.

"Think it'll do?" he asks.

"It will."

His face is a cool mask. "Remind me why we do these things again."

"Network. Prestige. Goodwill," Tristan says. "The company looks good. Acture Capital looks good."

Victor shakes his head. "I had to tell them to relegate all emails about this to my assistant. Do you think the question of what the catering company should serve really deserves the CEO's attention?"

I look past him to the preparations for the evening. Two technicians are on the stage, unrolling foot after foot of cords.

"Cecilia is good at handling that," Tristan says. "It's the one thing I miss about Exciteur."

Victor's quiet for a beat. "You mean Miss Myers?"

"Yes, Miss Myers," Tristan says dryly. "Your assistant, previously mine."

"She does good work, I suppose."

I roll my neck, catching a crick. Last night had been another one with barely any sleep.

Tristan bumps my elbow with his. "Tell us how the match-making company is doing. Have you found your ideal woman yet?"

I shake my head. "I still can't believe I'm the one who got this assignment. Should have never lost that poker game."

"Well, it's not like you're too busy with anything else, are you?" Victor asks, answering emails on his phone. His words are spoken matter-of-factly.

Because it is a fact. I don't do much else these days, not when I can handle my business from my home office.

"We're turning it into an app," I say. "Should have the company turn green in a matter of months."

"Gutting staff?"

Summer's face flits through my mind. "No. They have expertise, and they're a small operation already."

Tristan nods, a thoughtful look in his eyes. "We're going global with it, right?"

"Yes."

"There could be something there. Hosting elite singles parties worldwide."

"Like the Gilded Room?" I ask.

Tristan frowns at me. He doesn't like it when I mention his past habits, despite the fact that I'd once accompanied him to one of those parties. Especially not in public. I *know* he doesn't like it, yet here I am, needling him.

When did I start wanting to watch the world burn?

"In a way," Tristan says, lowering his voice. "But more... respectable. An app launch with a purpose."

"Could work."

Victor clears his throat. "Are you bringing any family members tonight, Anthony? Your brother?"

I stare at him long enough that he looks up from his phone.

Ice-blue eyes are cold as they stare into mine. "That's a no," he assumes.

"That's a no," I repeat.

He shrugs, returning to his phone. "A shame. Your connections could help us."

Tristan and I watch in silence as he strides off to the event coordinators. They stand straight as pins when he instructs them on what is doubtless minutiae.

"Remind me," I say, "why we tolerate him again?"

Tristan sighs. "He brings in a shit-ton of money."

"It's almost not worth it."

"Almost not," he agrees, and turns so he's standing by my side. We look out over the ballroom. "I'm glad you're coming tonight."

I make a noncommittal sound. Hate that he, too, has started to walk on eggshells around me. It's bad enough whenever I speak to my parents. Bad because I know it's not my impending blindness they're careful not to bruise themselves against, not when they have no idea the thorn is there. It's my temper they're wary of.

"Glad you don't have to spend those fifteen minutes alone, you mean."

He snorts, more to humor me than in any real amusement. The silence between us shifts, deepens, and his voice drops. "You know I care about you, man."

I close my eyes. "Don't."

"I have to," he says, and his eyes are on mine. "Is everything all right? Truly?"

It's the first time he's outright asked. Not just commented on my singleness, or my lack of social life, or my temper. But actually asked me for a response.

The truth rises further up my throat than I'd anticipated. Further than it ever has with my family.

But the thought of what comes after stops me. The questions. The well-meaning advice. The suggestions for a second opinion, for technology, for fucking Braille and guide dogs and *how are you feeling's?* The altered behavior. How I'd turn from a friend and business partner to someone you pity.

He'd inevitably ask the question that burned like acid in my stomach whenever I thought about the future. How long do you have left until you can't work anymore? Until my time as an equal partner at Acture Capital is over, until I become a burden, obsolete to everyone I know.

"I'm great," I say.

My answer might be dishonest, but the silence between us isn't. Tristan hears the lie and I know he does.

But he just nods. "All right."

My nerves are so frazzled that I curse out loud when my phone rings twenty minutes later. The cleaning lady before me in the hotel corridor jumps and I mutter a muffled "sorry" as I pass by. Pick up my phone to turn it off.

And see the name on the screen.

"Yes?"

"Oh, hi? Mr. Winter? I hope I'm not calling at a bad time," Summer says.

I force myself to take the edge off my voice. It's not her fault that I'm about to put myself through a charity event in a ball-room filled with strangers.

Despite what I'd said to Victor, it's not impossible that one of my family members will be here. Isaac Winter is the king of schmoozing when he thinks it will benefit my family's hotel empire.

"It's not a bad time. Do you have a date set up for me tonight?" I hope she doesn't. My energy feels strained enough as it is.

"Unfortunately, I don't. I'm so sorry, but I haven't been able to find someone I believe would be a good match. I know I waited too long to let you know, but I had hopes for one last client… but no. I apologize, Mr. Winter."

"Well, stop," I say. It comes out rougher than I'd meant it. "It's all right."

She breathes a sigh of relief and I feel like an asshole. An asshole for going through this charade when she won't win the bet.

But then her voice slips into a teasing note, soft through the phone. "Trying to strike the right balance between serious and silly with you is difficult."

"I imagine I'm not the easiest client you've ever had."

Summer laughs on the other line. "No, I can't say you are. But you're not the most difficult either."

"Are you sure about that?"

"Well," she admits, "you're among them, but not the worst, no."

"Yet."

"Yet," she agrees. "Are you really sure you'll be all right without a date to your event tonight?"

A wicked idea takes form. One I shouldn't speak out loud. But the interaction with Tristan has put me on edge, on a day where I'm already dancing with my demons. Why not add one more? "I'm not sure, Miss Davis. You did promise me a date, and so I haven't set up one on my own. But there is a way you could make it up to me."

"Oh?"

"You could take her place tonight."

Complete silence on the other line.

"Mr. Winter, I'm not sure if that would… I mean. Huh." A cleared throat. "What is this event?"

"It's a charity auction, hosted by Exciteur Consulting at the Halycon Hotel. There will be canapés. An open bar."

Her chuckle sounds nervous. "An open bar?"

"Is that a key selling point?"

"No. If I go, Mr. Winter…"

"Anthony."

"Anthony," she repeats, her voice soft. "It wouldn't absolve either of us from the bet. I'd still be looking for a third perfect date for you."

"I wouldn't expect anything less from you."

Her voice strengthens. "Okay, then. I'll go. It'll be professional, right?"

Her fears make sense, and I curse myself for being another form of asshole, too. Three for three. It really isn't my day, and it's not even noon yet.

"Yes. You work at Opate Match, Summer. I'm not asking anything more than some company at a function."

"I'll be there," she says. "Will you text me the address?"

"I'll pick you up," I say, my strides lengthening as I head through the lobby. Back out to the beckoning New York streets, the place I'd grown up, and the city that would one day become a deadly obstacle course for me.

"You don't have to—"

"I'm the one asking you for a favor," I say. The words flow easily, following a script I'd once known intimately. "Let me send a couple of dresses over to your apartment."

"Mr. Winter, I can't possibly accept that."

"I'm the one who asked you," I say. For someone who worked at a matchmaking company priding itself on catering to the elite, she seems unaware of its trappings. "I'd do the same for any woman I'd personally invited to a function."

"Okay then," she murmurs. "I'll text you my address."

"And your dress size."

"Um, yes. Okay."

We click off the call and I find my feet steering me in the opposite direction of my apartment, toward Bergdorf Goodman. I'd meant to make a phone call. Tell them to pick out three dresses.

The way I'd often done for Shelby, once. She'd always liked it when I did that.

But I'd never set foot in the store myself. Savoring the light of the New York summer sun on my face, illuminating the world to a brilliance that makes my eyesight feel normal again, I wonder why I hadn't.

Picking out the colors and shapes that would look good on Summer doesn't seem like a nuisance at all.

7

SUMMER

When I come home, there's a delivery man waiting outside my apartment building, shifting from foot to foot like he's waiting for the chance to bolt.

"Do you live here?" he asks, hoisting up three garment bags on his arm.

"I do, yes. And I—"

"Do you know who Summer Davis is?"

"That's me, actually."

He breathes a sigh of relief. "Thank God. This place doesn't have a doorman or a concierge."

"No, it doesn't. Oh, all right. Thanks?" I accept the parcels, and as I recognize one of the designer names on a box, my stomach nearly drops out beneath me. Apparently this is just what Anthony Winter does when he invites a woman to an event.

Par for the course.

"I can't sign," I tell him. "My hands aren't free."

The delivery guy chuckles and takes them from me again. "I should have realized. Wait, let's do it this way… here. Sign this."

A few minutes later he takes off down the street, hurrying to where a delivery car is double-parked.

I shake my head and head upstairs. Greet Ace who has been

home all day, his tail wagging so hard it nearly knocks a glass of water off the sofa table.

"I know, buddy. I couldn't bring you in today." I take him for a walk to the nearby dog park before finally allowing myself to open the parcels spread out on my bed. A glance at my watch tells me I only have a few hours before Anthony will be here to pick me up.

Nobody has ever *picked me up* in New York before. For a dazzling, daydreamy moment, I feel like I'm one of the women I regularly take on as clients. They date men like Anthony Winter. Men who run this city, or at least know the ones who do.

But I'm not one of those women.

I sit behind a desk and help them find love instead.

Tugging on the delicate wrapping paper, I open the first box. Run my fingers over the red, satin fabric beneath as if in a daze.

A certainty settles in my bones. He hasn't picked these out personally. Can't have, if this is something he does regularly for women.

The realization bolsters me. I open the others and pull out the three options. A red, spaghetti strap one. A black sheath that falls to my knees. And a dark green option with only one shoulder, narrow at the waist before it flares out.

My hands shake as I read the designer label.

Vivienne would absolutely adore this. It's exactly the kind of grand, over-the-top gesture she'd love.

Would she love that it's our new owner who sent them to me?

I flip the question over in my mind as I shower and straighten my hair, re-doing my makeup. Dark brown eyeliner, soft against my light coloring, and a touch of red lipstick. I stare at the three dress options on my bed.

Slipping into the dark green, one-shouldered dress, I find that it fits.

"Wish me luck," I ask Ace. He rubs his head against my hand, the soft, silky fur sliding through my fingers. "You know how long it's been since I went out with a man."

His tail wags.

"Thanks for being here with me, too, by the way. I know Mom has a giant yard you could play in."

He licks the back of my hand.

"You too, buddy," I say. "You too."

My phone chimes and I give him a farewell pat. The text is simple. *I'm outside.*

A dark Town Car idles by the curb and one of the passenger doors opens as I step outside. Nerves flutter in my stomach. Professional favor or not, he's not an easy man to be around. It doesn't help that I'm not even close to figuring him out.

But I paint a wide smile on my face as I get into the car. Anthony's waiting in the backseat. The dark tux he's wearing blends in with the dark leather seat. Dark hair. Dark clothes.

"Hello," I say.

He inclines his head. "You live close to the Halycon Hotel. Both are in Soho."

"Yes, I suppose I do." I fasten my seat belt. "Was it still okay for you to pick me up? I hope it didn't delay you."

"Of course not."

I open my mouth to tell him that I'm not used to this. Blurt something out about the dress. The car. The night.

"You wore the black," he comments.

I glance down at the dark green fabric. In the dim lighting, I suppose it looks almost black. "The green one, actually. Thank you. Or should I thank a personal shopper?"

He turns away from me, jaw working. "You're welcome."

The ride to the hotel is quiet. I open and close my clutch twice to double-check I brought my phone, just to have something to do other than glancing over at Anthony.

Long fingers drum against his thigh when the car pulls up outside the hotel. Is he nervous? I am.

"We're here," I say.

He nods and gets out of the car, his jaw working again when he comes to my side and finds me already on the curb. He buttons his dinner jacket and extends an arm to me. "Let's get this over with."

I take his arm and make it my personal mission to get one smile out of him tonight. Just one.

"A charity auction," I say. "Will guests be bidding on luxury items?"

"Yes."

"Do you have your eye on anything in particular? Oh, look, they have a brochure."

His voice is dry as he hands me a glossy pamphlet. "I suppose I have to buy something, but I haven't looked."

"You *have* to buy something?"

"As one of the partners of Acture, I'm technically a co-owner of Exciteur."

I swallow. "Right. The consulting firm throwing this party."

"Yes." Anthony steers us through the open double-doors and into a bustling ballroom. A string quartet plays from a podium, soft music permeating the air. Anthony's tux blends right in, and thankfully, so does my dress. I'm glad I didn't go for the red one.

"So?" I ask him. "What's the charitable cause they're raising money for?"

He's quiet for a beat. "I don't remember."

Unable to help myself, I laugh. "You were really involved with the planning for this, weren't you?"

"I had my hands full with all of your dates," he says.

"Two measly dates took up that much of your time?"

"There was a lot of prep work," he says. "Takes me hours to get ready for a date."

My eyebrows rise and then I burst out laughing. His rough, scowling handsomeness is entirely natural. I wondered if he even runs a brush through that thick, dark hair of his. Not that he needs to.

Anthony looks away, but not before I catch a faint tug at his lips. *Almost.* "Let me get you something to drink. Champagne?"

"Yes, please."

A few minutes later, the two of us lean against the bar in the corner of the ballroom. He'd opted for a brandy and has a crystal tumbler in hand.

I look out over the crowd of people. Fancy dresses. A string quartet. Waiters carrying trays with champagne. Anthony takes a drag of his brandy.

"Not a fan of mingling?" I ask.

He shakes his head. At his height, and so close, the cut of his jaw is sharp. "I can't stand small talk."

I grimace. "God, neither can I."

The sound he makes is skeptical.

"What?" I ask. "You disagree?"

"You're the definition of someone who loves small talk," he says. "What do you do with all of your clients? Small talk."

"Oh, that's different."

He turns his torso my way, his dark gaze landing on me. "Is it?"

"Yes. I have a purpose. It's all about finding out more about the person, never about just making idle chitchat. People reveal a lot when they think they're saying very little."

"So you're a good judge of character."

"I like to think I am. In my line of work, you certainly have to be. We're all about the personal touch at Opate."

Anthony narrows his eyes. "And yet you thought I'd hit it off with that model. Ciara."

"It was a *possibility*," I say, taking a sip of my champagne. "Tell me I'm wrong, though, and that men like you would never enter a dating situation like that."

He looks at me over the edge of his brandy glass. Something burns in his eyes, but then he relents. "I know men who would have taken the bait," he admits.

I beam at him in victory. "Right. Before I suggested Ciara, I had no way of knowing which camp you belonged to. And now I do."

"So it was a reconnaissance date? Your tactics are more refined than I'd expected, Miss Davis."

"Oh, I have a ton of tricks up my sleeve."

His gaze drops to my lips, lingering for a second before it falls to the brochure in my hand. "Rainforest conservation," he says. "That's the charitable cause."

"Oh!" I set my now-empty champagne glass down on the bar and open the brochure. "I like that."

"It's inoffensive," he says. "The perfect non-political choice. I'm surprised they didn't choose orphans or cancer research."

"Are you always so cynical?"

"Are you never?"

I bite my lip to keep from smiling and open the first page, scanning through the list of items and experiences up for auction. My eyes widen at the starting prices. "You're really going to bid on these, are you?"

"I'll have to buy something."

"It's all for show?"

"Something like that," he says, staring out at the crowd again. "We're four co-owners, and we all should, really. Buying will look good in the papers, not to mention encourage others here to bid, buy and donate."

"Hmm." I look through the list, the small print, the images.

"Find anything good?"

"The starting bids are very high," I say. "I mean, significantly higher than what these things might retail for."

"The markup is what makes it charity."

"Well, I suppose so. Oh, I don't—thank you. Okay," I say to the waiter, accepting another flute of champagne.

"Read it to me," Anthony says.

"The brochure?"

"Yes."

I clear my throat and start from the top. Detailing paintings, jewelry and vacations. A twenty-year-old diamond Cartier watch.

"Christ, they're asking... I can't tell you how much they're asking for this."

"Try me," Anthony says.

"Eighty-five thousand dollars."

"Is it pretty, at least?"

"Yes, it is," I say, smoothing my finger over the picture. It's something my aunt would wear, gifted to her by a lover from one of her travels. I've never met a more hopeless romantic than my aunt, but she combines it with a shrewd sense of business. I had the one, and was trying to foster the other. "But not eighty-five-thousand-dollar pretty."

"Think about the rainforest," he says.

"All those cute monkeys."

"Exactly."

"I hope I'm not expected to bid on anything? Oh, there's a china set here that I could... no. Definitely not."

Anthony takes a sip of brandy. Is it to hide a tug of his lips?

"Not to mention I wouldn't dare use it if I paid this much for it," I say. "Oh God. It has pheasants on it."

"You're not a fan of pheasants?"

"I don't think I've ever given them much thought."

"Tell me," Anthony says, turning toward me, "what is your favorite fowl, Miss Davis?"

The dry humor in his tone makes me laugh. I hadn't expected him to have so much of it. "Are you using my own tactic against me? I should add that to the list of prompts we ask potential clients."

"It would be original."

"It sure would," I agree. "You told me to call you Anthony. Doesn't that mean I'm Summer?"

He leans against the bar beside me, crossing his arms over his chest. Looking back out over the crowd. "Summer," he agrees.

"Good." I take another sip of my flute, only to find it near empty. I should slow down. "Are there canapés around here somewhere?"

"They should start serving them soon."

"Good."

His voice drops. "Oh, joy."

I follow the turn of his head to the two approaching men.

Similar in height, but one has brown hair, the other light auburn. Both in tuxes. Both coming straight here.

"Friends of yours?" I ask.

"Business parters," he says, and then, murmured beneath his breath, "and friends."

I smooth a hand over the dark green silk of my dress. "That's exciting."

Anthony has time to shoot a dry look my way before his business partners are upon us.

"Have you seen what's on offer?" the auburn-haired one says by way of introduction, an arm against the bar. The quick smile on his face makes up for a crooked nose... had it been broken once? "What the hell am I supposed to bid on here? A sixteenth-century French futon?"

"It would liven up your bachelor pad," the dark-haired one says. His eyes find mine and I can tell he clocks how close Anthony and I are standing.

"Yes, but a futon?"

I clear my throat. "There's a lovely set of china," I say. "With a pheasant pattern."

Anthony snorts at my side, reaching for his glass of brandy. The crystal hides the twitch of his lips.

"China," the auburn-haired one repeats. "Victor has lost his mind about this whole thing."

"I'm guessing he has no idea what's actually being auctioned here tonight. Anthony, why don't you introduce us to your date?"

He puts down his drink. "Gentlemen, this is Summer Davis. Summer, this is Carter and Tristan. We work together at Acture Capital."

I shake their hands. Neither of them tries to hide the looks they shoot Anthony. Is it surprise? Shock? Regardless, I give them my widest smile.

"It's a pleasure to meet you both," I say. "I've heard a lot about the work Acture Capital does."

"A china expert and a venture capitalist fan?" Carter asks.

"Anthony, where did you meet this woman, and can you point me in the same direction?"

"Much like a sixteenth-century French futon," Anthony says, "Summer is one of a kind."

I have to smile at that. He'd sidestepped the issue of me working at Opate, hiding it in the guise of a compliment.

"But unlike a sixteenth-century futon, I'm not usually sold at auction," I add.

All three of them chuckle. "What a shame," Carter says, putting down his glass. "Should we… oh. It's showtime."

A hush settles over the gathered guests as the MC takes the stage, tapping the mic a few times. He introduces the CEO of Exciteur to polite applause and a tall, dark blond man strides across the stage. The illusive fourth partner of Acture Capital. A glance at the brochure gives me his name.

Victor St. Clair.

"Let's have a seat," Anthony murmurs by my side. A moment later a large hand rests on the small of my back.

We find seats at the back of the room. His business partners sit two rows ahead, giving us privacy. I wonder if we should have made it clear that it's not like that between Anthony and me.

The bidding kicks off with an abstract painting no bigger than my hand, by renowned-artist-I've-never-heard-of and at a price-too-high-to-comprehend. I sit in awed silence as items and trips are auctioned off at hair-raising prices.

Anthony doesn't bid on a single one of them.

I lean toward him. His aftershave is pleasant, a hint of pine and musk. "Which one are you waiting for?"

He's close enough that I can follow the raised arch of his eyebrow. "I'm going to get you your china, of course."

I grin at the obvious joke. His gaze drops to my lips for a second before returning toward the stage.

"Now time for item number fourteen…" the auctioneer says. "A twenty-four-karat diamond watch from Cartier in the classic Panthére design."

Anthony raises his hand.

I look at him, but he keeps his eyes on the rapidly speaking auctioneer. Two others bid as well, but Anthony's arm rises another time. Then a third.

By the fourth time, he's the only one still with his arm up. The price is north of a hundred thousand dollars.

"Sold to Mr. Anthony Winter!" the auctioneer calls to the sound of applause. I just stare at him.

Anthony turns to me. "Well, you recommended it."

I just blink at him. "It's a woman's watch."

"So it'll make an excellent gift," he says, lowering his voice. "Think about the monkeys, Summer."

"Right. You're very generous."

"That's exactly it," he says. "And now they'll all remember it."

We stroll around the room after the auction, and he supplies me with another glass of champagne. I finally get my hands on some canapés, even if they're no bigger than a bite. Several guests approach Anthony, and he speaks to them in low, authoritative tones. No small talk and no jokes of the sort he'd exchanged with his business partners.

I drink my champagne and nod and smile to each of them. Toast to rainforest conservation. Drink. Toast to a lovely event. Drink. Toast to the summer weather. Drink.

Anthony's voice is dry when he finally steers us back toward the bar. "I'm done."

"You don't want to network some more?"

"I never want to network again."

That makes me chuckle. My heel catches in an uneven patch of carpeting and I sway slightly in response.

Anthony's hand locks around my elbow. "You okay?"

"Yes. That was the carpet."

"I believe you."

"But just in case, I don't think I should have any more champagne."

"A wise decision."

We make our way to the exit, his hand on my low back, as he calls his driver to bring the car around. My head swims in the most delicious way. I'm just the perfect amount of tipsy. I'm also hungry.

As soon as we get into the car, I inform Anthony.

He gives a half-amused sigh. He does that a lot, I've realized. Rare are the laughs. "You should have had more canapés."

"Well, I would have, if there were more to go around," I say.

"Disappointed with them?"

"Yes. Don't get me wrong, they were tasty. Flavors well-balanced, and I liked the presentation—"

"The caterer is not here to overhear you," he says.

"—but they were too small. I can't survive on that alone."

"What are you getting to eat, then?"

"There's a place down my street that sells pizza by the slice, or by the... whole? By the pizza? I don't know what you call an entire pizza. A wheel of pizza?"

The corners of his lips tug in earnest now. "A pie. It's called a pie of pizza."

"Oh, that's a New York expression."

"Yes, I believe so."

"That makes sense. You're smart."

"So I've been told on occasion."

The Town Car pulls up to a smooth stop outside my building and I can just make out the neon sign of a single slice of pepperoni further down the street. My body has an itch only melted cheese can fix.

Anthony clears his throat. Straightens his shoulders as if he's retreating inwards.

"Don't you want pizza too?" I ask him. "You can have a slice or a pie. My treat. As thanks for the evening, not to mention the dresses. You like pizza, don't you?"

"Yes." He's silent for a moment. Then he puts a hand on the front seat and leans forward. "Todd, feel free to take off for the night."

"Yes, sir."

8

ANTHONY

Buying a pepperoni pizza wasn't part of the plan for tonight. Neither was following Summer Davis up the stairs to her Soho condo. My body is wired tight, needles beneath my skin from the pointless networking I'd been forced to engage in. But my feet take me forward. Following the gold of her hair up the dimly lit stairwell.

Fuck, this is such a dumb idea. Like putting my hand to the flame or walking out on a tightrope. Challenging the demons to a duel in front of an employee… and it's Summer, nonetheless.

"This is my place." Her voice is just as cheerful as usual, made softer around the edges by the champagne. Her hair has slipped over her shoulder, revealing silky skin. "Do you have the pizzas?"

"I haven't dropped them yet."

She laughs and pushes open her apartment door. I step in after her into the darkness and stub my toe against a step. Bite down my lip to hide the curse.

"God, they smell good. Let me get the lights… here we go. Oh, hello, buddy."

I blink at the infusion of warm, beautiful light. Her place is small and cluttered, a frayed oriental rug thrown over hardwood floors. Two large couches take up most of the space, relegating a tiny kitchenette to the corner. An old chandelier hangs from the ceiling.

"Yes, we have a visitor," Summer is telling her dog. "And he's in a really nice, really well-fitted tux. So no jumping."

I glance down at my clothes. Well-fitted? "Where do you want the pizzas?"

"I'll grab them. Have a seat, why don't you? I'll get us something to drink..." Summer tosses her clutch on the tiny kitchen counter and opens her minifridge. "Do you want... water? Or juice?"

I run the back of my hand over my mouth to hide my smile. "Water, thanks."

"Yes, I suppose that wasn't much of a decision, was it?" Her voice drops to a soft muttering. "Here I am offering you juice, like we're twelve and having a sleepover."

A cold nose bumps against my hand. Two baleful, serious eyes look up at me, a tail wagging softly.

I know, I think. *No sleepovers. You don't have to remind me.*

Her dog sinks down onto his haunches and abandons me in favor of his owner. She hands me one of the pizza boxes and curls up on one of her sofas, kicking off her heels. Stretches out her bare legs on the linen.

"There's nothing like a bit of post-champagne pizza," she declares and opens the lid. The scent of mozzarella and pepperoni fills the small room. I shouldn't be here, surrounded by all of her things, her warmth, her life. Basking in her casual ease. Galling her optimism.

"Are you going to eat standing up?" she asks.

"You never let me off the hook, do you?"

"I just want you to feel at home."

The words are effortless, spoken around a bite of pizza. This is a woman with friends, with a life, and to her there's nothing unusual about what we're doing.

I sink down onto the couch opposite her. Pop open my own

pizza box. As I chew, my gaze travels around her living room. I make out an elephant lamp in the corner. A heap of books unorganized on a shelf. A homemade throw in varying colors.

"You're inspecting," she tells me. "I can see it."

"Inspecting?"

"Oh, yes. Making judgements, too, I'm guessing."

I raise a pizza slice her way. "It's not like you to be suspicious."

She laughs. "I'm just realistic."

"You don't need to worry. I'm not an interior designer."

"No, you're a venture capitalist. Which means you're a little of everything, aren't you? You wear a lot of hats." Summer props up a pillow behind her head and leans back. She looks like a mischievous goddess, a model divine, in her silk dress and gleaming eyes. The blonde hair is a tumble of curls around her shoulders. "Actually, have you ever worn a hat? I think you'd look good in one."

I shake my head. "You've had a lot more champagne than I realized."

"I'm not drunk."

"Sure you're not."

"I'm just… elevated by the juice of the grape."

I raise my eyebrows and she laughs. "I read that in an article once. Isn't it a great way to say drunk?"

"Sure. It's also six words too long."

Summer laughs. "You have a lot more humor than I thought the first time I met you."

"Well, I'm glad I can surprise you."

She smiles and grabs another slice of pizza. I take a bite of my own and breathe in the comfortable silence. It's been a long time since I sat like this with anyone. Despite the charity auction, despite the meaningless fucking small talk I'd had to engage in, the pressure behind my eyes is absent.

A good day, in the middle of a bad year.

"So," Summer says.

I raise an eyebrow. "So?"

"This wasn't your official third date or anything. The bet is still on. But if it were, how did I do?"

"You want a performance review?"

Her smile flashes again. "Yes. A debrief, like we've done before. What did you think of the client I fixed you up with tonight?"

I turn my face to the windows and the darkness beyond. The pathway to effortless conversation feels rusty. "She was serious when she needed to be. Silly when she could."

"A good mix of the two?"

"Yes, I'd say so."

Summer gives a low *whoop* of victory, startling Ace, lying beside her on the couch.

I roll my eyes at her. "I'm not that difficult to please."

"Sure you're not," she says, but she's smiling. "What else?"

"Is this a debrief, or are you fishing for compliments?"

"A debrief. I only have one date left to convince you that Opate Match, a business you believed in enough to buy, by the way, is based on a sound business idea."

"Oh," I say, "I know your business idea is sound. I just don't think it's the same one as you do."

"Right, because I think it's to help people find love, and you think it's… remind me again?" She stretches her legs out on the couch, long and elegant. "Arranged marriages for the elite?"

I snort. "I know that's what it's for. People who want to find a partner for status or prestige, rather than an actual relationship. Can you honestly tell me you don't have clients like that? Ones who'd decline to go on a date with anyone who earned less than a six-figure income?"

Summer takes another bite and looks at her dog, burying her fingers in his fur. "They exist, sure. But on the whole… I don't see it that way at all. These people come with their own set of difficulties. Some can't even date in public—we've had a few famous people as clients, actually. Others are older and wealthy and want to meet an equal, but it's harder to trust when money comes in the way. It's true that some come to us with a shopping list of criteria. But…" Summer's face softens, her voice growing warm.

"All that melts away when two clients like each other, when we've found a good match. Those are the best debriefs. I'll talk to both of them after their first couple of dates and it's there in their voice. The excitement, the nerves, and suddenly the preferences they *thought* were important don't matter anymore. The only thing they can see is the person in front of them. It's beautiful."

Her gaze returns to mine, and the joy in her eyes is real. "Anyway, I love my job. You're free to consider me a hopeless romantic."

"I do," I say, looking away from her. The old rancor burns in my chest. It's been a long time since I believed in anything like that. I doubt I ever truly have.

"I have a question for you," she says.

I force my voice to lighten. "I'm not answering any more of those prompts."

"It's not a prompt, I swear."

"I don't believe you."

"It's something completely different."

I lean back on the couch and drink her in with my gaze. The teasing smile. The warm eyes. "Fine. What is it?"

"Why don't you believe in true love?"

I groan, staring up at the ceiling.

"It wasn't a prompt!"

"It might as well be."

"I don't mean to pry."

"Sure you don't," I say, but there's a smile in my voice. Even I can hear it.

A second later and I'm hit squarely in the chest by one of the colorful throw pillows. I look over at Summer. She's staring back at me with a gaze that's half shocked, half challenging.

"Sorry," she says. "That didn't hurt, did it?"

Hah. My hand curls around the pillow, hurling it back at her.

She dodges it easily and breaks into laughter. Ace gives a single, low bark of surprise beside her.

"Is this how you treat your clients when they won't respond to your questions?" I ask. "No wonder Opate Match is in dire straits."

"I don't have pillows in my office," she says. Crosses one smooth leg over the other and shoots me a triumphant look. "You're avoiding the question, which is fine."

I push away my half-eaten pizza and lean forward. "How can you believe so strongly in it?"

"In true love?"

I nod. It's almost like we're in her office, talking about something rational and not here, in her home at midnight, discussing love over pizzas. I should leave.

I don't.

Summer sighs, and it sounds like music. "My parents have the perfect relationship," she says. "They work together, yet they never argue. Or rather, when they do, it ends in laughter because they both realize how ridiculous they are." Her hand traces the curve of Ace's head beside her on the couch. The dog looks like he's in bliss.

"They've gone through a lot, too. They had problems having children, and I was always destined to be an only child, but that only knitted them closer together. My dad bought my mom her dream house a few years back and they spend their weekends renovating. It's like they're a newlywed couple."

"You miss them," I murmur.

"Yes. I love living in the city, but it's far away from them," she says with a smile. Shakes her head. "Anyway, that's why I believe in true love. I've seen it with my own eyes."

Such honesty, it makes my chest tight. She'd answered my question without censure or artifice. Like I'm an actual friend.

"Your tactic worked. You avoided the question yourself."

"That," I say, raising a hand, "is because I know the way you work, Summer. You'll use my answers to win the bet."

"I'm not that clever," she says. "How was your pizza?"

"Delicious."

"You got the pepperoni, right?"

"Yes."

She throws her legs off the couch. "Do you still have any left?"

"Several slices."

Summer pads across the oriental rug on bare feet and sinks down beside me on the couch. She pushes thick, blonde hair back and opens the pizza carton. "It's not that I'm unhappy with my choice of only buying two slices," she says.

"Right."

"But these just look so good."

"Have one."

"If I do, will you tell me I should have gotten more than just two myself?"

"I would never," I say gravely.

She smiles as she pulls out a slice of pepperoni and takes a big bite. The smooth skin of her shoulder looks golden beneath the lights, her legs are only inches from mine. "That's deeee-licious."

There's a roaring in my head, one that rises to a deafening level when she turns her head toward me.

"How did you describe me to your personal shopper?" she asks. "All three of the dresses fit perfectly."

The true answer has no business being spoken aloud. That I'd picked them out myself, held the fabric up and pictured her form in them.

"Anthony?" she asks.

I push up from the couch and turn away, looking at the obvious coziness of her apartment. Sitting next to her on a couch is more temptation than I can bear.

Two pieces of paper pinned to one of her walls give me a convenient excuse. I step closer, like I'm examining them. Waiting for the pounding in my blood to abate.

"Oh, that," Summer says with a sigh. "You're seeing my whole life's plan right there. Promise me you won't judge?"

I can barely make out what the list says in the dim lighting. "I won't judge."

"I wrote it about a year ago. I had... well. I'd just gone through a really bad break-up, and it struck me that I had to go after what I wanted, or it wouldn't happen. Life is short." The scent of her perfume washes over me and she's standing right beside me. Soft and warm and light. "So I made a bucket list."

Fuck my worthless eyes in this lighting, because I can't make out more than a few letters, it's printed with such small font. There's nothing standing in the way of me learning more about Summer, other than my own inadequacy.

Oh, the irony.

"They're not very big things," she admits, sounding almost shy. "Try windsurfing. Learn how to horseback ride. But some are, I guess. I'd like to travel to all fifty states."

I nod, taking a step toward the front door. "It's good to have goals."

"It is." Summer rocks back on her heels, looking up at me. "Hearing some of your bucket list goals would help me, you know. To get to know you better."

"That's a much better prompt than asking if I'm a cat or dog person."

"It's on the list, too," she says with a smile. "Won't you at least give me one teeny, tiny goal?"

"You never give up, do you?"

"Getting to know you better is my life's mission."

It's an exaggeration, a joke at best. So it doesn't make me panic. If anything, it makes me...

No.

It's time for me to go now.

"Thank you for tonight," I tell her. "For accompanying me to the auction."

"It was my pleasure," she says, and the softness of her voice makes it seem like she genuinely means it. Like I hadn't coerced her through the bet.

I reach for the doorknob and speak with my back to her. There's no reason to say anything more, and I don't know where I find the words. "Whitewater rafting," I say. "That's one of my goals."

9

SUMMER

The enormity of what we'd done doesn't hit me until the next day, when the pleasant buzz of champagne has gone and left an aching head in its stead. Anthony had come up to my place, on my insistence. He'd seen where I lived. The mess, the trinkets, my open bedroom door and unmade bed. That stupid bucket list. He'd seen it, read all of the things I'd put down on paper as a way to convince myself to think big.

My ex-boyfriend's voice hasn't rung in my head for months, but it does again this morning. His subtle put-downs, reminding me I shouldn't be too much, too forward, that it would be better if I let him do the talking. I try to shove Robin back down, just like I'd finally, eventually, shoved him out of my life.

Anthony is a world apart from Robin, the two as different as two men could be. One quiet where the other couldn't stop talking; one stoic where the other was smarmy.

While Anthony can be intimidating, I can't imagine him saying the sort of things Robin sometimes did. Insults wrapped in words of sweetness. No, Anthony wouldn't do that.

I hadn't gotten a smile out of him yesterday, but it had been close. Next time, then.

My own thoughts give me a start. I should be focused on

saving Opate, and not intrigued by the mystery that is Anthony Winter.

Not even if he gets more interesting by the day.

He isn't set to come to the office until Wednesday, to go over the proposed creation of an Opate mobile app. I find myself counting the days until he does. Looking at the couch where he'd sat, too large in my too small apartment, a dark eyebrow raised at me. Like he couldn't quite believe he was there, himself. Like he was as intrigued by me as I was by him.

When Wednesday rolls around, nervous energy dances through my veins all morning. It rises to a crescendo when the clock finally strikes eleven.

I hear his voice before I see him. Deep and cool and just faintly hoarse, reaching me through the door.

Suzy responds. "She's in her office."

My spine straightens, gaze flying to my half-open door. But he doesn't enter.

Vivienne, then. Of course he's going to my aunt first. I grab my notebook and head across the office to join them.

Vivienne waves me into her office. Her camel wrap dress fits her like a glove and she gives me a warm smile. "Mr. Winter has brought a host of suggestions for how we can transform the company. Come, I want to hear what you think, too."

I close the door behind me and meet Anthony's gaze. Across the room, in his suit, it's like the other night never happened. Like I never stole pizza from him because I'd ordered too few slices for myself.

His fingers drum against the table. Dark stubble traces the sharp line of his jaw, and I wonder what it would feel like beneath my fingers.

"Our changes are outlined in the document. We've taken your request for personalization into account."

Vivienne pushes a copy over to me and starts *humming* as she reads through it. I try to focus on the paper in front of me.

"A dating app," I murmur, reading. "Singles parties in cities around the world?"

"You're skeptical," Anthony says.

"No, she's not," Vivienne interjects. "My niece is protective of the business, and to tell you the truth, so am I."

"As you have every right to be," Anthony says. "You've built this on your own, and you know it best."

She nods. "Yes, and I understand the need for growth and expansion. But what makes us work is that we put clients together based on what they want, not what they *think* they want."

I smile down at the table. I'd told Anthony the exact same thing.

"Given complete free choice, most people will be far more selective on dating apps than they would be if they met the same person in real life. They don't like her hair? It's a no. His eyes aren't the blue you'd always envisioned? It's a no." Vivienne gives an elegant sigh and crosses her legs. I've never looked up to her more than I do right then, as she pushes the paper with suggestions across the table to Anthony. It's a clear rejection to the man who owns a fifty-one percent stake. "I'm not against digitalization or expansion, but we need to ensure there's still an element of exclusivity and control. One where we might pair you up with someone. If not, our success rates will drop, and with them, our profits."

Anthony's jaw works as he flips the paper over. Jots down a few notes. "I understand," he says. "You have a lot of experience in this field. How do you think we could digitalize while keeping the personal touch?"

It's over thirty minutes later when our brainstorming session ends. I've caught Anthony rubbing his temples twice, resting his chin in his hand. There are rings beneath his eyes that speak of sleepless nights.

"I'll take this back to our development team," he finally says. "Thank you for your input, Vivienne."

With the meeting finished, Vivienne thanks Anthony for his time and then turns back to her computer in a clear dismissal. I catch the wry twist of his lips at that. She might only own forty-nine percent of the business, but she won't let anyone forget who started it.

Suzy isn't in the reception when we come back out. I cross the space to my office and push my door open. "Want to come in?"

Anthony nods. I leave the door ajar, with another glance to where my aunt has shut hers.

I clear my throat. "I wanted to say thank you for the other night."

"You're the one who did me a favor," he says. Sinks into the chair opposite my desk, a hand at his temple. Ace rises from his usual sprawl to say hello and leans his head against Anthony's knee.

"You mean I stepped in as a replacement," I say. "Anyway, the dresses, the car, the pizza... Thanks. I had a great time."

"All for the rainforest," he says.

"That's right. Your business partners seemed nice."

He raises an eyebrow. "Nice, yes. The two you met are nice."

"The fourth isn't?"

"Not particularly, no." Anthony shifts his gaze back to mine. "Summer, I wanted to say—"

Suzy sticks her head into my office and announces in a sing-songy voice, "the delivery guy will be here soon!" Then she notices Anthony and gives us both a chagrined look. "Oh, I'm sorry, Mr. Winter. Didn't mean to interrupt your meeting."

"That's not a problem."

She ducks out, leaving the door ajar.

Anthony looks down at his hand, curled around the armrest. "The delivery guy?"

"Oh. That's nothing, really. She's just... well. The delivery guy who comes each week asked me out a few days ago. I said no, of course. It wouldn't be appropriate."

"It wouldn't? The two of you don't work together."

"No, I suppose we don't."

"Then why not give love a chance? Don't tell me you don't believe in it anymore, Summer." His gaze is daring, but there's a tiredness beneath it. Like he's forcing himself to banter.

"I do believe in love," I say. "But…"

"But what? Is a man working as a delivery guy below your usual standards?"

"No, not at all."

"So?" He's taunting me now, an edge in his voice.

"Fine," I say.

"Fine?"

"Yes, fine. I'll ask him out for coffee when he drops by. You're right."

Anthony's gaze widens, but then it crystallizes into his usual aloof hardness. "Great."

"Yes."

"What of my third and final date?"

"I'll find you someone for this weekend."

Anthony leans back in his chair, fingers drumming along the armrest. "Well, look at that. You'll go out with the delivery guy, and I'll have my third date, and we'll see who has the most luck."

"Sounds perfect."

He stands. Buttons his suit jacket. "I'm looking forward to the end of our bet."

"Looking forward to shooting down my third candidate, you mean."

His eyes flash. "I'll give her a chance, Summer. I told you I would."

I don't for a second think he will. It's there in his eyes, in his demeanor, so much more abrasive today than it had been last weekend. Had I imagined the friendship between us? Or had he come to the conclusion that it was just as inappropriate as I had?

But it's no excuse for rudeness. My voice turns to icy professionalism.

"I'll text you with the details, Mr. Winter."

"Thank you, Miss Davis."

Ace's ears are pulled back as he watches Anthony leave my office. I can only imagine that mine would do the same, if they could.

10

ANTHONY

I don't know why I pick up the phone that Friday, seeing who's on the caller ID. Not when the headache pounds behind my eyes and bitterness tastes like ash on my tongue.

"Anthony," my mother says on the other line. I close my eyes at the censure in her tone.

"Hello," I say. The obligatory small talk we're forced to exchange is bothersome, but nothing like the irritation that flares up inside me when she starts on the one subject my family can't help but discuss.

"Did you receive a Save the Date for Isaac and Cordelia?"

"Yes, I did."

"It was very well put together, I think. They could have made their names slightly larger, but overall, it was a good card."

"It was," I say.

She hears the reluctance in my voice, of course. I haven't kept my dislike of my brother's fiancée particularly well hidden, but then again, my moods have lived right beneath my skin ever since the diagnosis.

"You are coming to the wedding, Anthony," my mother says. It's not a question. "I know Isaac hasn't spoken to you about the best man position, but I—"

"He'll give it to one of his friends. I'm aware."

A pause. "Well, I know he thinks… as do we all, Anthony, that we're not quite sure where you are at the moment."

It's a delicate way of phrasing my mood swings. My hand tightens around my coffee cup like a drowning man's around a rope. I know I'm not treating any of them the way they deserve. Not my brother, not my parents. Perhaps not even myself.

"You know I'll be there, Mom."

"At the wedding?" Her voice lightens. "Oh, I never doubted you would."

The well-meaning lie almost makes me smile. As if that isn't the reason both she and my brother have been contacting me about the wedding.

"That reminds me, Anthony. I saw the Winthorpe girl the other day. Shelby."

My hand spasms around the coffee cup. "Yeah."

"She's engaged now, I heard. To one of Farnham's boys."

Ah, yes. It doesn't surprise me. The lack of pain in my chest at the words does, however. Good for her. She deserves someone who is whole and has a full life ahead of him.

"Wasn't she lovely? I'm not sure I understand why you let her go."

She'd been the one to break it off, a month after we learned about my eyesight. And this, right here, is why elite match-making is all about prestige. People like my parents, or Shelby's parents or Cordelia's or the Farnhams, expect a certain caliber in their children's partners. The plans are dynastic, the breeding stock carefully vetted.

"We weren't right for each other," I say. "Look, I have to go, Mom."

"Okay. Whatever you need." She pauses, like she's not sure she should say what comes next. "We're having dinner with Isaac and Cordelia tonight at the Montauk house. Would you like to come? You can make it if you drive up now."

So I'd stopped being invited, too. Once, I'd been included in that sort of thing in the family text group. They probably have a new text group now. One without me.

"Thank you," I say. "But I have plans tonight."

For once, it's not a lie.

"All right, Anthony. Take care."

"You too. Say hello to Dad for me."

The brief pause betrays her surprise. "Okay, I will."

We click off and I push the phone away from me on the table, just like I push away the confusing guilt and anger I feel about distancing myself from my family. It's become second nature these days.

The guilt grows into frustration as I shower and dress, putting on the suit for tonight's date. Summer's text had been cordial and curt. Informed me who I was to meet and where. The *good luck* she'd added had lacked an exclamation point, and by now, I'm familiar enough with Summer's way of speaking to know that it really was lacking.

It's a Friday afternoon. Is she getting ready for her own date with the delivery guy? Despite my own words in her office, of course he's not good enough for her. Not with her optimism and humor. Not with the rosy-colored way she sees the world. Nobody could be.

The needles crawling beneath my skin intensify when my driver drops me off outside the restaurant for the evening. I'm there first, like I always am. Lean against the building and cross my arm across my chest.

Soon enough, a smooth voice speaks from my left. "Anthony Winter?"

"Yes." I extend a hand to a diminutive brunette, her eyes clear and curious. "Layla Garcia?"

"Yes, that's me. It's a pleasure to meet you." She waves a hand toward the restaurant. "Shall we?"

The restaurant is poorly lit, with candles sending flickering light up the walls. No overhead lighting. I bump into a waiter on our way to the table, and damn it, my peripheral vision is shit in situations like this.

Layla's voice is pleasant enough and had I been another man, or in another time in my life, she might have charmed me. But all

I can focus on is the tiny fucking print on the menu that might as well be Greek for the sense I can make of it.

I'd need a flashlight to see in here.

"What are you having?" she asks. "I can't decide."

"I'm not sure yet," I say, and likely never will be.

When the waiter comes, I tell him to give me tonight's special.

Layla's eyebrows rise. "You're adventurous," she says.

Fuck. Have I ordered frog legs or snails or something? Should've asked, but no, I just had to take my chances. Sometimes I'm not sure what I hate more. My failing eyesight or my pride.

Layla's a psychologist with a degree from an Ivy League school and parents who summer in the Hamptons. She asks the right questions. Doesn't comment on the fact that I apparently ordered couscous salad with candied goat cheese.

For each passing minute, I feel worse.

For wasting her time. For not engaging in the conversation she's trying to draw me into. And for my mind's constant path back to Summer and her potential date.

"You're a psychologist," I say.

Layla smiles, pushing her plate away. "Oh no."

"I'm not asking you to diagnose me."

"Good," she says. "I'm not allowed to outside of hours."

"But would you tell me why you find it interesting? Isn't it depressing to listen to people's problems all day?"

The look she gives me is one far too knowing for my liking. She cocks her head and reaches for her glass of wine. "It can be," she admits. "But most of the time, it's very rewarding. Most often, people just need to speak their thoughts aloud and know that someone is listening. What I say matters only half as much as letting them hear themselves speak out loud. People are beautiful and problematic and if I can be a part, in however small a way, in someone turning their life around... well. That's worth listening to difficult things once in a while."

"It's admirable," I say, and I mean it. But so is skydiving, and I have about as much of an inclination to do either, which is zero.

By dessert, the headache behind my eyes has erupted into a blinding pain. She notices too, which means I have to explain myself.

I ask for the check. "I'm sorry, Layla. This has been great—"

"No, you don't think it has," she says. "You can be honest."

Is that the tone she takes with one of her patients? Fuck me, but I find myself sighing. "I'm not in the best state right now. I thought I was, thought I could do this, but I don't think I can."

She's not angry with me. Instead, she reaches out and puts her hand on mine with professional courtesy. "I understand. It's good that you tried, though. Thank you for tonight."

The grace humbles me. I leave the restaurant on foot, walking the streets of New York aimlessly, thinking of her words. My mother's words. Summer's. A couple in love walks past me, their hands intertwined and their step quick. Laughter hangs in the air behind them.

With a sigh, I pull my phone out of my pocket. Layla will call Summer soon and give a report, and I know the conclusions Summer will draw. That I sabotaged this night. That I would never admit she'd done a good job.

Better to get there first.

I dial her number and hold the phone up to my ear. Cross the street and glare at a cab that brakes too late.

"Anthony?" Her voice is high. "I don't know what to do. God, I don't know what to do."

"Are you all right? Summer, are you hurt?"

"No, no, I'm at home. Ace just ate an entire box of chocolate." Her voice goes into hyperdrive again. "I don't know what to do!"

I turn on my heel and nearly crash into a middle-aged couple, heading in the direction of her apartment. "You need to get him to a vet."

"Yes, I've found one, but I don't... Can I take a dog in a taxi? He's fine now but at any moment.. Oh God."

"I can be at your place soon. I have a car. Until then, you call the veterinarian and warn them that we're coming in, okay?"

"Yes, I can do that. I'll do that. When will you be here?"

"In ten, maybe twelve minutes. I'll text when I'm downstairs with the car and you'll come down with Ace. Okay?"

"Okay," she whispers.

When I arrive, Summer is already downstairs. She has a bag slung over her shoulder and Ace in a tight leash at her side. The golden looks no worse for wear, sitting on his haunches and keeping an eye out on the street, like he's determined to keep her safe. I approve.

"My driver is on the way," I tell her.

She nods, the panic in her eyes leashed. Determined. "I've spent the last ten minutes on the internet. As long as he gets there in time, he should be fine."

"Good."

Her blonde hair is pulled back in a ponytail, dark smudges under her eyes from the panicked tears I'd heard on the phone. But now she's all business.

I don't ask about the hows or the whys. There will be time for that later.

My driver doesn't comment on the dog in the backseat, or the destination. He just floors it. I hold the door open for Summer when we arrive at the emergency clinic, and thanks to having called ahead, they're waiting for us. I have a seat in the waiting room while Summer follows a bespectacled veterinarian into a treatment room. Ace trots by her side, his tail tucked between his legs like he knows what's coming.

I feel for the guy.

I lean my head against the wall and let my eyes wander over the framed images of pets along the wall. The fluorescent lighting is a godsend compared to the dimly lit restaurant, even if the only thing here for me to study are pictures of hamsters and cats.

It's a long while before the door opens and Summer comes back out. She looks like an angel with her blonde hair beneath the fluorescent light, her eyes shimmering with relief. "He'll be fine," she says.

"He will?"

"Yes. They'll keep him overnight for observation and I will pick him up tomorrow afternoon. They've given him medication, and active charcoal that's meant to counteract the chocolate, and..." she buries her face in her hands. "I can't believe I was so careless!"

I step closer and throw caution to the wind, wrapping my arm around her shoulders. It takes me several long moments to find the words. "Well," I say. "You did the right thing by getting him here so quickly."

Summer nods into her hands and leans into me, like she's grateful for the support. Like I'm actually comforting her. "Thank you. I don't know what I would have done if you hadn't called right then."

"You would have figured it out."

She takes a deep breath and lifts her head, shimmering eyes meeting mine. "Oh God, you were on your date. Did I interrupt you?"

"I called you," I remind her, "and no, it was no problem. Let me take you home."

She nods and puts her hand on my arm, fingers curving, and lets me guide her to the door. "Thank you, Anthony. Truly."

11

ANTHONY

For the second time in a week, I find myself in Summer Davis's living room near midnight. It's a dangerous habit.

She's kicked off her shoes and taken her hair down and is now lying on the couch across from me, turning a ruined box of chocolates over in her hands.

"Dave brought them when he came by to pick me up," she says. "I put them on the hallway table. Ace must have knocked them off somehow, but he's never done anything like that before."

"Hard to resist if chocolate truffles are scattered all over the floor."

She pushes up from the couch and throws the remnants in the trash with firm movements. "Never again," she says. "From here on out, my household will be one hundred percent chocolate free. I'll never own a piece again in my life."

"Drastic," I say. "You couldn't have it in, like, a sealed Tupperware container?"

Summer pours us a glass of water each before sitting down on the couch opposite me again, pulling her legs up beneath her. "You're good at thinking rationally, you know."

"Thank you."

She drains half of her glass and pushes back a tendril of hair. "Today was far too much excitement for me."

"Do you want to talk about him?"

"Ace?"

"Yes. Why do you bring him into the office most days? Actually, why do you have a golden retriever in central New York?"

She sighs and looks down at her hands. "He might be happier upstate. But he does alternate between living with me and with my parents, so I think he gets the best of both worlds, but... well. It's kind of a funny story. He was supposed to be a guide dog."

"What?"

"Yes, a guide dog for the blind."

My jaw tightens. "Is that supposed to be a joke?"

"No," she says, eyes intent on me. "I mean, unless you find it funny? But no. My parents have raised retrievers for as long as I can remember. There are always one or two puppies in each litter that my mother earmarks as guide dogs. She'll foster them, too, before they go to the Foundation for the Blind for advanced training. Anyway, Ace failed halfway through his."

She turns her glass around, voice growing warm. "He was seventeen months when they withdrew him from training. Too easily distracted, you see. But he has the biggest heart, and he had so much training still in him... So my parents adopted him right back home."

The tight, suspicious fear in my chest softens at her words. A coincidence, then, that her dog was once destined to help guide the blind. Yet the reminder of blindness is unwelcome. It doesn't belong in this warm space.

Not around her.

"Your parents sound idyllic," I say.

"You think?"

"Perfect marriage, perfect kid, raising dogs... yes, I do."

Her smile widens. "Perfect kid?"

"You can't have been difficult to raise."

"You're making assumptions."

"Yes," I say, "but tell me I'm wrong?"

"You're not," she admits. "And they are pretty great. Over the last year, I've really wanted Ace with me here, too, and they've understood. He's helped."

"Helped?"

"Yes, with… well. I told you I had a pretty bad break-up a year ago."

"You did."

"Having Ace here has been lovely." She looks down at the glass of water in her hands, twisting it around. And just like that, I have to know more.

"Sorry to hear about the break-up."

She shakes her head. "Don't be. It was good, that it happened. I shouldn't have been with him."

"Then I'm happy to hear it."

"Yeah. I'm happier now, too." She puts her glass down and takes a deep breath. Gives me a look that makes it clear we're changing the subject, my insatiable curiosity be damned. "So, how was your third and final date? I understand that you might be trying to spare my feelings because of Ace… but put me out of my misery, will you?"

There's a smile waiting in the corners of her lips. Whatever acidic words I'd once longed to spew at the end of the bet are gone. They've withered in the presence of her light.

"She was lovely," I admit.

"Wow," she says, eyes on mine. They're impossible to read. "I didn't expect such a rave review. Was that why you called me? To admit defeat?"

I just look at her.

"Oh. There's a but here, right?"

I spread my hands wide, and I don't know if it's the weight of the day or the memory of her panicked voice in my ear, but more words spill through my cracks than I'd planned for.

"It's me, Summer. I'm not fit for a relationship. I'm not fit for dating. You could find me the goddess of love herself and I wouldn't ask for a second date."

"Why?" she asks.

I shake my head. Offer a piece of the truth, but like so often these days, it's the tip of an iceberg. "My last break-up wasn't the best either."

"Ah," Summer says. She leans back on the couch, the cut-off jeans she's wearing revealing a sliver of smooth skin at the ankle. "Look at us, then. You own a matchmaking company and I work at one, and neither of us seems capable of dating."

"Neither of us? What happened with the delivery boy?"

"Dave," she says. "His name is Dave."

"Dave," I repeat.

She looks down at her hands, twisting them over to play with one of her nails. "It was good. He was nice and funny. We went to a Korean barbecue down the street. But I just couldn't… I don't know. I couldn't get into it."

My gaze zeroes in on her face. Is she blushing, or is the light playing tricks on me again? "But you liked him?"

She shrugs. "Well enough, I suppose. But I don't think I'll go out with him again. It doesn't seem fair, really. To be honest, I haven't thought about him once since I came home and saw that Ace had eaten all of his chocolate."

"Poor guy," I say. By no fault of his own, he'd become associated with poisoning her dog. Perhaps I'm a bastard for it, but I can't find it in me to feel sorry for him.

She pushes off the couch with a yawn, and damn, I should go. She wants some peace and quiet, and not her boss hanging around, overstaying his welcome.

But she beats me to it, walking barefoot across the oriental rug to the kitchenette. "I'm about to make some tea. Would you like some?" she asks. "You don't strike me as a tea-drinking kind of man, but you know, I don't want to assume."

My hand relaxes on my thigh. "I'll have whatever you're having."

"That means chamomile tea with a drop of honey."

"Great." I can't remember the last time I drank tea, or had someone make me… things.

My gaze snags on the bucket list still pinned to her wall. With her back to me, I cross to it and turn on the flashlight on my phone. Bathed in artificial light, I can make out a number of items.

Learn how to windsurf. Swim naked in the ocean. Learn to speak Spanish. Visit all fifty states. Record a demo in a studio.

I put my phone down just in time. "Oh, you're back at the list," she says. "I should take that thing down."

"No you shouldn't. I didn't know you sang?"

Summer puts my mug on the coffee table and curls up on her couch, legs crossed beneath her. A sheath of blonde hair falls forward as she stares into her mug as if she's trying to read her fortune. "I used to."

"You used to sing."

"Yes. I majored in business in college, but with a minor in music. I can't play an instrument to save my life, but... I've been singing for as long as I can remember."

I raise an eyebrow, but Summer holds up a hand. "I know exactly what you're going to say. Don't."

"Do you?"

"Yes, you were going to ask me to sing something."

"Maybe, but maybe not. And even if I were, would it be so terrible?"

She gives a mock shiver, but there's real censure in her eyes. "Yes. I won't sing on command."

"All right, little canary," I say, taking a sip of the tea she's prepared for me. It's not half bad. "I'm not surprised, you know."

"That I sing?"

"You seem like the type." Golden, glorious, smiling. She should be a cartoon princess, walking through the forest with woodland creatures trailing behind. Hell, I feel like one, sitting here in her apartment for no apparent reason for the second time in a week.

"I don't know what to make of that," she says.

"It was a compliment, I think."

"Then thank you," she says, smiling. "I think."

We look at each other for a long moment, her smiling, me lost. I'm acutely aware of the fact that it's past midnight and she's in a pair of tight jeans and a tank top.

But then she sits up pin straight. "Do you hear that?"

"Hear what?"

"It's raining! Damn."

I watch in astonished silence as she flies up from the couch, grabbing towels that had been stuffed behind the couch. She rolls them up tightly and fits them against the windowsills.

"They leak?" I ask.

"Yes. The caulking is bad, I think. Anyway, every time it rains, without fail, I have wet windowsills."

"Summer," I ask, "how long has that been the case?"

"Oh, a few months, at least."

"You haven't told your landlord?"

"I have, but she's busy."

I narrow my eyes at her, but she gives me a serene smile, sinking down on the couch again. "You're renting from your aunt?" I guess.

She nods. "Vivi will fix them."

"You should remind her."

"I will," she says, stretching her legs out. I'm about to insist when she gives a soft sigh and leans her head against the back of the couch, closing her eyes. "This is nice."

My gaze returns to my mug. Surprised to find that I actually agree with her on that.

"You know," she says, "I have a few great friends in the city, but most of them are from college, and they have their own lives. I don't spend as much time with them as I'd like."

This is when I should leave. I know it in my bones, but my body is glued to the couch. Perhaps she's a siren.

Capturing men, soul after soul.

"I don't with mine, either," I admit. Somehow, it doesn't sound quite as pathetic spoken out loud in her warm apartment.

"You have your business partners," she points out.

"I do, although we mostly work together." Not to mention all my friendships have an expiration date.

"You grew up in the city?"

"Yeah."

She makes a soft humming sound, and I crack open one of my lids to see her regarding me thoughtfully. I can only imagine I look a sight, sprawled in my suit on her couch, holding a tea mug with peonies painted on it.

"You're thinking about something," I tell her.

"Yes," she admits. "Just that you're very fascinating, Anthony."

I close my eyes again. "Sure."

"I mean it, though. You're full of contradictions. You never say or do what I expect you to. You don't react to the women I set you up with the way I'd planned. You buy a matchmaking company you despise."

"I don't despise Opate."

She chuckles. "Right. You like my dog, despite pretending you don't."

"I've never pretended not to like your dog."

"Mmhm, sure." Now there's laughter in her voice. But I don't mind being the object of her fascination, or her laughter.

"And now I'm here in your apartment after midnight," I complete for her. "Drinking tea."

"Yes. You're fascinating, that's all."

"Happy to entertain." I give a half-bow from the couch and she chuckles again, turning back to her tea. This time, I'm fairly certain she's blushing. No trick of the lights here.

"You're part of one of the city's most illustrious families," she continues, "but you didn't mind eating pepperoni pizza out of a box with me. Right after, mind you, spending more money than most people earn in a year on a watch you can't wear."

"Hey," I tell her, something in me drawing tight at her words. "I would look great in a woman's diamond watch."

Her answering smile is too blinding, so I close my eyes again.

"And you're funny, too. But I don't think you joke too often, and I think your laugh is rarer still."

"I'm not one of your clients," I say, meeting her gaze. "No need to keep trying to figure me out."

Summer's mouth opens on a soft exhale. "Perhaps I just want to learn more about a friend."

"A friend," I repeat, running my thumb around the rim of the mug. Looking at her and knowing I'll never be satisfied with just that, but unable to ever offer her more.

12

SUMMER

"Want to see him again?" I ask my parents. I don't wait for the reply, turning my camera around to show Ace on the video call. He's sprawled on the rug, a chew toy between his front paws. He lifts his head to look at me. *Yes?* it says. *What do you want me to do?*

"Oh, he really does look great," my mother says. "I'm so happy your friend could help get you to the veterinarian so quickly."

"Was it Posie?" my dad asks. "Someone from college?"

"A new friend, actually. Through work."

"That's great, honey. You need friends in the city."

"You sure do. Hey, don't forget to give him nice, gentle food tonight and tomorrow, okay? His stomach has been through a lot. White rice, oatmeal, chicken."

"I will, Mom."

Ace returns to his chew toy, healthy and hale again. It's the sweetest relief. Never again, I think.

"Have you spoken to that vocal coach again? The one you contacted for singing lessons?"

I shake my head, and my mother sighs. "You used to sing all the time, honey. You sang before you could talk!"

"That was a long time ago."

"Not that long," she says.

"I'll look into it," I promise, not knowing if I will. Singing has been... difficult since Robin. During his time, too. The little comments about my pitch and my breathing. The smirk as he listened for something to comment on. He'd sucked all the fun out of it.

He'd done that with most things.

"That's good. Your cousin Frida is getting married in a few months, you know. I'm sure she'd love it if you sang there."

I groan. "Mom."

"Okay, okay. I'll lay off."

My dad peeks over her shoulder. "How's the new boss? The one Viv sold the company to?"

"He's okay," I say, shrugging. The picture of casualness. "He's a venture capitalist. He wants us to make more money, and that's pretty much it."

"I'm not sure Viv is taking too kindly to that," my dad says. His gaze locks on something over my shoulder. The towels, still rolled and pressed against my windowsills. "What's behind you, sweetie?"

"Oh, the windows leak when it rains."

"They do what?"

"It's an old building."

"That's not an excuse. You need to tell your aunt. She's your landlord," my dad says. "Typical of my sister to not schedule inspections. How long has it been like that?"

"A few months, I think. Maybe more."

"Have you mentioned it to her?"

"Yes," I say, but I'm smiling. "You know how she is, though. Razor sharp but as distracted as they come." Not to mention she's been gone a lot, lately. Taking long lunches and three-day weekends.

"I'll talk to her if you like," my dad offers.

"Thanks, but I'll bring it up again this coming week."

"You do that, sweetie. Remember, you're paying her rent, not getting to live there out of charity. So you demand what you need to. Vivienne will remedy it in a heartbeat if she actually listens to the problem."

"Yes, Dad."

He smiles. "That's my girl."

When we finally hang up, right after Mom gives me a virtual tour of the new kitchen garden she's planted and let me say hi to the dogs, homesickness is a tight knot in my throat. The place is most beautiful in the summer, and it's already halfway through June.

I clean up the remnants of my Sunday-breakfast-turned-brunch-turned-lunch and grab the two tea mugs still left out on the coffee table from Friday night. His, with peonies, and mine, with a cartoon dog. I look down to watch Ace lying comfortably on the floor, alive and pain-free.

Grabbing my phone, I write him a quick text.

Summer: Thank you so much for your help the other night and for staying a while after. I owe you.

I stare at the text and fight against the quick beating of my heart. It's absurd to care this much—that him reading my words, looking down at his phone, matters this much.

But it does.

He'd been calm and steady on Friday… and the way he'd sat on my couch that night? With his dark hair tousled and long legs stretched out in front of him, he'd looked like a lazy god. One constantly passing judgement on those around him.

One with layers and layers of secrets.

His response comes ten minutes later, sending me vaulting over the couch to where I'd thrown my phone.

Anthony: You're welcome. How's Ace doing?

I sink down onto my couch and let my fingers fly over the phone. Picture him staring down at his, waiting for my response.

Summer: He was tired when I picked him up yesterday and has been sleeping a lot. But today his mood is up and he's been playing a bit with his toys. Almost back to normal!

Anthony: That's great. Have you told the delivery guy what happened because of his chocolates?

Summer: No, of course not! He might feel terrible, when he did nothing wrong.

He doesn't answer that. I look at my phone for an embarrassingly long time.

Not ready to let this be the end.

My heart in my throat, I cast out for anything to say. Anything that might keep this going. When I'd walked back home with Ace yesterday, a woman had handed out flyers for a beer tasting. Would that be overstepping my boundaries?

But he hadn't objected the other night when I called us friends. Spending time with him is fun. Challenging. Taunting the cynic from his shell, his presence steady and his humor surprisingly dark.

My phone chimes again. He's sent me an image.

A packet of chamomile tea sits on the dark wood of a kitchen counter.

Anthony: I got a new toy to play with, too. It was all right when you made it.

I'm smiling as I respond.

Summer: Happy I converted someone to tea! It's great for helping you sleep, too.

Anthony: So I've gathered.

Throwing caution to the wind, I type an invite. Prepare

myself for his immediate refusal, or worse, silence.

Summer: If you're in the mood for something stronger, though, the bar on my street has a beer tasting tonight. Want to join?

It takes a few minutes for the response to come, and when it does, it's only two words.

Anthony: Just us?

Summer: Yes.

This time, his reply is instant.

Anthony: Text me the address.

———

"I had no idea it would be so crowded here," I say, pushing my way past a group of students. One of them is wearing a home-knit beanie, the other a crop top. Not exactly Anthony Winter clientele.

He mutters behind me. "Really poor lighting in here."

I suppose that's true, but it gives the place some charm. Cozy, instead of seedy. I stop at one of the few empty tables. "Is here all right?"

He nods and we have a seat on rickety chairs. A single, fake flower dangles precariously on its equally fake stem in a beer glass on the table. "How'd you find this place?" he asks.

"They were handing out flyers on the street when I walked past and I took one."

Anthony shakes his head. "Only you would actually stop to accept one."

"Hmm. You wouldn't?"

"Definitely not. I doubt anyone raised in New York would."

"Imagine all the things you miss," I say. "Beer tastings in

college bars? Invitations to dodgy underground clubs?"

"The horror." His eyes glitter with dry amusement, but they turn sharp as a waiter approaches us. He has a towel slung over a shoulder and a stack of menus in hand.

"Here for the tasting?"

"We sure are," I say.

"Great, welcome guys. Here's the list of lagers, ales and IPAs we'll be serving tonight." He hands us a menu each, slightly sticky to the touch. "There's a scorecard tucked in there somewhere, too. We'll be serving them in twenty-minute intervals."

"Okay, awesome," I say. "How about… oh."

He's already retreating, weaving through the crowd to attend to other newcomers.

"Excellent customer service," Anthony says dryly. He's wearing his usual scowl, but for the first time, I'm seeing him in something other than a suit.

A grey sweater stretches across his shoulders, clinging to muscles previously hidden. A thick watch rests on his wrist, no diamonds on it. He runs a hand through his thick, dark hair absently and stares down at the beer menu. I want to reach over and trace his bearded jawline. See if it would tickle against my hand.

He closes the menu. "Read about the first beer, Summer."

"Read aloud?"

"Yes. I enjoy your voice."

"Okay. Yes," I say, smiling. I tell him about the nutty character of the first pale ale, glancing up at him every so often.

He notices, of course. "What's the matter?"

"Nothing. I'm just…" I put the menu down. "I want to say thank you again. This beer tasting is on me, by the way. All of it."

He shakes his head. "No."

"I insist, Anthony. Please. You helped me with Ace, and without your car… thank you."

"You're welcome," he says, dark gaze softening. "But under no circumstances are you paying for this, Summer."

I sweep a hand out at our surroundings. "Please? Look, I know this isn't your usual scene, and I had no idea it would be this crowded. Please let me."

"Not my usual scene?"

"Yes. It's not exactly a place we'd set up an Opate date at, you know."

Anthony crosses his arms over his chest, but the look in his eyes is anything but agitated. "Who do you think I am, exactly? I'm not like one of your customers."

I smile down at the menu.

He catches it, of course. "You think I am?"

"Maybe, yes."

He shakes his head, but there's a smile lurking in the corner of his mouth. "You once told me you were an excellent judge of character. I'm strongly doubting that."

"Perhaps I let a few things I'd heard about you influence my thinking," I admit. "But in my defense, you bought a Cartier watch on auction that you can't wear. Does it even fit you?"

"No."

"See? You've had a hand in creating your own reputation."

"You said you'd heard a few things about me."

"Yes, well, I'm not allowed to talk about what clients tell me after dates."

His eyebrows lower. "But?"

"But, hypothetically, I might have been informed about certain connections your... well, your family has."

"My surname," he says. "Surely you made the connection before either of my dates pointed it out to you?"

I give an apologetic shrug. "I didn't. I'm sorry?"

Anthony shakes his head and looks up at the ceiling. "My grandfather would be rolling in his grave if he heard that."

"He would? Oh, I'm sorry."

But then his gaze returns to mine and it's bursting with silent laughter. "Honestly, how do you work at a place like Opate and not know this? Not care about it?"

"You know why," I tell him archly, but I'm smiling. "I'm in it for the *right* reasons."

"Ah, yes. True love."

"Exactly."

"You know, I thought you were just feeding me a line the first time I met you."

"And now?"

"Now I know you actually believe it. I don't know if that makes you honorable or naive."

I laugh, crossing my legs beneath the table. The movement settles my leg next to his.

Neither of us shifts away.

"Can't I be both?"

The waiter arrives with our first two beers, one each, and gives us pens for our scorecards. I gaze over the rim of my beer at Anthony. He commits fully, taking a deep drag of his ale and commenting on its flavor. Even adds little x's to the scorecard.

We drink and talk, and it's surprisingly pleasant, drowning out the sounds of students singing along to an indie rock song at the table next to us.

One of them ambles past us someway through the third beer, aiming for a stool. He gets on it with a wobble. "I was just dared!" he yells, "by my lovely girlfriend, that I had to tell you all… no, just wait a moment. Just give me a moment!"

He's escorted out by our waiter, another burly man on the other side, his beanie askew.

"Christ," Anthony mutters when they're gone.

I lean back in my chair and laugh. Laugh at the idea of him, sitting here in this place, going through the motions.

He raises the third beer to me. I raise mine in response, feeling the pleasant buzz of alcohol in my head. "To friends," he says.

"To friends," I agree. Keep my eyes on his as we both drink. My stomach flips once, twice. "That reminds me, actually. Is it odd to be friends with your boss?"

"I'm not technically your boss," he says, voice deepening. "Your aunt is."

"That's true. I haven't told her, by the way. Not about our initial bet and not that I was your date. Perhaps we shouldn't be spending time together like this, but..." I shrug and look up at him. Give him a smile.

"You don't have to worry about me, Summer."

"I don't?"

"No. I'm not out to ruin your aunt's business. I won't say a word to her about the bet, or that we apparently go to beer tastings together. And I will only give you chocolate in hermetically sealed bags."

I laugh at that, and his mouth softens. Curls up into a half-smile.

"Will you tell me something?" I ask.

"I know better than to indulge you."

"I won't ask you about your first kiss or where you'd like to get married. No prompts this time."

"Thank God."

"But I am curious. Why do you want to be friends with me?" I hold up a hand. "Don't get me wrong, I'm absolutely terrific. But it does seem like someone with your connections could walk into any room and be welcome."

"I could say the same of you," he says. "You smile at absolutely everyone, Summer. Have you noticed that?"

My fingers tighten around the pint of lager in front of me. "I hadn't, no."

"I gave you no reason to, but you still wanted to get to know me." Anthony looks from me to the crowded bar, watching the waiter weave between parties. His jaw works once. "So I'm the one who should ask you that question. Why you want to be friends with me."

"You're funny," I tell him. "Perhaps you don't think you are, but that's the truth. You're very difficult to predict, too."

His gaze returns to me. Eyes narrowed, but not in anger. In thought. I've learned to recognize the signs now. "You have no expectations of me," he says.

"I don't?"

"Very few, if so. Or if you do, they're different. All those people in the hypothetical room you mentioned? They would expect me to be one thing or the other. They all did, when we were at the charity auction."

"And I don't." Slowly, a smile stretches across my face.

"And you don't," he says. Tugs at the collar of his sweater. "No need to look smug about it."

My grin widens.

"Drink your beer," he mutters, but he's smiling down at the table. "We'll be getting our last one soon."

"Mmm. You know, it's dangerous to have a beer tasting without offering us any food. Nothing, not even a little bowl of pretzels or a tray of olives."

"A *tray* of olives?"

"A pitcher, then."

"You're losing it," he says.

"A trough," I suggest.

"A cylinder," he adds, but then shakes his head. "We've lost it."

I feel like I'm breaking inside, but in the best possible way, like a layer of ice shattering and thawing. "That's why we should have had food with this. We would have been so much better with words if we had."

"You're tipsy again."

"You're not?" I ask, looking at him over the rim of my beer glass. "I get that you have a higher tolerance than me, but come on."

"I'm not tipsy," he says. "I have at least a foot of height on you, not to mention I drink more often."

"Hey, you don't know what I do in my spare time."

"I know enough to be sure it's not downing beers like there's no tomorrow. Careful there, shorty. I'll finish the last of your final beer."

"How self-sacrificing," I say.

"That's me. Noble to the core."

Anthony, the sneaky bastard, pays while I'm in the ladies'

room. He listens to my protests with half a smile, shoving his wallet into the pocket of his dark slacks. "You have to be quicker around me, Summer."

"Next time," I warn him.

"I'll be on alert." He opens the front door and I step into the mid-summer warmth. The air is humid, but the heat of the day has softened, pleasant now.

"We forgot our scorecards!"

He chuckles. "How will we be possibly go on in life?"

"But I liked that second beer. The one from the little brewery in Montana. What was it called?"

"Green Eagle Ale."

"That's it," I say, snapping my fingers. "I'm going to have to get a keg of that."

"A keg? Summer, how much beer do you usually drink?"

"Honestly?"

"I'd prefer it, yes."

I laugh and he slips a hand down my back, steering me around a streetlamp that suddenly, and quite rudely, appears in my way. "I don't drink a lot of beer at all. It's not really my favorite."

He's silent for what feels like forever as we walk down the street to my apartment.

"But you suggested a beer tasting," he says.

"Yes, well, I thought it would be fun. It seemed like something friends do in the city."

He snorts, but there's something soft in the tone. The cynic is gone for tonight. "Next time, suggest something you actually enjoy, Summer."

The two beautiful words spread like warm honey through my veins. *Next time.*

"Okay, I will. Next time. But I had fun tonight."

"So did I," he says. We reach the door to my apartment building far too soon. It had felt smart to choose a bar on my street, but now, it strikes me as a grave error. The walk was too short.

I look up at him. "Anthony."

"Summer," he says.

I run a hand over the back of my neck, where tendrils of hair stick to my damp skin. "Let's play around with a hypothetical."

He raises an eyebrow. "Okay."

"Hypothetically, if you weren't my boss, and we weren't just friends, do you think we'd ever…? Well?"

Something swirls in his eyes before they drop to my lips. They linger there for so long I feel lightheaded with anticipation. "Don't go there," he murmurs.

"Why not?"

"Because we're friends. Because I'm not a romantic, Summer. You know I don't believe in love or relationships. I'm not… like you. And I don't want to hurt you."

The soft denial feels rote, and so completely at odds with the way his body curves toward me. Like it knows what it wants despite his words.

"Okay," I whisper. Not a surrender, but a strategic withdrawal.

"Okay?"

"Yeah, okay."

Our eyes hold for an eternity-long second. A strand of dark hair has fallen over his square brow, like it believes in his stoic facade just as little as I do.

"Summer," he says.

I sway closer. "Yes?"

He bends down and my eyes flutter closed as he presses the briefest of kisses to my cheek. The soft scratch of his beard against my skin sends goose bumps racing along my arms.

"Don't think I haven't thought about it," he murmurs.

"Oh," I breathe.

When I open my eyes again he's smiling to himself. He gives me a nod and walks away, hands in his pockets. I watch him until he disappears into the New York crowd, a man amongst many, before I finally open the front door to my building.

It takes my heart far longer than that to calm down.

13

ANTHONY

I don't meet my own gaze in the mirror as I give my suit one last look. Tug the collar into place. Ignore the reason I'm really going out today.

I could ask my assistant to drop off the papers to Opate. I could post them. I could even wait until the meeting in two weeks with the app developers, when Vivienne Davis will be there too.

But the sky outside my windows is a vivid blue, and perhaps a walk wouldn't be the worst thing in the world.

Neither would seeing Summer again.

I don't call my driver or hail a taxi. The streets beckon and the city's pulse feels in tune with my own. The sweet smell of candied almonds mingles with exhaust and subway wafting up from the grates beneath my feet. A cabbie yells to a pedestrian across the street.

It's a testament to everything I will one day lose.

New York, the city I love down to my bones, will become a deadly obstacle course for me when I can no longer see. It will evict me, brutally and with force, if I don't leave it first.

And all the fucking things the doctor pesters me about won't do a thing to help me, even if I'd consider them. *Have you looked into learning Braille? A guide dog? A cane?*

But doing that meant giving in. Surrendering. Accepting my fate, relinquishing, submitting, dying.

Will I forget what the city looks like one day?

The knowledge is like a sharp, angry weight in my chest. One that reminds me all too well why I'd told Summer what I had outside of her door the other night.

I can never tell her.

And yet, dating her without her knowing would be unforgivable, too.

Friendship, then. It's been a very long time since I tried to tread that line.

The receptionist looks startled when I arrive, hands fumbling with the lip gloss she'd been applying. "Mr. Winter?"

"Just here to drop off some documents for Ms. Davis."

She looks from Summer's half-closed door to Vivienne's open one.

"Vivienne Davis," I clarify.

Suzy nods. "She's out for lunch, but I'll be happy to put them on her desk and let her know you came by."

I hand her the envelope and keep from glancing at Summer's door. She'd been right to be concerned about our interactions making their way back to this office. As much as I hate it, I know how it would look, too.

But then her door creaks as it's nudged open, nails clicking against hardwood floor. Ace winds his way around my legs, a cold nose pressed against my hand.

I rub my hand over his silky ears and his tail wags softly, dark eyes looking up at me. Reminding me that I might one day need someone like him.

"Hello." Summer is standing in the open doorway to her office, her golden hair braided into a rope down the side of her neck. "My aunt is out at the moment."

"So I gathered, yes." I nod to her office. "Have you had a chance to look over the suggestions the app development team sent over?"

"Yes. I actually have a few thoughts on it, if you have a moment, Mr. Winter."

"I do, in fact."

"Excellent." She beckons and I join her in her office, the door shutting behind us.

Summer gives me a slow smile. "Hello."

"Hi," I say. Glance from her to the sad, half-eaten salad on her desk and the summer weather outside her window. "Come out and have lunch with me."

"Really?"

"Yes, really."

Her smile widens until it becomes a physical thing aching in my chest. "All right. You leave first and then I'll join you downstairs?"

I bend and give Ace a pat to hide my smile. "Yes."

Fifteen minutes later we're walking into the park next to her office building. Summer steers us right to the lone bench unoccupied by office workers and sinks down on it with a thankful sigh. Like a sunflower, she turns her face up to the sky.

"This was exactly what I needed," she says.

My hands tighten on the sandwich I'd bought on the way, the flimsy excuse to spend more time with her. I look away from her beauty before I'm tempted to forget it's not for me.

"You often eat lunch at your desk?"

"Sometimes," she admits. "We hadn't been doing so well before you guys bought us. I mean, you know that."

"I do."

"One of our problems is that we don't get repeat customers. If we've done our job well, they're settled into a relationship and will never need our services again."

"Kind of a flawed business model."

"My aunt should have thought about that before she started," she says. "Or perhaps we should just do a poorer job."

"That's always an option. Embrace mediocrity, Summer."

That earns me a laugh, one that sets off a tightening in my

chest. "This is coming from you, right? The embodiment of success?"

I turn my head. "I'm the embodiment of success?"

"Let's see," she says, counting on her fingers. "Co-founder of a wildly successful venture capitalist firm, rich beyond measure, part of the Winter family… do you want to add anything?"

"The epitome of male beauty," I deadpan.

She laughs again, reaching up to brush a tendril of blonde hair from her forehead. "I forgot about that one, of course. How could I embrace mediocrity when you haven't?"

I shake my head and lean back against the bench, closing my eyes against the sunshine. It's warm against my skin. "Don't compare yourself to me at all."

"That's an option, I suppose." I hear the tear of plastic as she opens the rest of her salad. "I bought a few of the lagers we drank the other night."

"Really?"

"Yep. They were in my local supermarket." She crosses her legs, the summer dress she's wearing sliding up over tanned knees.

I re-focus on my sandwich. "Your windows? Have you spoken to your aunt about them?"

"Yes, I have. She was horrified."

"Rightly so."

"They're getting fixed next weekend. I don't know how she got a hold of carpenters so quickly. I *think* she helped set up the meeting of the head of a construction firm with his wife, and that's why?" Summer chuckles. "My aunt knows more people than the Yellow Pages."

I'd gathered something similar from my time interacting with Vivienne Davis. Getting her on board with the changes to the company will be necessary if we're to succeed with it at all. She'll make for an excellent ally or a terrible enemy.

"I'll have to be out of the apartment for a day or two," Summer continues. She slides one foot out of her wedge sandal and buries her foot in the sun-warmed grass. "They'll mostly have to re-caulk the windows, but apparently some of the products aren't the best to breathe in."

"Where will you stay?"

"I'm not sure. I could go up to my parents' place, but it's quite far. My aunt would probably take me in if I asked."

"When is this?"

"Next week. Thursday to Friday."

"I have a place in Montauk, and I'm going next weekend," I say, making the decision to as I say it. "You're welcome to come along."

Her blue eyes hold genuine surprise. "Anthony, are you sure?"

"Yes." Not at all. "It's got more than enough space. Ace could run on the beach. Besides," I say, adding the pièce de resistance, "there are always windsurfers out there. I'm sure we could find you an instructor."

"Wow... are you serious?"

I shrug. "Yes. Unless you'd rather not, of course."

Her face splits into a smile that could rival the sun. "Oh, of course I want to! That's incredibly kind of you, Anthony. I don't know what to say."

"You can bring those beers," I say. "Print out a few scorecards."

"I've been dared by my girlfriend," she declares, "to tell you all that—"

I groan. "Please don't."

But she's laughing and shifting on the bench, her thigh coming to rest against mine. I can't believe I've agreed to this, let alone suggested it. Navigating the house at dark with her there to watch. The headaches have been good for the past week, but a migraine with her there and no way to explain...

"So you have a house in Montauk," she says, and the soft lilt of her voice brings me back. "How come?"

Oh.

The house is a test and a surrender. It's the one inch of ground I've given to the diagnosis, and having purchased a place for my future self, I've barely spent any time there. No one knows about the house who isn't my lawyer, accountant or assistant. They'll all ask why I bought it. And the answer isn't one I can speak out loud.

I need a place to live when the music ends, when the curtain falls, and the only thing remaining is darkness.

The place is gorgeous, with a view of the ocean that mocks me every single time I see it. Beautiful. And one day completely pointless. I could be living in a cave and not know it.

"As the embodiment of success," I tell her, "of course I have a house in the Hamptons."

Summer laughs, the sound sweeping away some of my fears. But I know they're only waiting in the wings for their cue. This show is one I can't stop watching, no matter how much I might want to.

14

SUMMER

My weekend bag slides through my fingers and hits the hard-wood floor with a soft thud. "Wow," I breathe. "This place must have cost you a fortune!"

Anthony gives a snort, turning from me to the windows that line the far wall. They open up to a patio, and beyond it, the beach beckons. Ace pads forward and does a sweep of the room, his head low and nose to the ground.

"I'm sorry," I say. "I know it's not polite to comment on finances like that, but… wow. This house is stunning."

"I don't mind. To tell you the truth, it was expensive."

"How are you not here all the time?" I run my hand over the marble kitchen counter, made with soft, rounded corners. Two giant cloud couches line the back of the room.

"Well, I have work in the city," he says. I hear the sound of running water, a glass being filled. "So?" he finally says. "Do you like it?"

"Like it? Anthony, this house is gorgeous. Can I?"

"Go ahead."

I open the doors to the patio. The midday sunlight is hot against my skin and a gust of wind tugs at my linen dress. "Oh my God."

"It is nice," he agrees, almost reluctantly.

I nudge his shoulder with mine. Well, I try to, but he's so much taller than me that it's his upper arm I get. "It's gorgeous. The beach is so empty, too."

"This part of Montauk is more secluded. People who don't live here don't generally come here."

I glance through the trees to my right, but I can't see the next property over. These oceanside villas are like entire ecosystems, existing on their own.

"You really like it here," Anthony says. Bends down to put a hand on Ace's flank, my dog leaning against his leg.

"Oh, yes. Who wouldn't? Were you doubting I'd be anything but impressed?"

His lip curls into that small half-smile. "Look to the left."

"No," I say immediately. "You can't have that too! It's not allowed."

"It was included in the purchase."

The clean lines of an infinity pool are nestled against the side of the house. It's the perfect size, complimenting the house rather than detracting from it. Emphasizing the ocean rather than competing with it.

"I don't know where to swim first," I breathe.

Anthony chuckles and heads back inside, like all this grandeur and beckoning glory is nothing at all. I suppose it's not, when you're used to it.

He picks up my weekend bag. "Your bedroom is down here," he says. "I'm guessing you won't mind an ocean view?"

"Okay, now you're just being blasé to annoy me."

The look he shoots me over his shoulder confirms it. "Is it working?"

"No, because while I'm here, I'm unannoyable. Nothing can take me down off this high."

"A fancy house, huh? That's all it takes to wow you." But there's genuine warmth in his voice, and as he pushes open the door to a bedroom, I forget my response entirely. It looks like a luxurious hotel room at an expensive resort. Beige wallpaper, a four-poster bed with fluffy white linens, and windows that over-look the deep blue ocean. It's like I've gone on vacation.

Ace nudges my legs to get a peek, too, and I step aside to let him explore.

"You're quiet," Anthony says. "Good quiet?"

"Very good quiet," I confirm. "Did you do the decorating yourself?"

"Very much not."

"Did you buy it furnished?"

"No."

"Well, whoever you hired really knew their job." A thought strikes me and I turn, his large form silhouetted in the door-frame. "Where's your bedroom?"

Anthony nods to the right. "The next door down the hall."

"Oh." My skin feels flush beneath the thin fabric of my dress.

Anthony reaches for the collar of his shirt and gives it a tug. "Yeah. Well… make yourself at home, Summer."

"Thank you again for letting me stay here."

"Of course. The fridge should be stocked and the wi-fi pass-word is out in the hall."

"Perfect. I'm thinking of going swimming and walking Ace along the beach. Do you want to join?" I ask, lifting my bag up on the bed.

"I have work to do."

"Always hard at work," I say. I dig through my bag and before I let myself overthink it, I pull my bikini out. Toss it onto the bed.

Anthony tracks the movement. "Like I said, make yourself at home. I'll be in the office down the hall if you need anything."

"Thank you."

But he's gone before I've finished the sentence.

I'm sundrunk, sandy and happy when I return to the house later that day. Ace is skipping along my side like he, too, has left all of his troubles behind in the city. What a place this is!

The only downside, the only thorn beneath my skin, has been the idea of Anthony spending the day working indoors.

"Stay here," I tell Ace. He sinks down onto his haunches and looks up at me like he knows what's coming and he's not pleased with it.

Reaching for the nozzle attached to the outdoor shower, I rinse him down, including paws and ears. He handles it with as much grace as he can and only whines softly once.

"There we go," I say finally. "You're salt water and sand free. But very, very wet."

I make it two steps away before Ace takes care of the problem himself. He shakes it off like he's dancing to a pop song, water droplets flying every which way. I laugh at his poofed-up fur.

"You look like a marshmallow."

He looks up at me, tongue lolling out.

"Yes, it's time for my shower too. Come on, buddy."

I spend too long in the giant en-suite bathroom, but with each minute beneath the warm water it feels like another worry melts away. My voice echoes against the tiles as I sing, massaging shampoo into my scalp.

My hair is still wet when I walk barefoot to the kitchen. He'd said there was a fully stocked fridge, hadn't he? I've just sized up its contents when Ace's tail starts wagging against the floor.

Anthony's changed into a linen button-down, but the black slacks are still in place. The scowl isn't. He puts his hands in his pockets and looks at the food I've lined up on the kitchen counter.

"Filming a cooking show?" he asks.

I give him a wide smile. "I'm trying to think of what we want for dinner. I also realized I don't know what you like to eat. I know you're not a vegetarian, but that's pretty much it." I lift a packet of fresh fettuccini. "Do you like pasta? I make a great pasta carbonara."

Anthony's gaze drifts from mine to the packet in my hand. He's quiet, and I immediately realize my mistake. I reach out and put a hand on his forearm. "Oh, I'm sorry. Do you not want to eat dinner together? Perhaps you meant for us to live more like roommates, you know. You do you, and I'll do me."

"Summer," he interrupts, "I'd love to have dinner with you."

Something about the way he says it sends shivers down my spine. "Okay," I breathe.

"Okay," he says.

I let my hand drop from his arm. Look through the drawers in search of a knife. I find it and clear my throat, fighting against the pounding of my heart.

"Do you have a cutting board?"

"I don't know."

"You don't know?"

"I'm not here often, and when I am I rarely cook." But he helps me look, strong hands opening cabinet doors and exploring. To my surprise, there are no wineglasses. Nothing but water glasses. Everything stacked neatly.

"Wow," I say. "Your interior designer really is a neat freak! She would hate to see my cabinets."

"Yes, she's something like that."

There are differently shaped knobs on each cabinet, too, which seems at odd with the streamlined decor.

He helps me find what I need and then stands there, by the kitchen counter, hands in his pockets. Like he's torn between staying or retreating to the office, lost, unsure of what to do and to say.

So I grab two of the lagers we'd both liked from the beer tasting and nod to the kitchen chair. "Keep me company?"

"Okay." He cracks open both of our beers and has a seat. Takes a long swig of his. "You know, you were singing while you took your shower earlier."

I nearly drop the spatula. "I was?"

"Yes."

"Oh." Blushing, I turn back to the stove. "I'm sorry, I didn't know you could hear me."

"Don't apologize," he says. "Your voice is lovely."

The bacon and cream in front of me turns hazy as I absorb the compliment, as it reaches inside and warms something I didn't know was cold. "Thank you."

"Tell me about the singing."

With my back to him, it's easier. "I always sang as a child. My mother likes to say I sang before I spoke."

"Recording a demo is on your bucket list."

"Yes. I used to sing a lot. Even had a YouTube channel, actually." I shake my head. "But that's over now."

"You posted your singing online?"

"Yes. Just for fun, you know. Not because I thought of myself as having a voice worthy to share or anything."

"It is, though," he says. "Are the videos still up?"

I shake my head. "I took them down a few years ago."

"How come?"

Shrugging, I turn up the heat for the pasta water to boil. Edging closer to a truth I don't know if I want to reveal. "Do you remember the ex-boyfriend I mentioned? The one I broke up with a year ago?"

"Yes. You said the break-up was a good thing."

"Well, he was a musician. And a sociopath, probably." I add a laugh.

But it's not really funny.

"How so?"

"Well, he had a lot of opinions, and he was great at expressing them in very convincing ways." I'm dancing around the truth here, but admitting to being manipulated in front of this man… He's so sure and stable and radiates the kind of *fuck-off* energy that tells people to not even try.

He would have seen Robin for what he was a mile away.

I add the fettuccini to the now-boiling water. "Anyway, he didn't like me putting singing videos online. Didn't like my vocal coach, either. It went from telling me I should practice more, to how it would be better if I focused my energy elsewhere. He implied people were just indulging me when they said nice things. That he was the only one doing me a favor by telling the truth."

Anthony's voice is glacial. "He said those things."

"Yes. I don't like to call people names, but he was sort of an asshole."

"He sounds like a lot more than just an asshole."

I force nonchalance into my tone and turn to where he's sitting, straight on the kitchen chair, his dark gaze on me. It's serious.

"It's on me for listening to him, in the end," I admit. "For not realizing what he was doing until it had already happened. He was very convincing."

"He was wrong," Anthony says, fury beneath his words. "Both about your singing and about whatever else he might have told you. You know that, right?"

"I know. Even if it's sometimes hard to remember."

His frown deepens. "You will, in time, and so much the better for the rest of us. You sing beautifully."

"Thank you," I say. "He did say I was wasting my time at Opate Match, and working for my aunt."

Anthony gives a low snort of derision. "Of course you're not. It's a well-paying job and the company is well-regarded. Give it a year and it'll be a much larger operation, too. Not to mention you're great at what you do."

Every single one of his words lights up something in me. Tugs at my lips until I have to grin. "Never thought I'd see the day," I say, "when Anthony Winter defends Opate."

There's a low scraping across the floor as he pushes the chair back and joins me by the counter. He holds the bowl as I drain the pasta into it, and we both watch as I add the sauce, combining the two into a mouthwatering dish.

"I don't have to believe in love," he says, "to respect the fact that you do."

Something lodges in my throat and I nod, keeping my eyes on his strong, tanned hands. Wanting to reach out and slide my fingers through his.

We grab plates and the food and head out onto the patio. Ace joins us and Anthony uncorks a wine bottle, pouring us a glass each.

"Thanks for not gloating," I say.

"About what?"

"I didn't get you love by the end of three dates. I know, I technically lost the bet."

He lifts one shoulder in a half-shrug. "I never expected you to."

"Ouch."

Anthony rolls his eyes. "Not like that. Like I told you, dating just isn't for me."

"I know. But anyway, thanks for not rubbing it in my face. My one and biggest failure."

He snorts and takes another bite of his pasta, his hair nearly ink-black beneath the evening sun. A sliver of tanned skin and dark chest hair peeks out from the V of his button-down.

"Like I said, Summer, you should embrace mediocrity."

"I can't," I say. "Not when you've invited me to a house that's practically the Garden of Eden come to life. How will I ever be able to settle for anything less?"

"Your apartment doesn't have a lot of room for an infinity pool," he points out.

"No, nor does it have an ocean view."

He clears his throat. "I called the windsurfing company earlier."

"You did?"

"Yes," he says. "They can give you a private two-hour session tomorrow. Would you like that?"

My fork and knife drop to the plate with a clatter. "You're serious."

"Dead serious, if you'd like to." But judging from the way he leans back in his chair with that half-smile on his face, he can already read the excitement on mine.

"Of course I want to! Where is it? Are you trying it too?"

He shakes his head. "No, this one is all yours. It's a beach close to here. We'll drive there."

"Windsurfing," I murmur, looking down at my plate. It had been an impulsive addition to the bucket list. The one I'd written

116

two weeks after I cut Robin out of my life. A way to reclaim myself and my goals and interests. To promise myself to push the boundaries.

Windsurfing had been a crazy, wild, totally unlike me suggestion. I was raised inland. But here it was, coming true.

"You're quiet," he says.

"Yes, because I can't believe I'm actually going to do this. I might be awful at it."

"If you've never tried before, you probably will be," he says. "All beginners are."

"That's true. Nothing to worry about then."

"The instructors are professionals. They've seen hundreds of beginners before."

I eat in stunned silence, contemplating my luck. The man in front of me. The weekend plans I have to look forward to. Anthony looks at me every now and then, like he knows exactly what I'm thinking.

At this point, I'm not surprised if he does.

The night is warm, but the breeze coming in from the ocean has more than a little freshness to it. Goose bumps rise across the bare skin of my arms.

Anthony notices. He reaches into a woven basket behind the patio door, pulling out a bundled blanket. "The decorator put them here for this very purpose."

"Thanks." I sweep it around my shoulders. "I suppose we have an early morning tomorrow, then. Windsurfing and all."

"You don't strike me as someone who usually sleeps in, regardless."

I shake my head. "Not usually, no."

He sighs and rises to his feet. I follow suit, running a hand through my hair. It's dried in a mess of disobedient curls, impossible to tame.

He reaches out, catching a blonde lock between two fingers. "Summer," he says.

"Yes?"

"Sing in the shower every day you're here."

My hands curl around the edge of the blanket and I sway on my feet. Reach up on my tiptoes and press a kiss to his lips.

He doesn't respond.

I fall back on my feet and take a step toward the open patio door. Embarrassment makes my cheeks burn. "I'm sorry. I didn't mean... sorry."

He catches my wrist and tugs me against him, tipping my head back and slanting his mouth over mine.

Anthony doesn't kiss me like it's our first time.

He kisses me like he already knows how I taste and is addicted to it. Like I might disappear at any moment.

It takes my breath away.

The blanket slips through my fingers as I reach out and steady myself against him. His shoulders are firm beneath my grip, a steady pillar amidst the roil of sensations inside.

His hand weaves into my hair and gives the softest of tugs. He's everywhere and I never want him to leave. Never want this kiss to end. I slide my hands up the skin of his neck and find purchase in the thick, dark hair. It's sleek through my fingers, a softness I hadn't expected.

He kisses me once, twice. Slow and soft before he lifts his head. My breath is coming hard and fast, and his isn't much better. Dark, wondering eyes gaze back at me. His thumb smoothes over my hip in the smallest of caresses before he releases me.

Takes a step back, chest rising as he gets himself under control. "Goodnight, Summer," he murmurs.

I run a finger over my lips. "Goodnight, Anthony."

15

ANTHONY

Summer has been knocked down by the waves more times than I can count. Sitting on a lounge chair on the half-empty beach, I have a front-row seat. Even if I should be focusing on the emails in front of me instead of the brave girl out at sea.

It's difficult, as it always is these days, when the latter draws my gaze so easily.

She'd been bang on the money yesterday when she'd marveled at the house and the money I'd dropped on it. It had been outrageously expensive.

Even more expensive if one factors in just how little time I've spent in it. After I'd hired an expert from the Foundation for the Blind to go through the place and blind-proof it, I've avoided it. It's impossible to forget it'll one day become my prison, the one concession I've made to the doctor's diagnosis.

There had been awe in Summer's voice as she'd looked at the place, the pool, the beach. She takes pleasure in everything around her, even making dinner in a place where I've only ever had takeout. Enjoying a pool I'd never swum in. Filling the contours of my life with color everywhere she goes, and rarely staying within the lines.

My hand tightens into a fist at my side. It's not fair. None of it. Not my fucking eyesight and not her, not finding her when I'm like this, when I have nothing to offer her.

Finding the one woman you want when you have nothing to give. If the universe has a sense of humor, I imagine it's laughing at me now.

"What a world," I mutter to the dog by my feet. Ace hasn't left my side since we arrived at the beach, despite watching the seagulls wading along the water's edge with a hunter's intensity.

"You failed at being a seeing eye dog, and I'm failing at being sighted. We're a solid pair."

His head turns up at my voice and dark dog eyes meet mine. *So what*, he seems to be saying. *We're on the beach. Enjoy it.*

Perhaps he's right about that, or perhaps I've lost my mind to be considering what a dog might be thinking. His mind is probably focused on belly rubs and meaty bones.

I shade my eyes and look out across the waves. Summer's wading in the shallows. She's in a wet-suit despite the warmth in the air, an instructor on either side of her. All three are laughing at the latest tumble she'd taken off the surfboard, their wet suits like second skins.

Not for the first time today, I'm wondering how the hell I was so stupid as to not book myself in for the session as well. Have I become such a fun-hating curmudgeon? Already?

She'd kissed me last night.

The tentative hope in her eyes as she did it, stretching up, taking the leap, had stunned me. Apart from the tipsy question she'd asked me after that beer tasting, my thoughts hadn't allowed me to consider the fact that she might genuinely want something.

Want me.

Or want who she thought I was, at any rate.

I should have let her run back inside, to safety, nursing nothing more than faint embarrassment. But after that first, tantalizing taste…

And now I can't concentrate for shit.

I close my laptop and surrender to the joy of watching her out in the water.

She's grinning when she walks up the beach to me later. Tendrils of wet blonde hair snake over her neck and hang in a braid down her back.

"That," she says, "was awesome."

"It looked like it."

"Were you watching the whole time? You must have seen me fall off a bajillion times."

I shake my head. "You did great by the end. Even the instructors thought so."

She snorts and looks over her shoulder to where they're disassembling the windsurfing board. "Brody has surfed since he could walk, and Luke has competed for the state. Twice. How did you manage to get *them* to instruct me?"

"Just made the right phone call," I say. Her smile makes it all worth it.

"That must have taken several phone calls. God, Anthony, I'm so full of adrenaline I feel like I could run along this beach or scale a skyscraper."

"There are none of those here."

She turns around, offering me her back, and lifts her braid out of the way. "Help me with the zipper?"

I grasp the metal between my fingers and tug the wet fabric down. It splits in a straight line down the curve of her spine, all the way to her red bikini bottoms. Two small dimples rest on either side of her spine, right there, at the low of her back.

"There you go."

She struggles out of the arms of the wet suit and laughs when it gets stuck. "These are great when they're on and awful pretty much all the time when they're not."

"I remember."

"You've surfed too?"

"Yes, but it was a long time ago."

"Can't be that long," she says, still grinning. "I've figured you out."

121

"You have?"

"Yes. You're only six years older than me, but you can't have spent all these years business-building. You told me you used to climb. What else did you do?"

"A lot of things."

"So descriptive," she says, and there's teasing in her voice.

"A bit of hiking. Kayaking. Skydived once."

"Whoa. That's intense." She sits down on one of the lounge chairs and peels her wet suit down long, tan legs. I look out onto the ocean. "Did you like it?"

"Yes. But I have no desire to do it again."

She chuckles. "I feel the same way, and I haven't even done it."

"How about windsurfing?" I ask. "Think it's something you'll do again?"

"Honestly, yes. I wasn't expecting to feel that way. It was something I added to my bucket list because it felt like a challenge, something completely unlike me, but it was fun."

I look back to her shaking off sand from the wet suit. Water droplets across her skin shimmer like diamonds under the sun. "Want to walk back?"

She tosses the wet suit over an arm. "Sure. Along the beach?"

"Yes."

"Let me just return this to Brody."

Because I'm shameless, I watch as she jogs across the beach to where the two instructors are working. If I'd had trouble being around her before, it's nothing to what seeing her in a bikini does. She has the body to match her wide, beautiful smile, and before I met her, I'd never thought of describing someone like that.

Now I don't think I'll ever want anyone else.

Summer shrugs into a sundress when she returns and takes Ace's leash from me.

"Thanks for watching him," she says.

"I didn't mind."

She puts on a pair of sunglasses and sweeps her wet hair to the side. "Did you get some work done, at least?"

"Some, yes."

"I feel kind of guilty for not working."

"But your aunt gave you these days off, didn't she?"

"Yes, but the company is in such a delicate state, I can't... No, Ace, don't touch that." She tugs softly on the leash and the golden trots away from a jellyfish resting on the shore. Her phone dings and she digs it out of her bag. "Oh, look at this," she says, showing it to me.

I have to shield my eyes from the sunlight to make out what's on the screen. "They're fixing the windows?"

"Yes, Vivienne stopped by to check on the progress."

"Where did you tell her you were this weekend?"

Summer smiles. "Well, I said I was with a friend by the beach."

"Right."

"So, not a lie."

"No," I agree. "Not a lie."

She pushes a tendril of hair back and turns to the shoreline. Slips off her sandals and carries them in her free hand. "I'm going to walk along the water's edge."

It's a moment's hesitation, but then I toe off my loafers and join her. The sand is wet and warm beneath my feet, the water reaching me cool and refreshing.

"Do you walk here often?"

I shake my head. The true reason we're walking back is practical. I'd given my driver the day off after he dropped us off here.

If she questions my use of drivers, Summer has never mentioned it. I don't know what to say if she does. That I'm no longer allowed to drive.

"My family has a house not far from here," I say. "So I know these beaches pretty well, even if it's been a long time since I spent a weekend here."

"They do? Did you spend your summers there?"

"Yes, most of them."

"Together with your brother," she says.

"With my brother," I confirm.

"That must be lovely. You know, having a sibling and all. You know I'm an only child." She kicks up water, and we both watch as Ace glances sharply that way. She does it again and he lunges after the wave, only to have it recede beneath his closing jaws.

"We were close growing up," I say. "Not so much anymore."

"How come?"

Because I'm not pleasant to be around anymore, I think, *and I don't know why I'm different around you. Why I like myself more when you're next to me.*

"We've grown apart."

"People do that sometimes," she says. "So, does that mean your brother is the one who works in the family business?"

"The family business," I repeat.

"Yes," she says, eyes sliding to mine with mirth. "You know, the one bearing your last name."

"Right, that one. Remind me, how long did it take for you to connect those dots?"

This time, the water she kicks is in my direction. I step away, raise my leg. Preparing to strike.

"No," she says. "Mercy!"

The splash I send her way barely reaches the hem of her dress, but she laughs regardless, the sound like the school bell ringing out for summer break. It's still softening my nerves when she sidles up to me again. "Why don't you work in the hotel industry, actually? Unless it's a sore subject."

"It's not." I put my hands in my pockets and turn my face up against the sun. That's something I'll still have, later. Not the light itself. But the warmth. "Do you know that company I worked on before Opate?"

"No."

"It was a small tech start-up. They were three college grads working out of a studio apartment in Brooklyn when we bought their company and gave them the financial and human capital to expand."

"They must have been so grateful."

"Grateful now, perhaps. Desperate back then. But... have you ever used Ryder, Summer? The app?"

"Yeah, of course. My friends and I sometimes use it to order food after a night out. Why?" She looks up at me, her eyes widening. "No, don't tell me."

"Yes."

"The three college grads were the ones who started Ryder?"

"They were. And while I was doing that, I was helping my business partners work on a medical company, a start-up within the finance industry, a consulting firm... My brother has spent the same years managing an already mature business. Sometimes, he'll scout locations for new hotels. Sometimes."

"You like the new," she says. "The untested."

"I like there to be stakes, and there are very few in managing the Winter corporation."

———

I'm standing with my back to the kitchen, hands in pockets, when Ace's claws against the hardwood floors signal Summer's arrival. He's rarely far from where she is. I keep my gaze on the sunset outside the window.

Ignoring the kiss between us had been difficult enough during the day. Spending the evening with her without demanding another will be torture.

But the idea of leaving feels far worse.

"You're done with work?" she asks. "How did it go?"

"It went well."

"Did you get something to eat?"

"Yes."

There's a soft rustle of fabric behind me. It's not difficult to imagine her snuggling up on the couch, bare legs pulled up beneath her. One vulnerable ankle peeking out.

"Thank you for today," she says. "Truly, Anthony, I don't

know how to thank you for this entire weekend. Letting me stay here, the windsurfing, I don't… well. Thank you."

"You shouldn't thank me."

"I shouldn't?"

"No." A low ache at my temples signal another migraine, an unwelcome reminder of what I'll never forget. "I've never enjoyed being in this house. But I have this weekend."

"Anthony…"

I turn toward her, unable to resist any longer. "Yes?"

She rises from the couch and covers the distance between us, bare-footed and with her blonde curls tumbling around her shoulders. Freckles dance across her nose and uncertainty is bright in her eyes. "Should I apologize for last night?"

"No, Summer."

"Are you sure? You shut yourself into your office as soon as we got back from the beach." She moves closer, and every nerve in my body lights up. "Anthony, I don't understand quite what—"

I kiss her.

Her soft gasp ricochets through me and a rubber band of want pulls taut and snaps inside me. My mouth moves over hers, again and again, teasing her full lips open. Her hands lock around my neck and fit there like they were meant to be.

Like she's always been made for my arms.

Her lips are too soft to tear myself away, but I do it, raising my head to meet her eyes. Needing to know how she feels.

She gives a dazed laugh. "Wow. So you do find me attractive."

"Of course I do." I shift my mouth to her cheek, wanting her soft skin beneath my lips. "It wasn't about that. Never about that."

"Then why… oh." Her breath turns shaky when I move my lips down her neck. Her hair is still damp from the shower earlier, and the scent of shampoo and Summer mixed together is the headiest of perfumes.

Knowing I shouldn't and unable to stop, I circle her waist

with my hands and blaze a path to her collarbone. Surrendering to her feels like putting down a weight I didn't know I'd carried.

Warm fingers slip beneath the collar of my shirt. They burn against my skin.

"Kiss me again," she murmurs.

And God help me, but I do. I kiss her until I know her lips better than my own, until the intimacy between us sings like a melody and the heat beneath my skin is a wildfire. I want her like I've never wanted before.

Summer smiles against me. I didn't think there was anything better than seeing that smile, but feeling it against my own lips tops it.

Her hands undo a button on my shirt, and then another. They sweep in soft, tantalizing strokes over my chest.

We make it to the couch, falling onto it like we've never done anything else. Like the time we spent lying on opposite couches was just practice for this.

Summer lifts a hand and runs it over my cheek, trailing over my stubble down to my neck. "I want you," she says.

I kiss her again and she falls back onto the cushions. The flimsy dress she's wearing molds to the curves of her body, and with me on top, I feel every single one. She shifts beneath me and spreads her legs to cradle my body. The simple, welcoming gesture makes me groan.

"Anthony," she murmurs again, arching up against me. Need hums in my blood. The urge, the one I haven't been able to shake for weeks around her, is at fever pitch.

I find the swell of her breast and smooth my thumb over a peaked nipple. Her soft exhale is like music to my ears, all of her a symphony I can't wait to listen to.

Can't wait to touch.

I undo the flimsy straps to her summer dress, tied around her neck. It comes undone and Summer smiles at me, eyes trusting, as she pulls down her dress. She's not wearing a bra.

It's like a collision in my mind, the two images. The heart-breakingly trusting way she's gazing up at me and the pink hardness of her nipples. Every part of my body screams at me to throw myself into this, into her. To ignore the gnawing guilt that I'm not doing right by her.

It's the painful twist in my heart that lets me get the words out. "Summer… You know I…"

"I know," she murmurs. "I know you don't do relationships."

"You deserve someone who does." The stark truth of those words is a sledgehammer against my skull.

"Perhaps. But I want you." Her hands are soft in my hair, pulling me down, and I can't resist. Not when she's warm and luscious beneath me and her breasts beckon. The graceful lines of her feel like a sucker punch I'll never recover from.

So I bend and take a nipple in my mouth. Summer gives a soft moan of pleasure and arches her back. Tending to her this way is enough, I think, flicking my tongue.

It has to be enough.

I switch over to the other side and relish the moment, focusing on the softness of her body beneath me. Ignoring the painful, aching need it's inspired in mine.

Even when she raises her hips. "Anthony," she murmurs.

I press down, giving us both pressure but no dangerous, dangerous friction. The contact alone is enough to make my vision dance. "Not tonight."

"Why not?" Her hands slide beneath my shirt and over the skin of my back, fingernails raking softly. My head swims at the sensation.

"Not tonight," I repeat, but I kiss her to soften the blow. It's one against both of us, with my body strung so taut it feels like the wrong touch will shatter me.

But I can't stomach the idea of taking Summer to bed, sweet, trusting, fierce, funny and true-love-believing Summer, while she doesn't know about what a wreck I'll become… the wreck I already am on the inside.

So I kiss her until both of us are breathless, until the fire in my blood is a painful companion and her gasps are committed to memory.

"I suppose we're not in a rush," she murmurs, smiling at me where we lie sprawled on the couch. Her hair is golden and glorious around her head. Eyes liquid blue.

"We're not," I say. Though it feels like parting with a limb, I push myself off the couch. "Which means it's time for me to say good night."

"Do we have to?"

"My self-restraint only lasts so long."

The smile she gives me is so hopeful it's like shards of glass through my heart. "You have too much of it," she murmurs.

"No," I say. "I don't have nearly enough."

She re-ties her dress and kisses me one last time, on her tiptoes. "I'm already looking forward to tomorrow," she says.

16

SUMMER

I sleep in the next morning, waking up to the summer sun announcing another beautiful day through the window. Sit up, check my phone, down a glass of water. Run a brush through my hair and try to calm my feverish cheeks.

Anthony and I made out last night. And he's right on the other side of the wall, in his own bedroom, only a few feet away.

In the bathroom mirror, my reflection looks back at me with the same level of excitement I feel inside.

He's no less intriguing now than he was the first time I met him. I don't understand the reason he's holding back, but whatever it is, I'm confident it's not related to me. Not with the way he'd kissed me last night. Like it was an art, rather than a sport.

I'd felt like something to be savored.

Ace nudges my ensuite bathroom door open and presses a cold nose to my hand.

"Sorry," I say. "Let's go for our morning walk."

He dances away on light paws with a doggish grin, and perhaps he can sense my mood, because I feel like dancing too.

Or running.

Which is what we do, the two of us on the beach, under the morning sun. I'm whistling when we finally return to Anthony's house. Scale the steps two at a time and wipe sweat from my brow.

The patio chairs are empty, as are the lounge chairs by the pool. He's not in the kitchen, either, when I've showered. The door to his bedroom is still closed.

A quick glance at the clock puts it at eleven. I wouldn't have pegged Anthony Winter as a late sleeper.

It's another piece filling in the puzzle of his character, added to the tableau already in place. The man whose humor is dry and black, who is hard-working and reserved. Cynical but kind.

I'm still humming to myself as I look through his kitchen cabinets. If he's sleeping, I might as well make us some breakfast.

Everybody likes pancakes, right?

Ace keeps me company as I cook. I sing old tunes as I find the butter, eggs, flour and milk.

Anthony must have called ahead and asked some anonymous staff member to stock the house for us. It's a small reminder of just how different a life he lives from me.

But, I tell myself, he'd sat opposite me at the beer tasting. He'd helped when I needed him that night, with Ace's chocolate poisoning.

When the batter runs out, I've got a high stack of pancakes ready. I set the kitchen table and find an unopened bottle of maple syrup.

But still no Anthony.

It's almost midday.

I send him a quick text. *Is everything all right? I've made pancakes for brunch.*

The minutes pass by in slow agony as I wait for a reply that never comes. Worry gnaws at my insides, warring with hunger. I pad down the corridor and stop outside his shut bedroom door. There are no sounds from within.

He doesn't strike me as the kind of man who stays in bed till midday.

I knock. "Anthony? Are you okay?"

A faint rustle on the other side, and then his voice. It's hoarse. "Yes!"

"Are you hungry?"

"No," he says. There's a long pause. "Coffee might help."

"I can get you coffee."

"Okay."

I make a cup in record time and return to his bedroom door. "Can I come in?"

It takes him longer than it should to answer. "Yeah."

I push open the door just as he props himself up in bed. The drapes are half-drawn and the sunlight that filters in sends uneven patterns across his king-size bed.

"Summer?" he asks. He's shirtless, dark hair dusting across his chest. The sheet pools around his waist.

"Yes, it's me. I've got your coffee. Here. Be careful, it's hot."

"Mmm." He closes his eyes as soon as he has the cup in hand and leans against the headrest. Raises it to his lips and takes a sip.

"Are you okay?"

He lowers the cup with a sigh. "Yes. It'll pass."

"What is it?"

"Migraine."

"Oh." I take the cup from him and put it on his bedside table, beside an ebook reader and a pair of glasses. I'd never seen him wear them. "Do you want me to pull the drapes?"

"No. Thanks." He sinks back down on the pillow, eyes closed. The lines of his face are drawn.

My mother used to have migraines. Not this bad, perhaps, but I remember what she used to do.

"I'll be right back," I say.

Anthony doesn't reply.

But when I return and place a cold towel across his brow, he lets out a low groan. "Is that nice?"

"It's very cold," he breathes. "Christ, I think I can taste blood."

Shit. I sit down beside him on the bed and he cracks open one eye. "Summer?"

"I'm here. Do you get them often?"

"Sometimes."

Had he been lying like this all night? A quick glance across the bed confirms what I already know. There's more than enough space.

"You don't have to stay." Anthony presses the heels of his hands against his eyes, teeth gritting together. "Shit."

I climb onto the bed beside him, sitting cross-legged. Grab one of his spare pillows and put it in my lap. "I can rub your temples, if you think it'll help?"

He peels his hands away from his eyes, but doesn't open them. "Fuck, Summer, you should be lying on the beach or something."

"I want to be here. Will you let me?"

"I don't understand why," he mutters, but shifts on the bed, lifting his head up. I scoot closer and he puts it back down in my lap with a soft groan.

I tug the cold compress into place and start rubbing his temples in light circles. It's been a long time since I did this for my mother, but I remember the motions.

He lets out a soft breath as I run my fingers through his hair, so I do it again. Dig my fingers into the muscles of his neck and shoulders. His skin is hot to the touch.

I don't know how long we sit there for, him in pain, and me trying to take what I can away.

Ace joins us. He's rarely allowed on beds, but he jumps straight up this time. Curls up beside Anthony and rests his head right next to Anthony's hand.

The next time I look up, Anthony's fingers are buried in Ace's fur.

"You're good at that," he murmurs.

"Massaging?"

"Mmm."

"Is it helping?"

"A bit, yeah."

I slide my thumbs over his cheekbones and down along the strong muscles of his neck. "Do you want a painkiller?"

"They don't work."

"Oh."

"Should be over… soon."

Despite his words, it's nearly an hour before his hand comes up to rest on mine. "Thanks."

"You're feeling better?"

"Yeah."

Ace lifts his head as we re-arrange, Anthony lifting his head and me scooting back. He removes the compress from his head with a groan. "I've never thought about doing that before."

"Did it help?"

"Yes."

I smile at him. "I'm glad."

He looks back, eyes dark, before turning them down on himself. The sheet is tangled around his legs and slants across his hips. A happy trail wanders across strong stomach muscles, disappearing beneath the sheet.

The outline pressed against it makes it evident he's not wearing underwear. Anthony cocks one knee. "Did you say you'd made breakfast?"

"Pancakes, yes. They're in the kitchen." I push off the bed, edging closer to the door. My cheeks feel hot. "Do you want some?"

"Yes, later. I think I'll try sleeping some."

"Okay. You'll let me know if you need anything, right? I'm here if you want more coffee or head rubs."

For a second, I worry he'll bite my head off. But then his mouth softens. "Thanks."

"Absolutely." I open his bedroom door and motion for Ace. "Are you in or are you out?"

Dark doggy eyes meet mine and he tilts his head, like the answer is obvious.

"Right. Are you okay with him staying?"

Anthony's hand finds it's way back into Ace's fur. "Yeah."

"Then he's all yours."

It's late afternoon by the time I hear footsteps from inside the house. I put my book down and get up from the lounge chair, double-checking my bikini is still in place.

"Anthony?"

"Yeah, I'm here." He steps out onto the patio and raises a hand, shading his eyes from the harsh sunlight. "Damn. I've practically missed the entire day."

"Not all of it," I say. "Are you hungry?"

"I just had some of your pancakes."

"You reheated them?"

"Yes," he says dryly, "I reheated them."

I sit back down on the lounge chair and give a tail-wagging Ace a welcoming pat on the head. "Do you want to join me?"

He looks from me to the calm, blue waters of his infinity pool. I wonder how many times he's been in it.

I wonder if he's *ever* been in it.

"Yes," he says.

Once we're both settled, my eyes drift from the pages of my book to him. He's almost too tall for the lounge chair and his feet hang off the edge. Dark waves of his hair fall over his brow, matted and disheveled.

He opens his eyes. "You're staring."

I bite my lower lip to keep from smiling. "I'm not."

"Yes, you are."

I put down my book. "Well, you're nice to look at. Are you feeling better?"

"I am." Anthony looks down at my hands, a frown marring his face. "You're too kind to me."

"There's no such thing."

"Yes, there is. Summer... I shouldn't have kissed you last night. Or the night before."

"Why not?"

"It was a mistake, and I'm sorry."

The words don't hurt by themselves. No, it's the absolute

sincerity in his voice that slides like needles beneath my nails. "A mistake?" I murmur. "That's really what you think?"

"Yes."

I can't sit here or the burning behind my eyes will give me away. I push off the lounge chair and turn toward the door, but a large hand around my wrist stops me.

"No, Summer... don't you see? I couldn't bear it if I hurt you. And I can't bear having you just to lose you, either. Do you understand?"

"I don't understand anything."

The pain in his eyes is more than I'd seen this morning. "Your friendship means a lot to me. More than I'd expected."

"So does yours," I whisper.

"I don't want to lose it, but God help me, I want you too much."

"You don't want to jeopardize our friendship? Help me understand, Anthony."

He pulls his hand away from mine with aching slowness. "I'm going blind, Summer."

"What do you mean?"

The words make no sense.

"I mean just that. I'm losing my eyesight."

"Your... oh. Is it connected to your migraines?"

He nods, jaw working. "It's one of the symptoms, yes."

I search his eyes for any indication that this is some twisted joke, but there's nothing but fierce focus in them. He's reading my expression as intently as I'm trying to read his.

"Anthony, I'm so sorry."

He closes his eyes. "Right. Yeah."

"When did you find out?"

"About two years ago. I complained about the font being too small on a menu, and my friend looked at me like I was joking. So I booked an appointment with an optician and figured I'd get glasses," he says with a snort. "I wish."

"What's the diagnosis? I mean, can the doctors do anything? Treatments or some kind of... what?"

He's laughing, but there's no humor in it. "This is one area where your optimism can't help, Summer."

His words sink in with a kind of nauseating finality, and I bite my tongue to stop the well-meaning, well-intentioned sentences that hover. My gaze falls to his hand, resting on his knee.

I grip it tight. "I can't imagine how you feel, Anthony, or how difficult it must be to reveal this news. Thanks for sharing it with me. If you want to talk about it, I'm a good listener. And if you don't... then that's fine too."

He nods once and looks down at our interwoven hands. Neither of us speaks for a long time. When we do, it's Anthony's voice that breaks the silence.

It's rough around the edges.

"Should we walk along the beach again?"

"You're sure you're up for it?"

He stands, hand sliding away from mine. "I'm not blind yet."

"Right. Yeah, that's not what I meant."

"Relax, Summer. I know it wasn't," he says. Aims a crooked smile my way.

But he's wound tight by my side as he locks the patio door and takes the steps down to the beach. Ace trails behind us, his tail-wagging muted. He's run on the beach enough this weekend to last him the summer.

We walk for a long time before I dare break the silence between us. He's staring straight ahead, jaw tense.

"Are there treatments?" I ask. "Ways of living with it? I think I've heard of technologies that might help. Voice-to-text, and devices you speak to and they turn on... Braille, too, right?"

Anthony's voice drips with bitterness. "Yes. All those things exist. My doctor keeps sending me documents about them. He likes to tell me I should familiarize myself with it while I still have most of my sight."

The venom in his voice is a warning, but I know down to my bones that it's not directed at me this time. "But you don't want to?"

"Of course I don't want to," he says. "If I do, it means I've accepted this fate. If I start doing that, I surrender."

"Ah."

"I know it doesn't make any sense."

"Some, I suppose."

"The house was the biggest concession," he says.

"The house? The beach house?"

"Yes. Haven't you noticed?"

I frown. "No. What?"

"The interior designer worked with a specialist on blindness. There are no sharp corners on tables or kitchen counters, no high thresholds. No high-stemmed wineglasses. Each knob on the cabinets is shaped differently." The tone of his voice drips with self-hatred. "Figured I might as well get a place ready for when it happens."

"When it happens," I repeat softly. "Do you know when that might be?"

"The million-dollar question. I don't, and neither does the doctor. Retinitis pigmentosa rarely shows up at my age, but when it does, it progresses fast. Most people have it diagnosed in childhood. It's genetic. Nothing I can do to change it. Nothing I did caused it."

My heart aches for him, and against it all, my eyes burn. I keep my eyes trained on the beach and fight against the instinct. If there's one thing he'd hate, it's being cried over.

"What's it like now?" I ask.

"My vision?"

"Yes."

"Tolerable, I suppose. Night vision was among the first things to go," he says. Memories click into place, of Anthony asking me to read menus. "Second is peripheral vision. I don't drive anymore, which you might have noticed." His gaze shifts to the horizon and the setting sun. The rays dance across the waves, setting the world ablaze in color.

"I thought you preferred drivers," I whisper.

He shakes his head. "Some days, I'd give anything to be allowed behind the wheel again."

I swallow at the knot in my throat. He clears his, breaks eye contact with me. We walk slowly, in silence, along the beach and the setting sun. None of the questions that hover on the tip of my tongue feel right. Not when he looks away from me more than he looks at me.

Blindness.

The weight of what he's just told me hasn't settled yet, but I can feel it. And if I can, it must be crushing him, strong as he is.

"Don't think differently of me," he tells me.

"I don't. If anything, I feel—"

"If you're going to say anything with the word compassion, sorry, or pity in it, don't. Summer, I can't bear it."

He's walking a knife's edge with despair, I realize. And each day is a new struggle to keep his balance.

"I wasn't," I lie. The edge feels close enough to cut me, too. "I feel grateful you told me."

Anthony doesn't reply. He turns his face back to the golden sliver of sun kissing the horizon. "We should start to head back."

"Sure." I whistle for Ace and he bounds toward us, as happy to walk back to the house as he was to walk away from it.

Neither of us speaks until we're almost at his house, and then only of practical matters. He goes to lie down again, and I order dinner for us. My eyes lock on the knobs in the kitchen when I've clicked off the call to the restaurant.

The quirky design choice is to ensure Anthony will be able to tell the difference between the cabinets by touch, one day. Tears slip down my face and I'm grateful he's not there to see them. I have the distinct feeling that Anthony gave me a gift tonight, by telling me. Life is unfair and ephemeral and yet so heartbreakingly beautiful, and I hope he'll see that one day, eyesight or no.

17

SUMMER

Anthony's mood is difficult to read at dinner. His eyes contain a challenge, as if he's daring me to regard him differently. Daring me to treat him with anything that resembles pity.

"So windsurfing is done," he says, looking at me over the rim of his glass. "But there's one thing on your bucket list you can do here that you haven't. Not yet."

"There is?"

"Skinny-dipping in the ocean."

Keeping his gaze, I put my napkin on the table. Put down the chopsticks and push up from the chair. His eyes track every movement and I let that steady me, despite the pounding of my heart. "You're right," I say.

He watches as I walk the short distance to the patio doors. As I push them open. The beach is covered in darkness, but that does nothing to stop the sound of waves lapping against the shore in invitation. Behind me, there's the sound of another chair being pushed back.

I lose my nerve halfway down his patio steps.

Anthony's deep voice rings out behind me, and not for the first time, I wonder if he's capable of reading my mind. "It's pitch dark out here," he says. "If there's moonlight to see by, it's not enough for me. I won't be able to see you."

My feet sink down into the still-warm sand and I pull off my dress in one smooth motion, letting it drop onto the beach. The wind feels soft against my skin.

"All right," I murmur. "Let's do this, then."

The rustle of clothing makes me turn my head. Anthony's hands are moving over the buttons of his shirt, undoing them one by one.

Fire shoots through my veins. "You're going swimming too?"

His hands pause. "If I may."

"Yes. Yes, of course." I don't need to add that my eyes are good enough in the moonlight that I'll be able to make out his form.

We both know that.

I look at him as I reach up to undo the clasp of my bra. He doesn't look back at me.

He can't see at all, I realize. The light out here is enough for me to make out the shapes and contours of things, but what had he told me? Night vision was the first to go.

"I'm almost done," I tell him.

He nods and reaches for his pants, and if he can be out here, if he can tell me about his diagnosis... then I can damn well do this.

My heart pounds as I drop my panties and stand naked as the day I was born on Anthony's beach in Montauk. The ocean is completely dark, ready to swallow us whole.

"I'm ready," I say.

"Let's, then."

We walk side by side out to the water, and I keep sneaking glances at him, but he doesn't seem to need any assistance. Maybe he'd bite my head off if I offered.

The water feels like ice around my ankles. "Wow. That's cold."

"Hesitating makes it worse."

"True. But maybe this is something we should do in, like, the Cayman Islands?"

Anthony snorts. "It'll feel better in a bit."

"You're saying we have to be in the water for a while?"

"Long enough to really merit checking this off on your bucket list."

I cross my arms over my chest as we wade deeper. No bikini top there, no, only my skin, reminding me just how naked I am. A quick glance down confirms what I already know. My nipples are hard from the chill of the water.

I don't dare look his way until we're waist deep.

Anthony groans. "Fuck, you're right. Cayman Islands it is."

"Too late. We're going to be swimming for a while." I brace my feet against the sandy ocean floor and in a smooth motion, I dive clear through the icy surface.

The water is dark and salty around me as I kick forward, a cold rush against my senses. I surface with a gasp. "Holy shit!"

"You're committed," Anthony calls.

I laugh, kicking water. The ocean is soft against my skin. Unhindered by a swimsuit, I feel completely submerged, one with the water. "It's nice when you get used to it!"

He mutters something and steps further into the water. Moonlight outlines the strong lines of his shoulders rising from the water's surface.

"Have you done this before?" I ask.

"Swum naked?"

"Yes."

"Sure, but it was a long time ago," he says.

I turn onto my back and float, taking in the stars in the sky above. Tiny pinpricks of light that stretch as far as the eye can see.

"You can't see me?" I ask. Adrenaline runs through my body, making my veins burn.

"No." Anthony's deep voice carries across the water. I cross the ocean floor to where he's standing. A soft current plays with my legs, too weak to do anything but tease.

"But you can touch me," I say.

"Summer?"

I find his hand, resting on the water's surface. It flips over and grips mine. "Summer…"

"Yes?" My toes bury themselves in the sand as I reach up and press my lips to his. Anthony kisses me back, lips opening mine, his free hand slicing through the water to find the curve of my waist.

He pulls me close.

The length of his bare body against mine feels electric, a shot straight to my nervous system.

His fingers dig into the skin of my waist, as if they're struggling to stay there. Mine know no such restraints as I explore his chest, shoulders, the nape of his neck.

A groan escapes him as I rake my nails through his hair. "Summer, we…"

"I want you."

He kisses me again, the force of it bending me backwards through the water. His hands lose their restraint and slide down to grip my ass, pulling me up tight against him.

My awareness drops to the hard length of him trapped between our bodies. It feels hot against my skin, despite the chill of the water. One of his hands trails up the side of my body and cups my breast, a thumb flicking over my nipple.

I hold on to his shoulders and jump up, wrapping my legs around his waist. He supports me, strong arms beneath my thighs. Clad in nothing but seawater and moonlight, pressed so tightly together I can feel the beating of his heart, our bodies learn one another.

"Summer," he murmurs. Bends his head to mine and kisses me with reverence.

I don't know when I first register the chilly wind on my lower back, or when the cold water on my thighs is replaced by night air. I only know that when he raises his head from mine we're no longer in the water.

He's carried me onto the shore.

"Let's go inside," Anthony murmurs.

I slide down his body and find my footing on the sand. He

groans at the friction, his hardness clear to my night-adjusted eyes. My mouth feels dry and my heart full.

"Yes," I whisper. "Please."

I bend to scoop up our clothing and walk toward the house. I'm halfway up the steps before I turn and see him, standing by the base of the stairs. Turned too much to the left.

My own idiocy leaves me shamed. In the darkness, he can't make out the first step.

"Here," I murmur and take his hand.

His jaw works but he says nothing, finding his footing. Letting me draw him toward the patio doors and the living room. My heart aches, then, with want and tenderness for him. I reach for the living room lights and turn them on.

Anthony shuts the patio door behind us and turns to look at me.

I feel electrified beneath his burning gaze, taking all of me in. He looks like an ancient general, a conquering hero returned from sea, a man who needs with every breath he takes. His body is the tall, strong form of a man who uses it for work. Chest hair. Strong thighs. Rugged features that I'd once considered plain.

How had I been so blind?

"You still want me," he says. It's a statement and a question, evident in the lines of his body and the way he's holding himself back.

Had he thought I wouldn't, after he'd told me about his vision? Had he thought I would turn him away?

"Yes. So much."

He reaches out and takes a strand of my wet hair between his fingers. "You'll catch a cold."

"No, I won't," I whisper. "I go to bed with wet hair all the time."

Anthony's lips curve. "In that case…"

My gasp of surprise turns into a breathless laugh as he lifts me up. Carries me through the living room and into his bedroom, shutting the door in the face of an all-too-curious golden retriever.

I slide down his body, feet touching the floor, but I keep my arms around his neck. His hands are reverent and soft over my naked skin. They sweep in arcs over my bare back and down my hips, like he's mapping my body.

I touch him the same way. Trace the strong, wide curve of his shoulders and the groove down his stomach. Grasp the hard length of him in my hand.

He groans against my lips, breath quickening when I start to stroke. "So it wasn't that cold in the water," I tease.

His answering chuckle is hoarse. He rests his forehead against mine, chest rising and falling with the force of his breathing.

I smooth my thumb over the blunt head and he groans. It's been a long time since I've touched a man like this, and he's deliciously soft and hard and silky at the same time.

He tips my head back and kisses me, tongue slipping between my lips, mimicking the movement of his hips against my hand. I'm so full of him my head is swimming and he's not even inside of me yet.

Anthony walks me back to his bed and lifts me again. Effortless for him, it seems.

He lays me down on the soft linen. I cradle him between my legs as he moves down my body, mouth tracing collarbones, across my breasts, finding the hard peak of a nipple.

He bites down.

I gasp, legs widening in a plea.

Anthony hears it. His hand slides up my inner thigh, closer, and closer still, until his fingers finally brush over my most sensitive skin.

He gives a low groan of approval and switches nipples, fingers moving. My breath hitches in my throat as his thumb brushes over the right spot.

He hears that, too, fingers returning without mercy to the swollen nub. Taking it between two knuckles and rubbing until I have to hold on to his shoulders for support. He presses his lips against my neck and whispers how hard he is for me, how good I feel, how much he longs to be inside of me.

I break apart with an ease I didn't know I could, cheeks flushing with the force of my orgasm.

Anthony kisses me and knots a hand in my wet hair. Reaches for a pillow and props it up beneath my hips, hands spreading my inner thighs, looking down at me.

He doesn't say a thing, but it's there in his touch, the reverence.

I've never felt more wanted.

I reach between my legs and grasp his erection again. Pull him forward, pressed against me.

"Condom," he says.

I hadn't even thought of that. And I always think about that. "Do you have one?"

Anthony nods and reaches for his bedside drawer. The crackle of foil follows and we both watch as he rolls it on in a smooth motion. Nerves and a throbbing ache mingle inside of me, watching as he presses my legs apart with his knees and reaches down to guide himself inside.

I sigh with pleasure at the first entry. It's like I'm welcoming him home, and as I wrap my legs around his hips and run my hands over his broad back, I realize it's never felt like that with anyone before.

Anthony braces himself above me, burying himself to the hilt with a groan.

I clasp his face between my hands and kiss him as he starts to move. Tears blur behind my eyes with the force of it all, my own pleasure heightening my emotions.

Anthony drives an arm beneath my neck and bends his head to my collarbone. Wet, salty hair falls against my cheek, but his breath is hot.

I hold him as his body surges with power, his hips speeding up. One of his arms locks beneath my knee and pulls my leg up, the fit growing deeper. The new angle sends waves of pleasure through my body with each quick thrust, until I'm hovering at the edge. It's Anthony's own pleasure that sends me over it. He loses control as he crests, thrusts growing erratic.

He groans against my neck with the force of his release and I grip him tightly through my own, my world beginning and ending with us, as close as two people can be.

18

SUMMER

"The round knob is for the plate cabinet," Anthony says, voice dry. "The triangle is for the glass cabinet."

I open both and take in the neatly organized plate-ware. Small beads are attached to the wooden cabinet dividers. I run my fingers along them. Two beads for water glasses. Three for bowls. Four for plates.

"Did they give you instructions for this?"

"There's a manual somewhere. I can't remember where I put it." He takes another bite of the omelet on his plate. "Come eat your breakfast, Summer."

"This is interesting."

"It's fucking depressing."

I don't let that stop me, though, not as I open the fridge. It had struck me as supremely well-organized before. Drawers with large labels and plastic bins. Now I see it for what it is.

A support system.

"You already took out the orange juice," he comments.

"That's right." I close it and sit down beside him at the kitchen counter, my bare legs against the leather seat. I fold up the shirtsleeves of his button-down and cut into my own omelet.

"We have one day left here," he says, reaching for his orange juice.

"When is your driver coming to pick us up?"

"Four."

"Hmm. What do you want to do?"

Anthony gives me a look that sends blood flooding to my cheeks. "I know exactly what I want to do," he says. "But I'll understand if you want to take in the scenery."

I reach for my glass of OJ and take a deep sip. We'd fallen asleep together in his bed last night. Woken up late, and gotten up later still after our decision to indulge in one another again. Anthony had entered me from the side, one of his hands on my breast and the other between my legs, until both of us were fully awake.

The memory makes me blush.

"Let's stay in," I say.

His lips curl. "Let's."

"But we have to walk along the beach again, and we definitely have to swim in the pool."

"I'm starting to think you have an addiction."

"To pools?"

"To swimming."

I hit him with my elbow. "Or I'm just trying to get *you* to swim. I still can't believe you've had this house for a year and never taken a dip in your pool."

"Well, I'm rarely here." He cuts into a piece of toast, the swell of his bicep flexing with the movement. "I think this is the fourth time I've been in the house since I bought it."

I put my fork and knife down. "The fourth time?"

"Yes," he says. "I told you how much I hate this place."

"No, you said it was your biggest concession. It's a beautiful place. The beach, the pool…"

He makes a dismissive sound and polishes off the last of his breakfast. Reaches for his coffee. "All of which I won't be able to see one day. This ocean view is a complete waste, and it probably accounts for more than half the value of this place."

"The view, perhaps, but you'll still be able to enjoy the beach when you can't see it." I almost stumble over the words, but they make it out in one piece. "You don't need your eyes to swim, and listening to the waves is lovely."

"I suppose so."

"How did your family and friends respond? Are they supportive?"

He pushes his plate away and turns on the chair, an eyebrow raised at me.

"Oh, I'm sorry. Was that an insensitive question? I'm really sorry."

Anthony shakes his head. "I'm not hurt," he says. "I'm just wondering how you'll fit in all your swimming if you're planning on spending the day asking me every blind question under the sun."

"Every blind question under the sun?"

"Yes." He picks up the last piece of toast from my plate and feeds it to me, his thumb grazing my bottom lip. "If I can choose between swimming, fucking you and talking about my vision, I know which one I'll rank last."

"Well, when you put it that way…"

"I do."

"Can I just ask you one last question before we head out into the sun?"

Anthony sighs, but doesn't object, turning my chair to face him. Skilled hands move over the two buttons on my shirt I'd managed to close. "I'll endure it," he says.

"Do you have a bucket list of your own? With things you want to see before it happens?"

He opens his own old button-down I'm wearing. Smooths his fingers over one of my breasts, his gaze on the nipple he's teasing into hardness between his fingers.

"No," he says, and the tone of his voice makes it clear the conversation is over. "Until I do, though, I intend to enjoy myself."

I slide off the stool and slip the shirt from my shoulders, intent on helping him do just that.

I cut through the warm, smooth water of the infinity pool to where he's lounging on the steps. His arms are on the edge of the pool, eyes closed, tilted up to the sun.

"You look like a lizard," I tell him. "Soaking up the rays."

"And you look like a siren," he responds, not opening his eyes. "Sing for me as well and I'll be lost here forever."

I grin. Shoot a glance to where my discarded bikini top rests on the lounge chair. "I'm not sure I want you to drown yet. I'm not done with you."

"Thank God," he says, "because I'm sure as hell not done with you."

I turn onto my back and float, the clouds dancing above us across the azure sky. This place is a private, privileged paradise, and as much as I love my apartment in the city, not a single part of me looks forward to leaving.

"Have you given those singing lessons of yours any more thought?" he asks.

I close my eyes. "No."

"Will you sing for me now?"

"Probably not."

"So I'll have to camp outside your shower. Good to know."

Laughing, I turn over and swim toward him, my strokes splitting the water. "You really liked it that much?"

"Yes. I've never known anyone who could sing. Can't remember the last time I went to a concert, either." He runs a hand through his wet hair. The sun has begun to darken his olive skin, hinting at the deep tan he'd have after a week of this.

"Well, who knows," I say. "If we put on some good music in the car on the way back home…"

He reaches for me and I settle on his lap, the water divine and temperate around us. It laps in soft waves over my exposed breasts and Anthony looks down, a soft half-smile on his face.

"Good thing you advised me to take my top off," I say. "Thanks for reminding me of the dangers of tan lines."

"I'm nothing if not altruistic." His hand cups my left breast, nearly covering it whole.

"Of course you are."

"I'm so generous, in fact, that I might just book you in for an open mic night without telling you."

"No, Anthony, you wouldn't dare."

"Wouldn't I?" He raises a dark eyebrow and meets my gaze. "You know, I'd very much like to have a word with that idiot ex of yours."

"He's not worth it."

"You're absolutely right he isn't," Anthony says, pulling me closer. I rest my cheek against his sun-warmed shoulder, his hand moving in soft sweeps over my bare back. I close my eyes and bask in the closeness.

It's a long time before he speaks again. I can feel the rumble of his voice through his chest and into mine. "I hated Ace when I first met him."

I turn my head to where my dog is resting in the shade, his tongue half-out and eyes closed.

"I noticed," I murmur.

"And then you told me he'd originally been trained as a guide dog," he says. "What are the fucking odds?"

I link my hands behind his neck and lean back. Meet his gaze. "Is that something you've ever—?"

"Don't," he says. "I can't. None of those things. I don't want to consider them."

"All right. We won't, then. But does this mean you hate Ace less now? Because I hate to break it to you, but he really likes you."

"He does?"

"Are you kidding me? Every time you come into my office his wagging tail gives him away. He's followed you everywhere this weekend."

Anthony's scowl softens, disappears, as he glances to Ace. He's flipped over onto his back, all four paws up in the air. "He's a good dog."

I grin at him. "Praise? From Anthony Winter?"

"I'm capable of it, in small doses." His hands slide down and grip my ass. "When something really impresses me."

"Oh?"

"Yes. Like you, for example. And this. Not to mention these two. Or here, where I—"

I cut him off with a kiss. His hands return to my waist and tug me close as I lose myself in him and he in me, in the beautiful place where time stops altogether.

We're both breathing hard when I lean back. Brace my legs against the edge of the pool and push away from him, back out into the deep.

"Running away?"

"Yes," I say. Look up into the sky with the largest, goofiest smile on my face. My heart feels like it might explode. "You're welcome to try to catch me."

"Mmm. I quite like the view from here."

I swim the length of the pool once, twice. Think about his words and his situation, my mind finds its way back to what he'd shared with me over the weekend.

"Why'd you choose Montauk for this house?" I ask him. "Was it because your family has a summer house nearby?"

He leans back on his forearms and tilts his head back to the sun. Eyes closed again. "It's close enough to the city. I know the place well. It came onto the market at the right time."

"Hmm." I push away from the wall and start on a third lap. "Must be nice to be close to them, too."

He doesn't comment on that. Takes a long time to say anything, actually. But when he does, it stops me mid-stroke in the pool.

"I haven't told them."

"About the diagnosis?"

"No, and I'm not planning to until I absolutely have to." The sudden tautness in his form is enough to set me on edge.

I swim toward him. "I imagine it's difficult news to share."

"I suppose," he says with a shrug. "I've only really told you."

The shock that ripples through me doesn't reach my face. I'm very careful about that. "Thanks for sharing it with me."

"Mhm." He reaches for me when I'm close enough and I find myself once again in his lap. Despite his relaxed features, the body beneath mine is rigid. We're in deep water again.

"Your business partners and friends don't know either, then?" I ask.

"No."

I walk my hands up his chest and wrap them around his neck. The knife's edge he's treading feels closer than it has for hours, within sighting distance. So I swallow my questions.

"I'm grateful you trusted me with it, Anthony."

He reaches up and cups my cheek, eyes inscrutable. It's not the first time I can't read him.

I doubt it will be the last.

"Thanks for listening," he murmurs. Kisses me again, and like so many times before, it derails my thoughts entirely.

I'm breathing hard when I lift my head. "So?" I ask. "What happens when we get back to New York?"

He groans. "Is it crazy that I wish we could just stay here? For the first time ever, I quite like the privacy of this house."

I push a lock of half-dried hair from his forehead. "I have couples to set up. Matches to make. Love to create and sparks to fly."

"Right. You have to shoot Cupid's bow."

"Exactly. Hey, does *this*, you and me, mean I technically won the bet? Because you did go on a date with me too, you know. I remember."

"Mmm, so do I. We saved some rainforest together."

"You saved it. Well, contributed to saving it."

"You were valuable moral support," he says.

"I accept," I say. "Now, does it or does it not mean that I was right? About Opate Match?"

Anthony grins, and it's a full-fledged smile, wide and true and dazzling. It takes my breath away. "Don't gloat, Summer," he says, but the way he kisses me is a clear yes.

19

ANTHONY

Summer's small bed is wedged in the corner of her too-small bedroom, and the linens are always rumpled. They smell like her, though. Of shampoo and perfume and warm woman.

The cups in her kitchen are mismatched. Her bowls are handmade, courtesy of a course in ceramics she took with her mother one summer.

And, as I've learned over the week since we got back from Montauk, she isn't all sunshine. No, she's not human until she has her first cup of coffee in the morning. Discovering that had been a balm to my own inadequacies, despite the mountain they represent next to her speedbump.

We're lying on her couch, her back pressed to my front, a discarded pizza box on the floor from her favorite restaurant. I close my eyes and breathe in the scent of her hair.

I've never thought I had an addictive personality, but clearly, I'd just never tried the right drug. Because Summer is all I crave. Here, in this small, eclectic apartment, the rest of the world doesn't exist. All the shit I don't like to deal with—the shit I ignore—can't touch us here.

Here, I have fun.

I'm alive.

The bitter contrast to my own dark and empty townhouse

was enough to drive me straight to bed yesterday, curtains drawn.

"Oh, listen to this," Summer says. She's reading the paper and has been entertaining me over the past half an hour by reading things aloud that she finds interesting.

She finds a lot of things interesting.

I find critiquing her findings interesting.

It's a solid combo.

"The city is hiring street artists to paint murals of famous birds in five different subway stations," she says. "Isn't that nice?"

"Birds? Did you say famous *birds*?"

"Yeah. You can vote online for which ones will be featured. Oh, should we do it? Let me find the website."

"That's the stupidest thing I've ever heard."

She nudges me with her elbow, but I lift my leg over hers, trapping her deliciously close to my body. "It's harmless and fun," she says.

"There are people with serious bird phobias. Anyone with half a brain who watched Hitchcock will have developed one. This will give people panic attacks on the subway."

"People aren't that afraid of *birds.*"

"Oh, yes they are. Who came up with this idea?"

"The mayor's office. Apparently it's in honor of Small Birds Awareness Week. It says here domestic cats have decimated a lot of our small bird populations and ornithologists are trying to get their numbers back up."

I close my eyes and slip my hand under her shirt, finding a bare hip. "Right. Well, I'm sure the Coalition for Worms and Bugs will have something to say about that. Their numbers have skyrocketed thanks to bird loss."

Summer laughs, her tummy shaking beneath my hand, and I wonder how it's possible to be so perfectly happy as I am in this moment. Not a twinge of a migraine, the darkness kept at bay by her sunshine.

I never want to leave this couch.

There's a rustle as she turns the pages. Re-arranges her head placement on my arm. "Oh, Page Six!"

"It's all garbage."

"Yes, but it's *fun* garbage."

I snort. My mother and Summer could have a field day over that. What was said and what wasn't was often the most important topic of discussion in the Winter household when I grew up.

"It's pretty tame today. Oliver Langston publicly apologized for his affair."

"Ridiculous," I say.

"Why?"

I snort. "He should be apologizing to his wife, not to the people of New York. He didn't wrong any of us."

"Well, we don't know how many other women he had affairs with," Summer says. "Perhaps this was the most convenient way to apologize to them all. You know, saved on his phone bill."

I laugh at that, brushing her hair away from my nose. "Imagine that."

She reads on. But then she sighs, a soft, surprised "oh."

"Another hypocritical politician?"

"It's about your family."

"So close enough," I say. "Read it to me."

"Well, it's a public announcement of the upcoming nuptials between Isaac Winter and Cordelia Jacobs. There's a bit of speculation here, too."

"Read it to me," I repeat.

She clears her throat. "One can't help but wonder if the joining of the Winters and Jacobs families is a dynastic move of premeditated proportions. Not unlike, in fact, the Winter Corporation's recent expansion to the Caribbean, where Robert Jacobs has built his famous golf courses. What came first, the chicken or the egg? The love or the business deal?"

I snort. "Clever."

A rustle and soft thud as Summer puts the paper down. "I'm sorry."

"About what?"

"Well, about them talking about your family like that. I mean, I don't know if I'd like it if my marriage was put in the paper with a heavy insinuation that it's arranged."

"You'd mind, because it wouldn't be true."

She shifts in my arms, turns over on her back. "It's true?"

"True enough." My brother had known Delia his whole life. So had I, for that matter, and my opinion hasn't changed much since I'd met her at sixteen. "But how my brother chooses to live his life isn't any of my business."

"Are you close?"

"Isaac and I?" I ask, as if there's a third brother she might be referring to. Buying me some time. I look down at my hand, smoothing over her flat stomach, circling her navel.

"Yes," she says.

"We used to be close when we were younger. It was us against our parents. Now we live pretty different lives." Not to mention I've been an ass around everyone who isn't Summer for the past two years.

It's pitiful how unused I am to having these conversations. Any conversation, really, that requires me to respond in more than monosyllables.

"Are you going to the wedding?"

"Yeah."

She nods, looking down at my hand. Covering it with her own and slipping her fingers through mine. "Families can be tricky. Friendships, too."

Does she have a sixth sense for when I need her to drop a subject? Because she manages every damn time.

"Yes. Well, not if you're Summer Davis, and your parents are the ideal representation of true love, raising puppies for a living."

She bursts out laughing and I prop myself up on my elbow, enjoying the show. Freckles decorate her nose, courtesy of the summer sun. "You make me sound like I have little birds helping me dress in the morning."

"Don't you?" I ask. "No, don't tell me. You would've, if domestic cats hadn't decimated their populations."

She bursts out laughing and I move my hand up across her ribs, tickling. Summer doubles up, shrieking.

Ace looks up from his sprawl on the couch opposite ours. Cocks his head.

"I'm just teasing your owner," I tell him, trying to keep a grip on a squirming Summer.

"No, he's not," she shrieks. "He's torturing me. Help, Ace!"

The golden puts his head down with a sigh. He's over our antics.

"No help is coming."

Summer pleads for mercy, finding my lips with her own. My hand smooths out on her skin. "Peace," she murmurs.

"Peace," I agree.

But then she slips out of my grasp and bounces away across her living room, a triumphant smile on her face. "Success!"

"Damn your wiles, woman."

She laughs and takes the few steps toward the kitchen. Opens her fridge. "Do you want a refill?"

"Sure. Thanks."

"I was actually thinking," she says, opening the half-drunk bottle of wine, "about this weekend."

"Were you?"

"Yeah. Should we go on a proper date?"

I turn onto my back and prop my hands behind my head, watching her pour the red. "Do you mean sleeping together in your apartment all week doesn't constitute a date? Shocking."

She sticks out her tongue at me. Her blonde curls are tousled around her face, and in her rumpled summer dress, she's the most beautiful thing I've ever seen.

"I was thinking we could go back to Montauk," I say.

Summer raises her eyebrows. "Really? I thought you hated that house."

"Yes, well, it grew on me last weekend. There's something

about seeing you swim naked through my pool that's really made it come alive to me. You were the missing furniture piece."

She laughs again, setting out wineglasses on the table. "You make a compelling argument."

"Well, I was in debate club in high school."

"You were?"

"Why do you sound so shocked?"

She shrugs, sinking down on the plush oriental carpet with crossed legs. Much too far away for my taste. "I don't know, really. You seem the quiet type."

"I was, but it looked good for college. Besides, I usually ended debates, not started them."

"Hmm. I can see that." She looks down at her wineglass, spinning it around on the long stem. "There's actually a thing happening this weekend."

"Oh?"

"Yeah. It's one of my best friend's birthday parties. She's invited a bunch of her friends to a bar in Midtown Saturday night."

"Sounds nice."

"Yes, I think it could be fun, actually. I haven't seen Posie in a while. The thing is…"

I know what's coming before she says it. Still, I ask. "What?"

"My ex-boyfriend will likely be there."

My muscles lock in anger, like she's flipped a switch. The fact that she dated someone who was so manipulative, who belittled and mocked and broke her down brick by brick… Her, this woman who deserves so much. Who deserves everything.

"I want to go for my friend. I don't want to go because of Robin." She shrugs, looking at me with an apologetic smile. "I'm sorry, I'm sure you don't want to hear about this."

I sit up and brace my arms against my knees. "I'll come with you, if you want."

"Are you sure?"

"I'm sure."

"Oh, Anthony, I'd really like that."

The thread of unease inside me lessens at her smile. It'll be crowded and dimly lit. My worst nightmare. But perhaps it won't be quite as bad if she's there.

"We don't have to stay long."

"We can stay for as long as you want," I say and wonder who I've become to be promising this. More than likely, I'll be miserable and in a bad mood from the darkness and the constant chatter of her friends. It'll be a headache-inducing experience.

"Thank you, Anthony," she says, smiling. It's filled with trust and hope and tenderness. No pity, either. So far, I haven't gotten the crushing sense of it from her.

Even if her optimism about my eyesight feels delusional at times. I envy her for it. And I like her for it.

She reaches up and pulls her hair back in a ponytail. "Do you want to sleep here tonight too?"

I gesture down to my rumpled clothing. The half-eaten pizza. The glass of wine.

She laughs. "So that's a yes, thank God. You're so much nicer to have in bed than Ace."

"Spare me the compliments, will you? You're making me uncomfortable over here."

Summer puts her glass down on the coffee table. "That reminds me! I have to show you something."

"You do?"

"Yes, I saw this article in yesterday's paper... you're going to love this."

"You mean I'm going to trash it."

"Exactly," she says, smiling. "I think I put it in my purse..."

She disappears into her bedroom. Ace gives a soft whine and flips over on his couch. The two of us, both obsessed with her. Both following her everywhere.

I shake my head and rise from the couch, stretching. Glance at the printed bucket list with her goals still proudly pinned to her wall.

With the lights on, it's easy enough for me to read it this time. She's ticked off windsurfing. Skinny-dipping, too.

But so many of the goals remain unfinished.

My eyes scan down the list, at the plans for a full, rich life, one with travel and experiences. A few years from now, and most of these things won't be possible for me anymore. I stop at goal twenty-seven. *Become a mother.*

Something I can't be a part of, either.

Just like my fucking vision, Summer's presence in my life has an expiration date. She might not realize it yet, but she will. The life she's dreaming of can't include me.

"You really love looking at that list, don't you?" she says, yesterday's paper tucked under her arm.

I reach out and wrap mine around her shoulders, giving the list a final glance over the top of her head. "Just looking for more things I can help make happen," I say.

Before I have to leave you.

20

SUMMER

Anthony is waiting for me outside the bar. He's leaning against the building, glancing left and right, hands in the pockets of his gray slacks. I can make out his clenched jaw, even from this distance.

It mirrors the butterflies in my own stomach. I pull my handbag up higher on my shoulder and step straight into his arms. "Hi."

His hands settle on the low of my back. "Hi."

"Did you have to wait long?"

"No."

"You worked from home today?"

He nods, tipping my head back. "Yes."

"Will I ever get to see your place?"

"One day, perhaps. If you behave."

"What if I misbehave in the way you like?"

"Then we'll go there first thing tomorrow." He bends his head and kisses me, a greeting and a promise. "How was work?"

"It was great. I met with two new clients all day, and I'm really excited about these two. They'd probably work well together."

His lip curls. "Romantic."

"Oh, yes. Definitely. Should we go inside?"

"Yeah."

"We won't stay long," I promise again.

"We can stay for as long as you want," he reminds me. I don't doubt he means it, but I also suspect he won't enjoy himself very much.

But he's here. For me.

The warmth in my chest as I slide my hand into his threatens to consume me. I want to be back in my apartment, have him lying beside me in bed or on my couch, and run my fingers through his hair. Or kiss him until he groans beneath me and begs, in that raspy voice, to touch me.

I'm so head-over-heels with this man.

He presses a kiss to my temple. "You look unbelievable in this dress, by the way."

"Thank you," I murmur.

A waitress leads us to the table Posie's booked. Or more accurately, tables. Raucous laughter rises from the group of people crowded around them.

My gaze snags on Posie's willowy shape. Her red hair is up in a messy bun, the same shade she's dyed it since college, the one that wouldn't look good on anyone else.

"Summer," she says, eyes lighting up. "You made it."

"Of course I did. Happy birthday!" I pull her in for a hug.

"Oh, thank you. I'm half-tempted to stop counting, really, but it might be too early. Is that when we hit thirty?"

"Yes, we're not quite there yet."

Her arm drops to my waist, effortlessly, the way it's always been with her. "And who's this?" she asks.

"This is Anthony."

He extends a hand. "A pleasure."

"A friend of Summer's is a friend of mine," Posie says, with a not-so-subtle glance in my direction. It says *tell me everything!*

I give a little shrug. *It's new, but yeah… he's amazing.*

Anthony sees it too. There's a curl to his lips as he tells us he's getting us something to drink. "Glass of white?" he asks me.

I nod, and watch him disappear toward the bar. Posie

wiggles her eyebrows. "Who is this, Summer? I didn't know you'd met someone!"

"It's new. Really new, actually. But it's going great."

She glances toward the bar. "He looks intense."

I chuckle. "Yeah, he can be intense. In a good way, though."

"How'd you meet him?"

"At work." I shake my head before she can finish the thought. "He wasn't one of my clients. He's more on the business side of things."

Which is certainly true. He owns the business.

"You look happy," Posie says, her hands sliding down to clasp mine. "That's the most important part."

"I'm really happy. He's... well. I'm head-over-heels, really." I laugh. "But how are you? How's Ben? Is he here?"

"Yes, yes, he's over there," Posie says with a nod to where her long-term boyfriend is mingling. Her voice drops, tugging me closer. "I didn't invite Robin, Summer, but someone dragged him along anyway. You know how it is."

I nod. "Yeah. I figured."

Anthony chooses that moment to return and my hands slide out of Posie's to accept the glass he hands me.

"Happy birthday," he says to Posie. "I heard you went to college with Summer?"

"I did, yes. We had a lot of music theory classes together."

"Posie's a virtuoso," I say. "Think Mozart or Bach, but better."

She laughs. "God no. Don't listen to Summer. I play a few instruments, that's all."

"Five, right?"

"Well, I added cello recently. I'm not competent yet."

"Your version of 'not competent' is another person's mastery," I protest. "So six instruments."

"I'm impressed," Anthony says.

"She plays at the New York Philharmonic."

"All right, now I'm even more impressed."

Posie laughs. "Summer, you've always been better at selling me than I do myself."

Anthony lowers his glass, glancing from me to Posie. "How was she in college?"

"Summer?"

"Yes."

Posie shoots me a wide grin. "Oh, she was popular. Great at managing her dual subjects of business and music. Charmed everyone with that voice of hers."

I shake my head. "Now you're overselling me here."

"Not in the least." Posie leans closer to Anthony, lowering her voice. "This girl right here used to sell out the student café when she was performing. She'd write mash-ups of the most popular songs on the radio and sing them, harmonies and all."

"She did?"

"Oh yes. I'd play guitar and she'd sing, sitting on a barstool with a single microphone, and bring down the house."

"That was a long time ago," I say.

"Yes, it was," Posie agrees. "Far too long. We should do it again, Summer. Find an open mic in the city and bring the place down for old time's sake. This time I can comp you on cello."

"I'll help," Anthony adds, voice serious. "I'm passable at playing the triangle."

We both laugh at that, and Anthony smiles, even if the look he gives me is full of speculation. He only knows me as the non-singing, post-Robin Summer. Posie is soon swept along on the tide of more friends come to celebrate her, so Anthony and I chat with some of my other college friends.

Well, I chat. Anthony chimes in on occasion, but he's mainly a quiet, stable presence beside me.

It's at least twenty minutes until I see Robin for the first time.

His hair is pushed back, disheveled flannel shirt front-tucked into a pair of jeans. I know they both cost more than they look.

My fingers tighten around my glass of wine. Anthony shifts, bending down so his mouth rests against my ear.

"What's happened?" he murmurs.

"My ex is here."

His hand slides to my low back. "The asshole."

The heartfelt epitaph falls naturally from his lips and I laugh, looking away from Robin to meet Anthony's dark gaze. "Yeah, that very one."

"How do you feel?"

"Happy."

His eyebrows knit. "Happy?"

"Yes. Happy I'm not with him anymore. Happy I'm with you."

Anthony's thumb rubs a small caress through my dress. "Ah," he says.

"That's it?"

His lip curls, but as he bends and brushes my hair back, the heat in his voice is unmistakable. "Yes, Summer. That's it. Unless you want me to show you how *happy* I am in front of all your college friends."

I sway a little on my wedge heels. "Let's go home," I tell him.

His eyes dance as he lifts his head. "Anything you want, but we can stay, if you'd like."

I glance to where Posie is sitting, Ben's arm around her waist and a colleague from the Philharmonic beside her. There are more than enough people here to celebrate her and we have a dinner scheduled in a few days, just the two of us.

"Let's go," I repeat, standing on my tiptoes to get closer to him. "Besides, Ace can't be alone for too long."

"Oh yes," he agrees. "Let's go home for Ace's sake."

I kiss him, loving the pleased surprise in his eyes. "Come on then, Winter."

We don't make it far before Robin intercepts us. He's holding a Whiskey Sour in one hand. I remember once drinking them reluctantly with him, because he so often ordered for me.

How had I ever been with someone like that?

The me I'd been with him feels like the memory of a dream, and not a good one at that.

"Summer," he says. His gaze slides to Anthony, and the calculating gleam in it is obvious to me now.

"Hi, Robin," I say.

"You weren't planning on leaving without saying hello to me, were you?" His smile doesn't show in his eyes.

"I was, actually."

He blinks. Looks back at me from his perusal of Anthony, and for the first time I remember, it actually seems like he's seeing me.

"Ah," he says. "Well, that's sneaky of you, Sum."

Anthony clears his throat and extends a hand to Robin. "Anthony Winter."

Well, that's not fair. He's breaking out his full name, knowing exactly what that thing does. I cheer him on silently.

Robin's eyes narrow. "Robin Whitlock," he replies.

"A pleasure," Anthony says in a bored drawl. "Now, we were leaving, so if you'll please…"

The hint of a flush rises in Robin's cheeks. Oh, I haven't forgotten how quick he is to anger when he feels shamed.

I give him a brilliant smile. "Take care of yourself, Robin."

We step past him toward the exit. If he responds, it's not something I hear. It's not something I want to either.

Anthony doesn't put his arm around my shoulders or tug me against his side. He just brushes the back of his hand against mine in a subtle invitation, and I know him well enough to know it's not accidental.

I curl my fingers around his in answer.

We walk hand-in-hand through the crowded bar, like we walk this way all the time. Like we're a confirmed item. My heart beats fast, and it's not only from the confrontation with Robin.

Anthony stops a few feet from the door. It's such an abrupt stop that I startle, looking up at him.

He's watching a couple in the opposite corner.

There's nothing special about them. A dark-haired woman is sitting in the crook of a tall man's arm. They look a bit mismatched, perhaps. He has a leather jacket on and she wears a tweed blazer.

As we watch, the man turns her face up to his and kisses her.

"Anthony?" I ask. The look on his face sets my heart into overdrive. He looks... outraged. Betrayed.

Confused.

"My fucking eyes," he mutters. "I can't be sure... I have to be sure, Summer."

"Sure about what?"

Barely taking his eyes off the couple, he pulls out his phone. A few seconds later and there's an image of a pristine young brunette on the screen.

"Is this her? Sitting over there?"

I look from the image of a smiling woman with pearl earrings to the couple across the bar.

"Yes," I whisper. "It's her. Who is she, Anthony?"

"Cordelia Jacobs," he says. "My brother's fiancée."

21

ANTHONY

I walk through the lobby of the Winter Hotel with quick strides. It won't be long until one or more of the concierges recognizes me, and once they do, there will be no end to the hello-ing and hi-ing I'll have to endure.

Worse, because they're people I'd once spent a lot of time with. Marcel at reception had looked after Isaac and me when we were children, letting us ride the luggage trolleys down the corridor sometimes when we visited.

The plush carpet gives way under my feet as I walk up the marble staircases. The railing is polished to gleaming. The way it's always been, and if my brother has a say in it, the way it'll always be.

The Winter Hotel is an institution.

It's my family's greatest accomplishment. It's also my family's ball-and-chain.

Isaac's office is on the second floor. He'll be here, because he's always here on Thursday afternoons, and my older brother is as regular as clockwork. My mother likes to joke that it started with his birth, with him arriving at noon on the expected date.

An attendant stares at me open-mouthed when I swipe my keycard to access the staff corridor. Perhaps I'm a ghost around here. A tale passed down to new employees, a name whispered. The lost son.

I give a nod and shut the door behind me.

Knock twice on Isaac's office door.

"Enter," he calls.

Ah, yes. *Come on in* is doubtless too many words. Not efficient enough.

Isaac's eyes widen when he sees me and he pushes back from his desk. "Anthony?"

"Yes."

"I didn't know you were coming in today."

"It's an impromptu sort of thing."

He nods. Glances to the chair opposite his desk. "Well, I'm glad. It's been a long time."

"It has."

"You're answering my email in person," he says, smiling. "Does this mean you accept?"

"Accept?"

"Being my best man."

My stomach sinks, and I do something I haven't done since this office belonged to our dad. I sit down in the chair opposite him. Wish I was anywhere but here. "Isaac, about that... I saw Cordelia yesterday. And she wasn't alone."

———

The taxi pulls up outside of Summer's Soho apartment. I pay him more than I should and wave away the change. My steps feel heavy and my head thick as I call her on the intercom.

"Come in!" she sing-songs.

But when she opens the door for me and sees my expression, the smile on her face is wiped clean. "It didn't go well?"

"Not particularly." I wrap my arms around her waist and kick the door shut behind me. Nestle my head against the crook of her neck. God, I adore the way she smells.

She runs a hand over my hair. "That bad, huh?"

171

"That bad."

"Well, I suppose there's no good way to tell anyone they're being cheated on."

"It was worse."

"Worse?"

I lift my head with a sigh and finally say hello to Ace, who is eager and bouncing around my legs. His ears are silky beneath my hands. "My brother didn't believe me."

For once, it seems like I've struck Summer speechless. She just stares at me.

"He didn't... what?"

I sigh. "He didn't believe me. Something smells amazing. Are you cooking dinner?"

"Yes, there's lasagna in the oven. You like that, right?"

Turning toward the kitchen, I have to fight a sudden burning behind my eyes. There's no way she'd understand how much this normalcy means. How rare it is in my life.

How much I'll miss it when it's gone.

"Yes," I say. "I like lasagna."

Summer says nothing, just runs a hand over my arm. Touching me casually. Easily. I bend to give Ace a final pat to get myself under control.

"Did he say why he didn't believe you?" she asks, opening the fridge. "Wine?"

"Yes, thanks." I sit down on one of her small kitchen chairs, stretching out my legs. She'll have to step over them as she moves around, that's how small this place is.

I accept the wineglass she hands me. "I've burned a lot of bridges with my family."

"Oh?"

"Yeah. More than... yeah."

"How come?" She arranges vegetables on a cutting board as we speak, searching for a knife. Making a salad. Asking me without looking at me.

I run a hand over my face and feel a century old. "I haven't been particularly nice since I got my... well. Since I found out about my eyes."

"You've been nice to me."

I'm quiet for a beat. "Yes. Well, you're an exception."

"You're nice to your business partners."

"I work with them."

"Still, nice. You were really nice to my friends the other night too."

My lip lifts. Yes, I'd made semi-pleasant small talk for forty-five minutes. It had been a small price to pay to be alongside her for the night.

"I'm capable, I suppose. But not always."

"And you haven't been nice to your family," she says.

"A year ago," I say carefully, "I was at a family dinner with my parents, my brother, and Cordelia. Mom asked me about the future. My dating life, specifically. And I nearly bit my mother's head off at the dinner table." I close my eyes, because the shame and self-loathing that floats inside of me can't handle Summer's gaze. "I didn't trust myself around them for a long time. Not sure if I do, still."

Summer's voice is soft. "It's okay to be angry about your vision, Anthony. To feel cheated or bitter."

"Yeah. Well, they don't know any of that. They only know I've become an unsociable asshole."

"Do you think they'd understand if you told them?"

I open my eyes to see her leaning against her miniature kitchen counter. She has a small tomato stain on her lilac dress and an expression so soft it slices through me.

"Yes," I murmur. "They would. But they'll also snap into fix-it mode. Start looking for ways to solve this problem or to adapt."

"And you don't want that," she completes. "Because adapting is surrendering."

"I know it makes no sense."

"It does, in a way. Even if it doesn't serve you." She brushes her hands down her thighs, a thoughtful tone to her voice. "Do you also want to protect them from it?"

"Yes."

"Hmm. I figured you might."

"It'll crush my parents. My mother, in particular. How could it not?"

She gives a slow nod. "As long as they don't know, they don't hurt. And as long as they don't know, it's not real."

I shift on the chair, feeling too hot. Too seen. "Yeah."

"Again, it makes sense, in a way," she says. "But I think they might appreciate you letting them in, and who knows? They might be helpful."

"Yes." The idea of being helped stings, though. So does the idea of becoming reliant on others. It's what I can't bear to let happen to myself.

Exercising that sneaky sixth sense of hers, she turns back to the salad. Hums a little melody in perfect pitch and sways her hips in tune. I lean back against the wall and watch her, drinking my wine.

Pushing away the words my brother had said. The accusations. *It's not enough that you ignore your family. You're trying to sabotage us now, too?*

None of that exists here.

Not to mention Summer is infinitely more interesting than me and my miserable future.

"How did it feel the other night?" I ask. "Seeing him?"

Her humming stops, but not her swaying, as if she's still singing in her head. "It felt great," she says. "Honestly. I didn't expect it to, but it did."

I cross my legs at the ankles and she jumps over them to reach the sink. "When I think of him and me, and of who I was when I was with him, it feels so long ago."

"Hmm." It's hard to see her shining goodness, her smiles and laughter and jokes, and imagine her with someone who told her she couldn't sing. It makes my blood boil. "Why were you together with him?"

"You're going to laugh," she says, but doesn't sound the least bit concerned that I might. "But I think I was more in love with the idea of us being in love, than actually with him. I was so in love with the idea of being in a relationship... that I didn't care about the red flags. Figured I could change him. Or he'd change because of me." She shakes her head, reaching up on her tiptoes to reach a bowl. "It was stupid."

I'm silent, absorbing that. Reminded of her love of love. Of true love.

"You know what, I really like that about you," she says. This time there's a clear smile in her voice.

"Like what? I haven't said anything."

"Yes, exactly." The look she throws me over her shoulder is warm. "You didn't rush in to tell me it wasn't stupid. Because I know you think it was. And that's okay."

I clear my throat. "I wouldn't have called it stupid. Hopeful, maybe. Even beautiful in a way. But no, I don't think believing love will change someone's shitty behavior is a solid strategy."

"I don't either. Not anymore. So I suppose I should say thank you to him, really."

"Maybe that's taking it a step too far. He's still an asshole."

She laughs, looking down at the chopping board. I can see the curve of her lips from where I'm sitting.

"You still believe in true love," I said. "He didn't... ruin that?"

"For a while, maybe," she says. She looks across the room to Ace, who's lying down and watching her move in the kitchen with attentive self-interest. "But I see it too much to ever doubt its existence."

"Your parents."

"My parents," she agrees. "But also in my friends, in stories I read, in the world. In every call I receive from one of Opate's clients gushing about the match we set up. It's everywhere, if you look hard enough."

"I wish I could see the world the way you do."

She puts down the knife and turns, eyes meeting mine. "You mean that?"

I run a hand over my face. "Yeah."

"How come?"

"I see it the way you do, I suppose. But in reverse."

"You see evidence that love doesn't exist everywhere?"

I shift in the seat, rearrange my legs. Run a hand through my hair. "Not everywhere."

Summer doesn't push. She finishes the salad instead. Puts two plates on the table and bends to check the oven. "Two minutes."

"My ex," I say. "It didn't end... well. I found out about the diagnosis and a month later, she told me it wasn't working anymore."

"Oh. I'm sorry, Anthony."

"Yeah. Well, I was pretty foolish, I suppose, to think she'd stay. Who'd want to shackle themselves to a man who'll need help for the coming decades?" I shake my head. "She did the right thing."

"You don't believe that," Summer says. "Not really, or it wouldn't have hurt."

I look down at the plate in front of me. Fiddle with the fork. "Yeah. I suppose."

"You talk as if you'll become paralyzed. You won't. There are ways to live—"

My raised hand stops her. "Please, Summer. I... please."

"I won't, then. Just don't talk disparagingly about yourself to me, okay? I happen to really like you, and no one talks bad to you in front of me. Not even you."

I roll my eyes. "My savior."

"That's me. Now, do you want extra parmesan with your lasagna?"

"If the question is between cheese and more cheese, there's only one answer."

Her smile lights up her face, a difficult topic dispelled. It must be effortless for her. "See, I know there's a reason I keep you around."

"My infinite wisdom, yes. Happy to oblige."

Our knees touch under the table as we eat, and talk, about everything and nothing. It's cramped. The table is tiny. But the wine is drinkable and her food delicious, impressive, home-made. Cooked for us. For me.

I insist on doing the dishes afterwards and endure her laughter. "You've never done this before?" she says, reaching past me for the dish soap.

"Of course I have."

"You fill the sink up *first.*"

"I just hadn't gotten to that part."

"Mhm. You've clearly never lived in a place without a dish-washer," she says. "It shows."

"I don't cook either."

"What do you live off of? When you're not at mine?" Our elbows rub together as we inefficiently wash a dish. My fingers graze over hers beneath the soapy surface.

"I order in, mostly."

"All the time? Like, for every meal?"

I shrug. "I suppose, yes."

"Wow," she breathes. Her hip bumps into mine, and I keep mine there, our bodies side-to-side. I'll never tire of hers. "I haven't thought about it much lately, but… there's such a differ-ence between us."

I glance down. "We're different in some areas, yeah."

"I meant financially," she says, shaking her head. "Sorry. Perhaps I shouldn't have used the F-word."

"F-word stands for finance? Man, I've always wondered."

She laughs, reaching for the plug. Drains the sink. "I just mean, when it's only the two of us here, I usually forget that you techni-cally own my aunt's business. That your last name is on hotels all over the country or that you can afford to order takeout nonstop."

I lean against the counter and watch her flit around the kitchenette. She needs to step past me every time she passes, and on one such pass, I catch her.

Wrap my hands around her waist.

"I think I prefer it when it's just the two of us here."

She runs her hands up my shoulders. "I think I do too."

"Does it bother you?" I ask. "The difference?"

Her hand smooths my hair back from my forehead, and this close, with the kitchen light, I can make out the flecks of gold in her blue eyes.

"No. Although… no."

"Although what?"

"I don't know how to tell my aunt. About us. I mean, technically, I don't really know if there's anything to tell yet? You said you didn't do relationships."

Her eyes are on the lock of my hair she's smoothing back. The tentative hope in her voice feels like a stab, the sweetest poison. In the end, I give her a compromise.

"Are you happy, Summer? With me?"

She nods and her eyes meet mine. "Yes," she says.

"I'm glad," I say, tilting her head up to meet mine. "I'm happy with you too."

22

SUMMER

I wake up to a warm bed, a warm man, and a door being softly nudged open. Ace's nose bumps against my hand a few seconds later. I turn my fingers into his fur. One hand on each of my boys, I think, tracing Anthony's arm around my waist with my other.

He's stayed the night, as he's often done. Carried me from the couch to the bed. Despite my cracked bedroom window, the summer air is stifling. Our bodies stick together in the heat.

Neither of us has moved away.

He grumbles behind me as I shift, arm flexing around my waist.

"Just checking the time."

"You don't need the time," he says, voice raspy. "It's Saturday."

"Saturdays are worth seizing."

"Christ. Have you ever just spent half the day in bed? Doing nothing?"

I turn onto my back, and his hand slips beneath my camisole, large hand splayed on my stomach. There's a thud as Ace lies down beside the bed. "Of course I have."

"Really," Anthony says. "When?"

"Well... do you want a specific date?"

"Specificity would help."

I turn and look at him. Disheveled hair, soft eyes. To think I'd sized him up as not for me. Unguarded and newly awake, he's glorious.

A secret only I get to know.

"See?" he says. "You can't think of any. You're a seize-the-day kind of girl."

"Guilty," I admit. "Take me away to the dungeons—I surrender!"

"About that. Where are your dungeons around here?"

"We haven't installed any yet. Working on it."

"Just what this place needs."

"Mmm. That reminds me. I still haven't seen how you live."

"Oh, I have plenty of dungeons."

"You do?"

"Yeah. That's why I haven't taken you there."

"Scared I'll run if I see them?"

He shakes his head. A lock of dark hair falls over his forehead and I smooth it back. "They're only something I show to true connoisseurs."

"I haven't passed the test yet, then."

"No. Doubt you'd like them either." He turns over, lifts himself onto his free arm. His right hand makes lazy circles on my stomach. "You're hopeless in the doom and gloom department."

"I could try. Dress in all black and start scowling. You could teach me that."

"I don't wear all black."

I raise an eyebrow.

"Not all the time I don't."

"At the office you always do."

"That's because I'm wearing a suit there."

"Suits come in other colors than black."

He looks up at the ceiling, like he's beseeching a higher power to give him strength, but he's smiling. I can tell. "It's too early to argue with you."

"Now, how would you know it's early? You didn't let me look at a watch."

"Outsmarted," he says morosely. Bends his head to kiss my neck. "Are you as warm as me?"

"Yes," I say, and hook my leg over his hip. It does nothing to keep either of us cool.

"I hate the city on days like this," he murmurs against my skin. "Do you have any plans this weekend?"

"No, not really."

"Montauk," he murmurs.

"Montauk," I whisper back.

It should feel strange packing my things with him in the apartment, or getting into the car with a driver he summons with a few clicks on his phone. But it doesn't. Not as he makes dry comments about what I pack that make me laugh, or when he's the one to leash Ace and give an approving click of his tongue when my dog heels.

Not as we arrive at the beach house paradise, the place he loathed for what it represented.

"Home sweet home," he says dryly.

I step past him into the kitchen. Set down the bag of groceries we'd stopped for on the kitchen counter. "Don't you think there's a way to still live in New York? After?"

"I can't imagine a more deadly situation than walking blind through the city," he says. I watch his back as he strides to the double-doors and opens them up to the patio and the white sand beyond. The ocean is a glittering blue in the distance. Ace weaves around his legs, tail wagging faster than I've seen it before, and Anthony bends down.

He's too far away, but I think I make out the words *you like it here, don't you, boy? That's a good dog.*

I smile down at the chicken filets we'd bought. My heart feels like it's doubling in size and constricting at the same time.

"I've seen people who were blind in the city before," I say instead. "On the subway."

"With a cane," he responds. Tugs off his jacket and throws it over the back of the sofa. The tone of his voice makes it clear that's not an option for him. "Come on. I want us to take a walk on the beach."

"You do?"

"Yes," he says. "What?"

"No, nothing. I'm down. I'm just surprised you're the one suggesting it."

He looks at me for a long moment, but then his lip curls. "Yeah. Well, I guess some of your seize-the-day nonsense has rubbed off on me."

I shut the fridge door with my foot. "Then let's squeeze all the juice out of this one."

The day doesn't complain, despite my brutal phrasing. We're both sweaty when we return with a sandy dog in tow. "Pool," I say, reaching for the hem of my T-shirt. "Now."

Anthony grins and reaches for his own. Here, beneath the sun, it's like he's a different person. The man I'd once seen sitting opposite me in the darkness feels a million miles away.

But I know he's not. He's here too, when he thinks I don't see him. The darkened eyes and scowl. Or, sometimes, the long looks when he's sure I won't notice.

I wish he'd share what he's feeling with me. To have a diagnosis like that, hanging like the sword of Damocles over one's future.

My heart aches. I wish he would let me tell him that, too. That he's worth staying with. Fighting for.

But most of all, I wish he'd believe that himself.

Anthony looks at me with those inscrutable eyes from the pool, his head slicked along his skull. I won't be surprised if he knows where my mind's gone. My parents still tease me about my lack of a poker face.

"Coming in?" he asks.

I nod, stepping out of my shorts, and dive into his arms.

It's late that night when I pull out the pièce de resistance, the thing I'd seen in the grocery store and been unable to resist. Somehow Anthony hadn't seen it in the checkout line.

"Marshmallows?" he asks. "And... graham crackers. Are you making some sort of dessert?"

"S'mores," I say. "We're making s'mores. How could you not have guessed that?"

He turns a chocolate bar over in his hands. "Right. I don't think I've ever had it."

"Please tell me you're joking."

"Okay. I'm joking."

"You're not very convincing."

He raises an eyebrow. "If it's so important to you, you should have asked me about it when you created my dating profile. It should make for a good prompt."

"I would've," I grumble, "if I knew I was planning on dating you myself."

Anthony laughs and reaches for one of the marshmallows. He pops it into his mouth and chews.

"These are really not that good," he says. It comes out half-mangled.

I laugh, pushing at him. "They're much better half-melted and gooey."

"Mhm. You sure about that?"

"One hundred percent. How have you never had these?"

He shrugs. "I've never been camping. But I trust you. You're a great cook."

The earnestness in his voice is what makes me blush. I make simple pasta dishes and know the incredibly complicated recipe for s'mores. But he's entirely genuine.

"Thank you," I murmur. "But it must be easy to impress a guy who mostly eats takeout."

His crooked smile is back. He reaches past me for the tray and we make it out to the patio. "I don't know," he says. "My mother used to cook a lot."

"Used to?" I ask.

"Still does, I suppose. But I haven't been there for a while," he says, pulling out my chair for me. It's such a quaint, old-school movement that I smile, but Anthony looks lost in thought.

I light the candles. Wrap a blanket around my shoulders and pull my legs up beneath me. The sun is setting, and it won't be long until the sky is star-filled and luminous.

"My parents have a family dinner every Sunday, without fail," he continues. "They'll invite people over. Aunts, uncles. Family friends."

"That sounds nice."

"Yeah. It can be."

"When was the last time you went?"

Anthony looks out to the ocean. "I think it was around Christmas."

It's July now. I swallow, looking down at the lit candles. My parents would be heartbroken if I didn't want to remain in close contact with them. So would I, for that matter.

"Anyway," he says, reaching for one of the skewers and turning it over in his large hands. "I imagine our childhoods were pretty different."

"You mean mine wasn't s'mores-deprived?"

His lip quirks. "Right. You probably sat at the campfire every summer evening with your loving parents, surrounded by a pack of well-trained dogs, and grilled s'mores."

"You make it sound so idyllic."

"Wasn't it?" he challenges.

I skewer a marshmallow. "Sometimes it was like that. There were certainly always dogs around."

"And your friends," he adds, "who your parents treated like their own kids. You were popular in school. But not in the cliquey kind of way, no, everyone just wanted to be your friend, and you found everyone interesting. "

I look at him, and he looks back at me, an eyebrow raised. "Am I wrong?"

"Not really, I suppose. I don't know if everyone wanted to be my friend, but I was friendly with most."

"That's a yes, then."

"Think you have me all figured out?"

"I had you all figured out the first day I met you."

I laugh. "Glad to be such a mystery."

Anthony doesn't laugh. He lowers his skewer instead. "You are, though. The mystery is how you do it."

"How I do what?"

"How you manage to stay happy, and optimistic, and willing to see the best in everyone."

"Right," I murmur, looking down. "And birds help me dress in the morning."

He knocks my marshmallow with his own. "Hey, I'm not mocking you. I know I've teased you about it before, but Summer... your optimism is genuine. That's the way you see the world. It's impressive. It's a complete fucking mystery to me how you do it, but it's breathtaking."

I meet his gaze, dark and earnest. I don't think a man has ever looked at me the way he does. Like he's trying to memorize my every feature. "I'm not always happy."

"I know," he says. "But you're always genuine."

"An open book, or so I've been told."

"You let people see you, Summer. That's strength."

This time, I reach out and take his hand. He flips his over and long fingers tighten around mine.

"You should let people see you too," I murmur. "Because you're amazing."

Anthony looks down at our intertwined hands. His thumb makes a slow, sweeping arc over my palm. When he speaks, his voice has dropped. "The more time passes, the more difficult it feels to... well. I know I have to tell people in my life about my vision. Fuck, of course I know that, Summer. But that will make it real. As long as I'm the only one who knows, I can pretend it's not happening."

My heart aches with the need to reach out and hug him. To say that everything will be okay. I sit still instead, listening. Bearing witness to his pain.

I think he needs to be listened to.

We talk as we eat s'mores, slow and haltingly. Anthony swears when molten chocolate escapes down his fingers and I can't keep from laughing.

"They're good," he admits. "Messy, and simple, but good."

"They're a summer thing, like watermelon and mosquito bites. You have to have them at least once."

He grimaces and pushes away the half-empty bag of marshmallows. "I can live without the mosquito bites. Come here, join me on this side."

I shift over to his side of the patio and sit next to him. There's a soft sweep of fur against my bare leg and I glance down. Ace is splayed over Anthony's feet, his face tucked against Anthony's ankle.

Thick as thieves.

"He loves you," I murmur.

Anthony looks down at my dog. A smile plays around his lips. "He's a good dog."

"They really are man's best friend."

"Yeah," he says, and I wonder if he's thinking the same thing I am. About guide dogs. "They are."

I nestle against his side and he snorts, lifting his arm and draping it over my shoulders. The night is beautiful, warm and calm, the ocean a soft sigh against the nearby shore.

"I love this place," I say.

Anthony's hand moves over my shoulder. "Then I'm glad I got it."

My heart feels full of love for more than just his house, but I don't say it. Not yet. The knowledge settles like warm honey in my stomach.

I rest my head against his shoulder and look up. The moon is a barely-there slice in the sky, surrounded by friends, their faraway light shining down on us in tiny pinpricks.

"Do you know any constellations?" I ask. "I've never been able to pick out anything apart from the Little and Big Dipper."

Anthony doesn't answer right away. When he does, his voice is thoughtful. "I can't remember the last time I saw the stars."

"You mean…"

"Yes," he says. "One night, the stars went out for me, and they'll never return. The night sky has gone dark."

I'm glad for the darkness now, hiding the emotion on my face. My heart feels like it's breaking for him.

"I'm thankful I saw you, at any rate," he murmurs. "Before it all goes black."

My eyes overfill. I don't know how he knows, but he does, his free hand smoothing the tears away from my cheeks. "Don't cry, Summer," he whispers. "Not for me."

I do anyway. "How can you bear it? How do you keep from despairing?"

He kisses my temple and pulls me close. "I don't," he says, the sound like a confession against my hair. "You just haven't seen it yet."

23

ANTHONY

I reach for the glass of scotch on my coffee table and nearly knock it over. The slippery thing has moved since I put it down last. It's safer to keep it clutched tight in hand.

It burns going down my throat as I drain it.

It's been a while since I last sat here, in this chair, in my own living room, downing booze. Racking my brain through the splitting headache is hard, but not impossible.

It was a few weeks before I met Summer.

Not terribly surprising, that. She'd been bright enough to drown out the darkness. Concentrating on anything else, including my own misery, was difficult with her around.

But she's not around now. No elephant lamp in the corner of her apartment, no thick oriental rugs or the chamomile tea she makes.

Tea. I'd bought that for myself.

I look toward the kitchen, but making it feels like too much effort. It would help me sleep, but so will the scotch, and it's closer at hand.

Perhaps it'll also help me forget.

Accelerating. That was Dr. Johnson's word this morning. Accelerating. I prefer it when it's used in relation to fast cars and not mentioned in the same sentence as retinitis pigmentosa, vision degradation, blindness.

It's like I'm in a fight, and I'm swinging, but my arms are getting tired. And I'm losing. And I know I'm losing, know failure is the only outcome, but I can't for the life of me give up the fight.

Not yet.

I pour myself two more knuckles' worth of scotch and lean back in the chair. Close my eyes. Blackness behind my lids. Will I see that, then, one day?

The doctor doesn't know. There's a ton he doesn't know, as it so happens. Not how quickly I'll lose my eyesight. Not how much of it I'll lose. If I'll retain the ability to differentiate between light or darkness. If I'll maintain tunnel vision. Or if I'll be blind as a bat before the year is out.

But he does know that it's accelerating, oh yes. He was very sure of that. *You've noticed the deterioration in your night vision?*

Yes.

How is reading for you these days?

It works if I increase the size of text. And have a very bright light. Up the contrast.

And printed text?

I'd shifted in my seat. If it's big enough, I'd said.

Dr. Johnson had done what he always did. Looked into my worthless eyes, taken notes on his computer, returned to my eyes. Gone through a series of tests, all of them already confirming what we both know.

I'd made a joke to the good old doctor. *You know,* I'd told him, as he peered at an enlarged photograph of my eye. *All of my worst memories include you.*

He'd laughed, because he meets people like me daily, sorry fuckers who are losing life one day at a time.

I drain half of my glass. Going too fast, too fast, both the drink and my eyes. Too fast. I'm supposed to have more time. More time with Summer. More time to tell people. To fucking *adjust,* as Dr. Johnson keeps telling me.

Adjust. As if anyone could.

Summer's out with friends tonight and I'm glad she is. Mostly. Jealous, too, if I'm being honest. I push up from the armchair and make my way to the en-suite by my bedroom in search of a little white bottle with pills. Painkillers. Blessed relief-bearers. They help with the migraines.

I get the twist cap open and pour out two into my empty hand. Look at the glass of scotch in my right.

I know this is a bad idea. But the part of my brain that cares is locked away. I can see it, but I can't feel it, and it sure can't reach me.

So I swallow the pills and drain them with alcohol. Set the glass down on the marble. Make my way to my bed and stretch out on the linens. They don't smell like Summer, because she has never been here. They smell like laundry. The cleaning lady must have been here recently. It's off, the smell.

Like I'm in a hotel or a rental.

I twist over on my back and close my eyes. Decide to see how long I'll last in the blackness before the crushing sense in my chest gets too much.

It's not a fun game, but it is preparation. And wasn't that what Dr. Johnson wanted me to do? Adjust.

Look at me trying, Doc.

———

I wake up to a room cast in sharp, painful light. The curtains. I hadn't drawn the curtains last night.

The pressure grip around the crown of my head feels like a steel vise. The alcohol, probably. Its wondrous effects are always short-term.

The sound of a doorbell being insistently pressed rings through the house. Was that what woke me up?

Summer.

I'd invited Summer here today. It's Saturday. I'm supposed to show her my place. Walk around the neighborhood.

Fuck.

I push myself out of bed and run a hand through my hair. Stop in the bathroom to brush my teeth. Close the door to my bedroom on the way out.

I hadn't forgotten. But it had been pushed to the back, too painful to touch, along with the realization that I have less time with her left than I thought. Accelerating, accelerating, fucking accelerating.

I reach the front door. Try, and fail, to take a deep breath before I open it.

"Good morning," Summer says. Her wheat-colored hair falls in waves around her face, bouncing as she holds up a paper bag. "I brought us bagels."

"Right. Nice."

Her smile shrinks, eyes zeroing in on mine. Seeing too much by far. "Are you okay, Anthony?"

"Yeah. You want to come in?"

"Um, yes. If that's okay?"

"Of course." I push open the door to illustrate just how okay it is. Ace is a tail-wagging, excited storm of a dog at my feet, pushing his nose against my leg. I bend down and give him a solid pat hello. "Good dog," I murmur and shut the door behind them.

Summer stands in the middle of my living room and takes it all in. I feel my stomach sink as I look at the place through her eyes.

I distinctly remember planning to tidy up yesterday. Dr. Johnson had derailed all those plans. His words had lured me back to a dark place with no way out.

I shove my hands into the pockets of my crumpled slacks and watch as she walks around the living room. The old marble mantlepiece. The leather sofas. The box of takeout on my coffee table and the half-empty bottle of scotch.

It's clean, at least, thanks to the house cleaners. But evidence of my life is everywhere.

"This townhouse is old," she says.

Not what I expected.

I clear my throat. "Yeah. Late nineteenth century, I think."

"Have you lived here long?"

"Yes. My grandparents lived here for a time when I was a child. We visited a lot. They moved to a different property a while back and neither my parents nor my brother wanted this place." I shrug. My mouth is running. With the headache and the darkness hanging over me like a cloud, the filter is gone. "I've always liked this street."

"It's a lovely area of New York. Very quiet."

"It is."

"You've got three stories for yourself?"

"Yeah."

She turns, smiling at me from across the room. The sunlight through the windows gilds her, the tan of her skin a beautiful contrast against her yellow sundress. "Doesn't that get lonely?"

I clear my throat. "Sometimes, I suppose. But I like my privacy."

"You sure do." She crosses the space and reaches for me, her arms wrapping around my waist. "Are you sure you're okay?"

"Don't I look it?" I ask. Take a tendril of her hair between my fingers.

"No," she says. "I'm here to listen if you want to talk."

I step out of her arms and head toward the kitchen. Turning my back on her hurts, but spilling out the truth hurts more. It feels like a flood inside me and the gates are already weak.

"Want something to drink?"

"Yes, sure."

I open the fridge. Close it again, and hope she didn't see. It's pitiful. I can't remember the last time I ate anything in this place that wasn't takeout, and for the past two weeks, I've spent more time at hers than mine.

Her place. I wish we were there now. Pizza and that stupid elephant lamp and Ace watching us from his sprawl on the opposite couch.

"Water's okay?" I ask. Stupid, Anthony.

"Of course." There's a rustling sound as she sits down by my kitchen table. "The weather is beautiful outside. It's ridiculously warm, really. We could go to the park later?"

"Good idea." I hand her the glass of water. Retreat to the kitchen counter and lean against it.

To think there'll be a time when I won't be able to see her, sitting right there in front of me, so beautiful it feels like my heart is being torn out of my body. The world creates beauty like this, and then takes my eyes away from me.

The cruelty of it is ripping me apart.

She puts her glass down. "Anthony?"

"My eyes are getting worse."

"Oh. It's progressing?"

"Quicker than the doctor had thought."

It's there, then. The look of pity and sorrow in her eyes. I can see it and it hurts like a freight train. That I'm the one causing her this. That I'm someone to be pitied. Both and neither, all wrapped up in one.

"Do they have a timeline?" she asks.

I shake my head and look past her to the beckoning sunlight beyond. "Nothing concrete, but he said a couple of years, most likely. Could be two. Could be eight. But it's not decades, at least."

"I'm so sorry, Anthony."

The soft-spoken words grate. I don't want to be someone she's sorry for. I want to be someone she can trust, someone she can turn to. A man she can see a future with.

Fuck, I haven't let myself think of the future in a long time. But I want it now, with her. I want it so bad it's like acid on my tongue. And I can't have it.

"It might be easier for you if we end this now."

"What do you mean?" she asks.

"It might be easier for you if you don't get too invested in this before I'm out of the picture. Ending it now as opposed to in a year or two."

"Anthony," she says, with infuriating calm, "you're not dying."

I have to smile at that. It's humorless, like me, like the pathetic existence I have to look forward to. "I might as well be. My way of life is dying. My career. My interests."

"You bought the house in Montauk as a getaway," she whispers.

"Yes, well, I suppose I should start learning where everything is. It'll be a prison soon enough."

She shakes her head. "Is this why you told me once you had no interest in relationships? In love?"

The words slip through my teeth like nails beneath a tire. Puncturing something on their way out. "I'm not going to be a burden on anyone, Summer. I refuse."

She pushes her chair back and stands. "You wouldn't be a burden. Anthony, you can't possibly think that."

"I can't possibly think that? So you'll never get tired of me not being able to navigate the house we live in? Never resentful that I can't take you places? That I'll slow you down, hinder your trips, stand in the way of all those dreams of yours. Your bucket list, Summer. I won't be able to tell you if your haircut looks good, let alone hike with you to Machu Picchu."

There's a stunned look on her face. She hasn't considered this, then. Good. I've had enough time to consider it for the both of us.

"There are ways," she murmurs. "Ways to learn to live with it. Guide dogs, white canes, braille... I know this won't defeat you."

"How do you know that?"

"Because you're stronger than this, Anthony. You're the strongest person I've met."

I shake my head at her. "You don't understand."

She buries her hand in Ace's fur. He's pressed against her leg, looking between us. "I don't. You're right. But that doesn't mean I don't want to be here, because I do, Anthony."

"You want children," I say. "It's on your bucket list."

The look she gives me is wide-eyed. She's not following, but she nods.

I tap a finger against my temple. "What kind of husband would I make? What kind of father?"

"A good one." A tear rolls down her cheek, and in the king of all ironies, I can see it with shattering clarity.

"A useless one," I correct her. "I refuse to become someone you have to take care of. Summer, I would rather die than be anything less than a true partner to you."

The small shake of her head is one of denial as her illusions shatter. Because the truth is I'll never be the man she wants me to be. Never able to live up to her fantasies of true love and two-point-five children.

"You should find someone else," I tell her. Nod to the door. "Use your own matchmaking service, Summer. Find a man who can take you on trips and give you children. Who doesn't spend the night passed out on painkillers and alcohol. You want a relationship like your parents have."

"It's my choice too," she says. "It's my choice who I want in my life. And I want you."

"Now, maybe. But you won't in the future."

She takes a step closer. Her eyes are wet, but the set of her mouth is sharp. "Stop telling me what I want! Damn it, Anthony. Would you rather your pride kept you company at night than me?"

"This has nothing to do with my pride."

"Doesn't it? Because I think it starts and ends with that." She shakes her head again, blowing out a breath. "I don't agree with you, Anthony. I don't agree with how you see yourself or your future."

"You will, in time."

"No, I won't." She reaches up and puts a hand on my cheek. I can't handle the emotion shining in her eyes, so I do what I usually hate.

I shut my eyes.

"I disagree with a lot of the things you've said today," she

195

says shakily. "Your life isn't over, and I won't let you throw the rest of it away. And as for me? Don't you dare make decisions for me about what I can and can't handle, or decide what I do or do not want."

Her hand slides off my cheek, and when I open my eyes again, she's back by the kitchen table. A flush is stark on her cheeks.

"I think it's best if I left for today," she says.

I nod. She should leave and never come back, if she knows what's good for her.

Her eyes fill again, like I've given the wrong response. But the vulnerability is gone as she turns on her heel and heads toward my front door.

Ace stays seated in the kitchen, a soft whine escaping his throat.

"Come on, Ace!" she calls out. I've never heard her use steel in her voice before when speaking to him.

He gives me one last long, brown-eyed look. "Go on, boy," I tell him.

He turns, shoulders down and tail between his legs, trotting to where Summer has already left.

24

SUMMER

I sink back onto my chair with a sigh. That was the longest meeting with a client I've ever had. He'd been meticulous about the details, and the fast prompts I'd given him had become opportunities for soliloquies.

But between the shyness in his expression and the depth of intellect his responses betrayed, finding a match for him won't be difficult.

I already have a few ideas, but I'll have to look through our client database to be sure. A tentative knock on the door to my office and Suzy sticks her head in.

We share a look.

"I was so close to coming up with a fake meeting for you, just to get you out of that one," she says.

"Thanks. We should have some sort of signal for that."

"We should. Like, if you call out to reception twice in quick succession."

"Or I can email you."

"Or you can email me," she says, grinning. "Did it go okay?"

"Absolutely. I think he's just anxious to get his responses right, and well... not everyone is comfortable with the idea of using a dating service."

"Very true." She steps into my office, leaving the door open behind her, and looks at herself in the gilded mirror. Runs a finger below her eyes to catch any falling mascara.

"You look great," I tell her. "I love this green dress on you."

She beams. "Thank you. It was a thrift-store find. Vintage Hermès."

"Really?"

"Yes. Had to get it dry-cleaned, but it was worth it."

"You should tell Vivienne about that store, if you haven't already. She might give you a raise on that alone."

We both laugh. My aunt's eclectic taste in everything expensive and historic is evident in the decor of our office, not to mention her own flawless outfits.

"I will," Suzy says. "She hasn't come into the office yet today, though."

"Not even while I had my meeting?"

She shakes her head. "Do you know what's going on?"

"No," I say, frowning. We haven't had one of our usual lunches in weeks. When I see her, she's usually leaving, or so am I, like ships passing in the night.

"Maybe she's just conducting more business outside of the office," I suggest. It's not unusual for Vivienne to meet with high-profile clients at restaurants or cafés. Hers has always been a casual touch.

"Yes," Suzy agrees. "At any rate, she'll be in this afternoon. Ryan is coming by to show us the latest prototypes for the app."

"Oh, he is?"

"Mmm." She pulls out a tube of lipstick and applies it carefully in the mirror.

I raise my eyebrows. "Suzy…"

"Yes?" she asks, all innocence. But then she breaks into a wide smile. "Okay, fine. He's absolutely delicious."

I laugh. "Of course he is."

"You've met him. Don't you agree? Oh, Summer, is it completely unprofessional if I ask him out? I know he's working for Acture and all, and they technically own us now."

I smile at her. There is nothing I can say to that, not when I've spent nearly all of my free time over the past month with Anthony. Suzy dating his employee pales in comparison.

I've been meaning to tell Vivienne that, too, but…

"Summer? You really don't think I should, do you?"

"No, I think you should go right ahead. You're brave, Suzy."

She beams at me again. "Thank you. What's the worst thing that can happen? That he says no."

So simple, and so true.

After she's left, I take her place in front of the large mirror. Smooth a hand over my dress and repeat her process of double-checking that my mascara hasn't smudged.

Anthony might come by together with his app developer.

Not that he's texted or called since we'd last spoken, that day at his townhouse. The argument has felt like a lead weight in my stomach ever since.

There had been such bitterness in his voice, the force of it sliding between my ribs like a steel blade. And truth, too. There had been truth in his words, in the way he looked at himself.

But it's not a truth I can accept.

Not when I've seen him at his best, at his truest, his freest. When he forgets to mourn what he hasn't yet lost.

When he lives in the moment.

I sit back down in my chair and call Ace over with a soft whistle. His tail wags low and he burrows his head between my knees, letting me wrap my arms around him. Bury my hands in his soft fur.

"What do you do," I whisper to him, "when the person you love refuses to love himself?"

A single, tentative lick to my neck. I close my eyes and fight against the sudden rush of tears.

He's losing his eyesight.

The man I love, the one who is complex and layered and sarcastic, who makes me feel safe and cherished and understood, is fighting against the weight of that diagnosis. And there's nothing I can do to take it away. To solve it. Nothing he can do, either.

Doesn't mean life isn't worth living.

Doesn't mean he should give up.

But I cry nonetheless, for what he's losing, and miss him with a fierceness that takes my breath away.

I'm still sniffling when I hear the sound of voices in the reception. Two voices. Suzy's and Ryan's.

Anthony's not coming to the office, then.

I'm reaching for a tissue when my phone chimes. It's him, and my eyes soak up the words, greedy for every piece.

Anthony: I'm sorry about the other day, Summer. Can I come to yours tonight to talk?

Yes, I think. *Yes yes yes.* Doesn't matter if the word "talk" is intimidating. If I have him in front of me, I have a shot, at least. A chance to convince him that we're worth betting on.

That I'm worth betting on.

I don't know why his ex didn't choose to stay when she learned about his eyesight, but I know I won't make the same decision.

Summer: Yes, please. I've missed you.

The last three words are impulsive, but true. He knows I'm an open book. Read me, I think.

The response is instant.

Anthony: So have I, Summer.

———

I buzz him up from downstairs, nerves dancing through my stomach. Ace greets him before I do. He greets my dog before me, too.

Both of us wary to look at each other.

"Hi, buddy," Anthony murmurs and runs a large, tan hand

through Ace's white-blonde fur. His tail is whipping so fast it's a blur.

Anthony straightens to his full height and gives me that close-mouthed, half-smile of his. "Hey."

"Hi," I say, and head straight to him.

He opens his arms and I surrender into them. Bury my face against his chest and breathe in the scent of him, the fabric of his sweater soft beneath my cheek.

"It's only been two days," Anthony says, "but it feels like forever."

"It does," I agree. "I barely made it through my days without someone narrating the newspaper for me."

"I'm sorry. I neglected my duties."

"It's okay," I say, taking a step back and finding his hand with mine. "You're here now."

His eyes soften, but he doesn't smile. "I am."

He kisses me for a long time after that. Lips moving over mine in insistent, familiar patterns. I lock my hands behind his neck and hold on through it all.

His eyes are glazed when he lifts his head and smooths a thumb over my lips. They feel swollen. "Let's sit down."

The simple words cut through my haze of lust with the sharp sting of reality. I follow him to my couches and we take the right one, the one we've laid entangled on so many times.

He sits down, but if he wants us to sit properly, I won't let him. I prop myself up against the pillows and throw my legs over his.

Anthony half-smiles, his free hand settling around my bare ankle. "You've been good?"

I nod. "You?"

"Yeah."

"Two days," I murmur.

He snorts. "Two days. Ridiculous."

"And yet," I say.

"And yet," he agrees. "Summer... I want to apologize for Saturday."

It takes me a moment to find the courage to say the next words out loud. But I do. "Do you feel bad for saying things you don't believe? Or bad because you didn't want me to hear them?"

He keeps his eyes on me for a long time, but I don't look away. Watch me stay, I think. Watch me not shrink from this.

"I still believe in everything I said," he finally says. "I can't see how it could be otherwise."

My eyes close on their own, like I can't stand to let him see the expression in them.

"Summer, while I don't see how it could be otherwise, I *want* to. Very, very badly. I was standing in line at the dry cleaners yesterday and out of nowhere I heard your voice. I don't even think it's something you've said to me, but I heard it so clearly you might as well have been standing beside me. *Why the fuck are you wasting your time on this?* That's what you asked me." He chuckles. "That's why I knew it wasn't actually you, by the way. You'd never curse."

"I do," I whisper. "Sometimes."

His fingers tighten around my ankle. "But you wouldn't in that situation. And I realized you were right. I've wasted so much time of however long I have left being pissed off. At the universe, at my eyes, at injustice. When I should have been living. Preparing. Seizing the fucking day, as you do."

My mouth feels dry, but I nod, watching as an animated flush creeps up on Anthony's olive cheeks. There are dark circles under his eyes, but his gaze is fierce.

"I don't know," he says, "if I can be the man you deserve. If I can fight this the way you think I can. It's very likely that I won't be as good of a... a boyfriend to you as someone else would. Someone who won't have my limitations. But by God, Summer, I'm going to try."

I reach over and cup his face between my palms. "I know you can. I know you will. Anthony, I—"

He kisses me, swallowing my words, and I fall onto the sofa. Pull him over me. His lips move with quiet urgency, pressing against my mouth like he's memorizing its shape. Like he's saying goodbye.

I knot my fingers into his shirt, but he breaks the hold easily, lifting both of us up again. This time, I slide onto his lap. Any space between us is too much.

"Summer," he murmurs. "I have to straighten myself out first, though."

"What do you mean?"

His answering smile is wry. "I have to go away for a little while. Summer, what you saw on Saturday… you haven't seen it all. How bad it can get. There have been days where I've…" He shakes his head. "I have to face it."

My fingers slip into the collar of his sweater and grip tight. "I want to face it with you."

"I know, baby."

"And I won't leave you because you'll one day lose your eyesight," I vow. "I know now, and I'm not about to run for the hills."

"I know," he murmurs. Runs a thumb over my cheek. "I have to fight this, Summer. You deserve someone who fights."

"Can't we do it together?"

"Not yet." He looks past me toward the windows, like he's embarrassed, the sharp cut of his jaw working. "It's like I have this darkness inside of me, this bottomless abyss, and sometimes it swallows me whole. I'll be having a normal conversation with someone and want to scream until my voice gives out. I can't fucking stand listening to someone complain. About anything. You lost your keys? Great. I'm going blind. It's self-pitying. And I can't stop it."

He shakes his head in a quick motion. "I don't like myself like this. It's not about the diagnosis, and you helped me see that. It's still the worst thing that's ever happened to me. It still a fucking tragedy. But this darkness inside of me… that's what's choking me, Summer. I don't like who I am when it's in charge. And it's in charge too often."

My fingers tighten around his neck. I feel like crying, and I try not to, but he sees it. He gives me a soft smile. "You've helped so much, Summer."

"I have?"

"Yes." He rests his forehead against mine, and I hold on, thinking about the bleak look in his eyes on Saturday. The half-drunk bottle of scotch and scent of despair in the stuffy town-house. "There's something worth fighting for now."

"What are you planning?"

"Everything," he murmurs. "And nothing. One step at a time. I'm going to tell my business partners, I think. Maybe call my doctor back and tell him I'm ready to start investigating... aids."

"Aids?"

"Canes," he says. "Dogs. Braille."

The words tear at him. I can see it, and yet he says them, eyes locked with mine.

"And you want to do it alone," I whisper.

"I need to, Summer. Until I know I have control of myself. I know that I lash out when I'm..."

"Hurting," I fill in.

"Mmm."

"Will you keep me updated? Come back to me when you're ready?"

"God, yes," he says, hands tightening around my waist. "Summer, this isn't a goodbye. It's not me walking away."

"Good."

"It's me saying I have to sort my life out. I can't hide in this apartment with you forever, however much I might want to."

"I know."

"I'll miss you every day," he murmurs. Touches my lips with his, and this time, the kisses are filled with words neither of us have spoken yet.

He stands, my legs locked around his waist, and walks us to the bedroom. I close the door and watch him through hooded eyes. He watches me back, the want and love stark in his gaze. I lift my dress over my head and revel in it. Shake my hair out,

204

undo my bra, tossing it away. He drinks me in, taking off his own clothes with fast movements.

I run my hand through his chest hair and he shudders. How many times have we done this before? And still, today feels different. Every touch laden with meaning.

He runs featherlight fingers up my bare arms. "I'm so grateful," he says, "that I'll have the memory of your beauty, for however long I get to keep it."

That's when my tears fall.

He kisses them away, and I kiss him back, pouring everything I feel into the touch. We're gentle with each other, each touch slow, like we're drawing it out. Like we don't want it to end.

When he reaches for a condom from my bedside table, I run my hand over his broad back. "I've booked an appointment with my ob-gyn next week."

He pauses, chest rising with his heavy breathing. "You did?"

"For birth control," I say. We haven't spoken about a relationship. About making us official. But that had been where we'd been heading, at least for me, and so...

I'd made the call.

Anthony shudders, eyes glazing over. He runs a hand down the inside of my thigh. "Very good thinking," he murmurs.

I watch him put the condom on with practiced hands, and then he's pushing into me with delicious slowness, both of us exhaling at the pleasure.

In the weeks since we first did this, Anthony and I have explored plenty. There have been fast times. Hard times. Ones where we both laughed afterwards at how loud it had gotten, or where my skin smarted from the force.

This isn't one of those times.

He holds himself above me as he moves, and I rise to meet him. Burying my hands in his hair and wondering if this is how it feels to fall in love with someone. To lose your footing, and plummet to that final depth, where you know you'll never be the same person again for having had them in your life.

Tears leak out of my eyes again, sliding down my temples and dampening my hair. Anthony feels them. Lifts himself up on an elbow to look at me.

The concern and emotion on his face undoes me. I tighten my grip on him. "Anthony," I murmur. "I love—"

He halt my words with a kiss and shudders in my arms. "Don't, Summer. Please. I won't be able... please."

"Okay," I murmur. "I won't."

He smooths my hair back with his free hand, still buried deep inside me. "Not until I'm back with you. Not until I'm better."

"Okay," I whisper. Lock my legs behind his back.

"It's not that I don't—"

This time, I'm the one who stops his words with my lips. They aren't needed. Not as we cling to each other in my small bed, chasing away the future one touch at a time.

25

ANTHONY

My grand dedication to change starts small. Minuscule, in the grand scheme of things. It doesn't involve a cane, or braille, or any of the things I've avoided in the dark, curtain-drawn cave of my townhouse.

It starts with taking out old take-away boxes.

They pile up in the weeks between the cleaners, for no other reason than I don't care about this place. Or about myself, really, when I'm... well.

But I'm going to have to start.

Summer gave me permission to leave my baggage and failing eyesight at the door. To forget about the accommodations and timelines entirely, for five minutes, for an hour, for an evening.

She was brilliant escapism, a reminder of the goodness all around us, and a few of those rays landed on me.

But I want more than evenings in her apartment. More than her having to sneak about, worrying about what her aunt will say. I want her to do all the things on her bucket list, and I want to be there for some of them. Most of them. All of them, damn it.

So I take out the trash.

The futility of it in comparison to what I have left to do almost undoes me. Takes the wind out of my sails and leads me back to my computer or my bed, to the oblivion of work or sleep.

But I resist.

I throw the curtains open in the old townhouse instead, this place that had once been filled with life. I used to have friends over. Friends I'd neglected. Family. I'd neglected them, too.

My walk around the grocery store is pathetic, but I do it. Buy some of the things I've seen Summer use. Stock my fridge.

And then I stare at my phone, at that scary, silent glass object resting on my kitchen counter.

Call Dr. Johnson is the one point on this little to-do-list of mine that I don't want to do. Correction—one of the many. But it's at the very top.

I can't see myself walking with a cane. A fumbling idiot on the street, that'll be me. Having to rely on the world at large for my safety. What do I do if I'm lost? Hold up my hand and wear a placid, come-help-me smile?

Dear God, I'll be at the complete mercy of voice activation on my phone. Siri already misunderstands me half of the time.

The floor sways beneath my feet, threatens to give out. This can't be happening.

But it is, I remind myself, fighting with the bottomless pit inside me. It is, and running from it won't make my eyes stop worsening. Won't do a damn thing.

So I reach for my phone.

Three hours later, I'm walking with Tristan in Central Park. He's staring down at his phone, sorting through email.

He's not Dr. Johnson.

He's also confused as to why I showed up at the Acture Capital and asked if he wanted to take a walking meeting. Hell, he's probably confused as to why I haven't said a word in the past five minutes, despite asking him out here.

I hardly know why myself.

"How's Freddie?" I ask.

He smiles, sliding his phone into his pocket. "Good. Great, actually. I've almost convinced her to move in with Joshua and me."

"Damn. That's great."

"Yeah, it is." He shakes his head, a fond smile on his face. "You know, I always thought the idea of sharing my life with someone would be difficult. Impossible, even. With her, though, it's been seamless. Sure, we've had to compromise on things, but on the whole... Seamless."

"I'm happy for you," I say.

"Thanks, man." He looks over and gives a chagrined shrug. "I was at a jewelry store the other day."

It takes me a moment. "A ring," I say. "You're thinking of proposing?"

"Yes. It's too soon, I know that, and she does too. Hell, she'll tell me off for proposing to her if I do it now. But I will. Sooner rather than later."

I put a hand on his shoulder. "That's fantastic. Truly. You know she'll say yes."

"Yes," Tristan says, smiling. "I do know that."

I've never once thought about engagement rings, but now I wonder what Summer would like. What's her style?

Understated, I think. Perhaps an original design. Something she can be a part of herself. I can already see her chatting up an attendant, the two of them becoming fast pals as they bond over precious gems.

"Anthony?" Tristan asks. "Was there something in particular you wanted to talk to me about? Is everything okay with Opate?"

"Yes. The app is almost ready to launch. We'll run a trial period of three months, iron out any bugs, and by then it should be ready to launch nationwide."

"Excellent," he says. "Keep us in the loop."

"Will do." I don't know how to say the rest. The words sit in my throat, choking me. With Summer it was... easier. But there's no way to start this conversation.

I find it, though. It's not surprising which path my mind takes. "There is something, actually."

"About Opate Match?"

"In a way, I suppose," I say. "I'm dating Summer Davis. The owner's niece."

Tristan's look is one of bafflement. Then he laughs, smile widening. "Anthony!" he says. "I did not expect that at all."

"Honestly, neither did I."

"How did this happen?"

I rub a hand over the back of my neck. "It's unprofessional."

"I dated an intern at the company I was CEO of," Tristan replies. "I'm not about to judge."

"Turned out great for you, though."

"Best mistake I ever made," he agrees. "So? Is this serious?"

"It could be, yes. I think it will be."

"But you're not sure," he guesses.

I look at the pond in the distance, the tall, summer-green trees that line it. It's been a long time since I've simply walked in the park for the joy of it. It's been a long time since I've done anything simply for the joy of it. Long before Summer.

"There's something I haven't told you," I say. "Two years ago, I had to go the doctor's. For my eyes."

"Oh?"

"Yes. As it turned out, I'm losing my eyesight. It's been deteriorating ever since."

He's quiet for a long moment, but so am I, both of us staring at the park teeming with life. A group of children run shrieking down a hill, one being chased, the others following suit.

When Tristan finally speaks, it's with such startling sincerity that it makes me laugh. "Well, fuck."

"Yes," I agree. "That was my immediate reaction too."

"There's nothing to be done to stop it?"

I shake my head. "Just monitoring it regularly. They don't know how long it'll take, but in all likelihood, I'll be completely blind sooner or later."

"I'm sorry. I wish there was something else I could say, but that's just… I'm sorry."

"Yeah," I say. "Thanks. Anyway, it'll have some consequences for the company."

"The company," he repeats.

"Acture Capital. I won't be able to continue, when... well. When it gets to that stage."

He's quiet for a beat. Then Tristan does something we haven't done in forever. He pulls me in for a one-armed hug.

I return it, thumping against his back and swallowing thickly.

"You're part of the company," he tells me. "Hell, you and I were the ones who started it. Of course you'll still be a part of it, if you want to. Perhaps your role will have to change, but there's technology for that, right? I don't know shit about what it's like to live blind."

"Neither do I," I say. He returns my grin, and we stand there, a hand on each other's shoulders, smiling fiercely.

"Two years," he says.

"Two years," I confirm.

"You should have told me."

"It took me a long time before I could bear to hear the words spoken out loud."

He nods, once, and lets his hand fall from my shoulder. "Well," he says. "I know now. Do you want to talk about it?"

I find, to my surprise, that I do. His advice has steered me right on countless business decisions before, just as mine has done for him. I remember sitting next to him, devastated, when he told me about the news of his sister's death. Of his decision to adopt Joshua.

I hadn't run away then.

He won't now.

I crawl into bed that night, exhaustion like a thick fog around me. The headache is back. I'd succumbed to takeout for dinner. But I fall asleep without a glass of scotch, without a painkiller, and without Summer beside me in bed.

Small signs of progress.

It gives me false confidence. After working for a few hours the next day, I surf the web for resources on how to live blind.

It's the first time I've voluntarily sought out the information. The first time I haven't run from my fate.

It starts good. Confidence-building, even. Ways to color-coordinate your clothes. Testimonials from people who lost their vision later in life and learned to compensate, to prosper. To evolve. There's a quote about how blindness can be a gift that makes me laugh. Yeah, no matter how you try to make lemonade from these lemons, it'll always taste bitter.

There's a link to a documentary about a man who lost his vision later in life. Went completely blind, without the bright pinpricks of light I might expect, to use Dr. Johnson's optimistic view of things.

My finger hovers over the play button for the trailer, but I hit play.

It's a mistake.

The trailer is beautifully shot. But as his raspy voice starts to speak, and as he narrates his descent into depression upon waking up blind… my blood turns cold.

He describes forgetting what people look like. Visual memories started to fade, until they became memories of photographs, memories of having once had visual memories. And as the years passed, he could no longer remember what his wife looked like. His parents. His children.

Himself.

I barely make it to my bed before the floor gives out beneath me and despair washes in, the taste of fear like ash in my mouth. I reach for my bedside table, not sure what I'm looking for. My phone to call Summer. My painkillers for the headache.

I choose neither, but I don't get out of bed for the rest of the day, either.

My self-imposed exile from Summer lasts for three more days. I call her after an hour of deliberation. Lie back on my bed and close my eyes, ready for the wonder of her voice on the other end.

"Hey," she says.

"Hi," I murmur.

"How are you?"

"Good. Working."

"On Acture?" she asks. "Opate?"

"On myself," I say. "And a bit on Acture."

We're quiet for a beat, both of us breathing. It feels like the first relaxing moment I've had all week.

"I saw the prototype for the app, for Opate," she says. There's a rustle in the background and I picture her lying on one of her sofas.

"What did you think?"

"It's good, Anthony. You... you created an app where Vivienne and I are still needed. Where we chat with new sign-ups and vet the candidates."

"Of course I did." She'd convinced me, after all. The human touch is necessary for Opate's magic to work. Candidates need to be vetted. Interviewed. Nudged. "If this works, you'll need to hire more personnel."

"Expanding," she murmurs. "Vivienne will be... I... well. Thank you, Anthony."

"I should thank you. You're the one who showed me how Opate truly works."

"Mmm. By setting you up on dates that *didn't* work."

"I'm very glad none of them worked."

"So am I," she says and sighs. "I miss not seeing you."

"I know, baby. Me too."

"Are you sure this is necessary?"

The bleakness of the last few days hangs over me like a cloak, still visible despite the warmth in her voice. I still haven't called Dr. Johnson.

"Yes," I say. "But things are getting better."

"That's good, Anthony. I'm here if you need me."

"That's why I'm doing this in the first place, Summer. To get back to you."

We hang up shortly after, and I carry her voice with me into sleep, waking refreshed for the first time since I'd made the decision to adjust.

———

Dr. Johnson's silence is incredulous on the other end. It has taken me another week to make the call, but now that I'm on the phone, he doesn't seem inclined to believe me.

"You'd like me to put you in contact with the Foundation for the Blind," he repeats. "Is that correct, Mr. Winter?"

"Yes," I say. My skin feels sticky with sweat, and it's not just from the sweltering July heat. "You told me you could recommend a specialist who can help walk me through what I might expect."

"I did, yes. I've emailed you his contact details. Twice, in fact."

"Right. Well, I deleted both emails."

His silence is incredulous again, but then he chuckles. "Of course you did. Well, I'm happy to send his information over again. He'll set up meetings with people who've gone through the same thing as you're currently experiencing. Many of them are happy to share how they managed."

"Yes. Good."

"You're too early for cane training, but a guide dog might be a good idea. It takes a while getting used to, and the bond is a great thing to establish."

"That's the first time you've said I'm too early for something. Usually, you like to say I'm advancing rapidly."

Dr. Johnson laughs again. "You've got time yet, Mr. Winter. But most importantly, you've got plenty of time after as well."

"Yes," I say. "I'm starting to realize that."

26

SUMMER

"I'm really glad we could do this," Vivienne says. "It feels like it was forever ago we last had lunch."

A pair of oversized, vintage sunglasses sits on her nose, at odds with the wide smile beneath them. I nod and reach for one of the breadsticks. Olive's next to the office has been our standard lunch spot for years.

"It does," I agree. "I think it was back in May, actually."

"Can't have been that long ago, can it, Summer?" She shakes her head. "I suppose I've been in and out of the office a lot this summer."

I nod and make my voice casual. "Ever since Acture Capital bought us, actually. Perhaps a bit earlier than that."

My aunt reaches across the table and puts her hand on top of mine. Her thick gold rings rest against my thin ones, an interest I'd gotten from her. "I'm sorry about that, dear. It's been a stressful time for Opate and I know you've been the one to step up. Thank you, Summer. Truly."

Smiling, I squeeze her hand. "I love Opate. I'm only happy to see it succeed."

"I'm glad. You're the... well." Vivienne's smile turns chagrined. "You're the daughter I would have wanted, you know, if I'd ever wanted children. If I'd ever had any."

"Wow. Thank you."

"My dear brother is good at many things, but he's the best at raising kids. You're a gem," she finishes, taking her hand back.

I don't know how to respond to that. Luckily, I don't have to, because Vivienne isn't done. She pushes her sunglasses up on her head. "Well, I can't keep this to myself any longer. I've met someone."

"You have?"

"Yes. In April. It's been a whirlwind, Summer, all of it. His name is Jerome."

"Jerome," I repeat.

"Yes. He's French. A widower. He didn't understand Opate at all in the beginning, let me tell you. Apparently he thought I worked in the escort industry when we first spoke. I told him that was a compliment, at my age!" She laughs, an excited blush coloring the apples of her cheeks. "He's retired. Retired himself, actually, and now mostly works in philanthropy. Oh, Summer, I don't recognize myself!"

"You're in love."

"Yes," she says, pressing her hands to her cheeks. "Yes, that's it. It's the first time I've felt like this after Patrick, to tell you the truth."

I smile, my throat closing up. My aunt is the most stylish, hopeless romantic I know. That's what makes her so good at her job. Like me, she genuinely believes in love.

But her own divorce had left scars.

"I'm so happy for you," I say. "Is that why you've been out of the office, then?"

"Yes. Jerome keeps telling me to work less. To enjoy the time we have together. Me, working less. Can you picture it?"

"Yes," I say. "I think I can, actually."

"I'd be climbing the walls after a month. Or painting them, perhaps. Do you think I could learn how to paint?"

"I think you can do anything you want," I say, and it's the truth.

Vivienne gives me another broad smile. "The best niece ever," she repeats. "What about you?"

"What about me?"

"Don't think I haven't noticed, Summer, just because I haven't been in the office as often. You look happy."

"Well," I say. Grab another breadstick and flip it over in my hands, as if it can tell me the right thing to say. "I have met someone."

"I knew it."

"He's... amazing. Unexpected. Not the type I thought I'd be attracted to."

Vivienne nods, eyes burning. "That's often the case, darling. Opposites attract and all that."

"Yes. I've seen it a hundred times with our own clients, but I still didn't believe it myself. But I really like him."

"How'd you meet him?" She reaches for her glass of white wine, eyes curious over the rim.

"Well, that's the thing. One of the things, at any rate. I'm not sure you'd approve. I think you will. But I'm not sure."

She smiles. "Oh, Summer. To be twenty-seven again and dating. Is he in a relationship with someone else?"

"Definitely not," I say.

"All right. Is he more than twenty years your senior?"

I snort. "No."

"And not underage."

"Of course not."

She leans back in her chair and crosses one leg over the other in a pose as nonchalant as it is elegant. "Then there's absolutely no reason why I wouldn't approve. Not if he genuinely makes you happy, and not like the weasel you dated before."

"They're nothing alike. And he does, you know. Make me happy." Even if the time he's taking for himself feels like it's stretching into an eternity. One phone call and a couple of texts hasn't been enough.

But he'd asked for time, and if it means he comes back to me ready to fight, I'm time's biggest fan.

"Then I'm happy for you," Vivienne says. "Look at us, both in love."

"To love," I say, raising my glass.

"To love," she agrees, and we toast our glasses together. "And to beautiful, brilliant nieces who will soon be offered a promotion."

I put my glass down. "Seriously?"

She laughs. "Yes. I spoke to Anthony Winter just yesterday about the new app they've designed for Opate. You've seen it, right? Suzy spoke about a meeting with Ryan."

"I've seen it." She'd spoken to Anthony?

"Once we move into the beta-phase, we'll need to expand. I'll be hands-on for a long while, but I'm thinking of cutting down on my hours a bit. Spend more time with Jerome." She nods my way. "Are you interested in taking on more responsibility, Summer?"

"Yes. Absolutely, yes. I'm ready."

"I know you are, dear," she says, eyes sparkling. "I trained you, after all."

Vivienne tells me to go home after lunch, and after two glasses of wine, I'm more than happy with that arrangement. Opate usually closes early on Fridays, anyway. That's when most of our clients go on the dates we've set up.

More work for them, less work for us.

Ace keeps close to my side as I walk the familiar path home. New York is unusually cool today, the temperature comfortable rather than sweltering.

I'm going running tomorrow with Suzy. On Sunday evening there's another get-together at Posie and Ben's, and it'll be Robin-free, she assures me. A fun weekend.

But Anthony won't be here to comment on my newspaper reading, to drink the last orange juice, or to heat me up to a toasty hundred-and-four degrees during the already warm nights.

I contemplate calling him again just to hear the rasp of his voice tell me something, anything. I'm so deep in thought that I nearly knock into a person handing out flyers on the sidewalk.

"Oh, I'm sorry," I say. "Really sorry."

The woman chuckles and hands me a flyer. "Not a problem. Caught your attention that way!"

I look down at the piece of paper in my hand. The enlarged microphone. The elaborate font on top that spells out three innocuous words. *Open mic night.*

"Huh," I say. "Thank you."

"Come on by," she says. "Either to listen or to perform."

"Yeah. I... yeah. Thank you."

I make it another block before I find my phone. Call Posie's number. She answers immediately, surprise in her voice.

"Hey, Summer. You're not cancelling Sunday, are you?"

"No," I say. "Tell me, do you want to play guitar with me next weekend? Like we used to?"

27

ANTHONY

I run a hand through my hair and glare at the tiny, folded plastic thing on my kitchen counter. So small. Harmless. But since I took it out of the packaging, I haven't been able to touch it.

It's too early for cane training, Dr. Johnson had said. But the specialist I'd talked to had told me to order one anyway. *Get used to it,* he said. *It can be a great mobility tool. It's freedom. You'll see.*

So here I am, staring at the thing like it might attack me, and wondering how the hell it'll give me freedom.

All we need to do is get acquainted, I think. Shake hands, so to speak.

Perhaps I'm pushing this. In the afternoon, I have a meeting with a man who has the same diagnosis as me, but ten years down the line.

I'd started writing a list of questions for him yesterday, and by starting, I mean I'd stared at a blank notepad, a pen in hand, and felt like dying.

So yeah. No questions prepared.

But I'm going. That's the goal for today. Touch a cane and talk to a blind man.

I wonder if I'm similar to the guide dogs for the blind Summer's mother fosters. You sat down? Here's a treat! Oh, you can shake paw? Here's a treat!

There's only one treat I want for doing all of this, and though she might be too big to eat in one bite, she's delicious.

I reach out and grip the folded cane.

Nothing happens. It's cold, hard plastic. It's almost as if all of my combined fears *aren't* imbued in this one inanimate object. Who would have thought.

The doorbell rings and I drop the cane like it might burn me. But halfway to the door, I change my mind, and toss it into a cupboard. Just in case she's here. I don't want her to see it.

But it's not Summer on my doorstep.

It's my brother, and the scowl on his face mirrors my own. We haven't spoken since the harsh words in his office.

"You were right," he says in greeting and steps past me into the house.

I shut the door. "Ah."

"You were fucking right," he repeats and strides into the living room, only to stop dead. "You don't keep your booze in the same place Granddad did."

"The cabinet to the left. Top shelf."

He finds my scotch and pours himself a glass. Tugs at his collar again. It's sweltering outside, but Isaac is in a three-piece suit.

"For what it's worth," I say, "I wish I wasn't."

His lip curls in wry non-humor as he drains the glass, pouring himself another. "I just found out. Came here straight after."

"You confronted her?"

He looks at me like I'm an idiot. "I asked Cordelia about it right after you told me. She denied it."

"Hmm."

"But once I knew enough to suspect it, it was easy to look for the signs. I pushed her on it just now. Right after she dragged me to a meeting with a bakery to taste cakes. Why is it so warm in here? Anthony, do you still have the heat on? It's July."

"It's August first," I say, "and the heat is off."

"You know what really gets me? I thought she loved me. Not

221

in the exuberant, infatuated kind of way. We've never been like that. But I thought she loved the life we were committing to enough to stay faithful. I've made the same sacrifice."

"Right."

"I'm sorry, by the way," Isaac says. Gets up from the couch and pours me a glass of scotch, handing it to me. Even distressed, his manners are impeccable. "You came to me and you told it to me straight, and I didn't believe you."

"Well, I can see why you might not. I haven't been the best brother for the past two years."

His eyes meet mine. "No, not really."

"I'm aware," I say. "Take off your jacket, Isaac. You look like you're melting."

"Yes, because I couldn't get a cab from the damn bakery and walked all the way here." But he does what I've told him and tosses it over the back of the couch. "You never liked us together."

"No," I say. "I never did."

"I thought you were an asshole because of it."

"I know you did."

"Now I wonder if you were the smartest of us all," he says, running a hand through his hair. "I wonder if old Rupert Jacobs will still want us to partner with his golf courses. Is that sad? That the first thing I thought when she confessed to cheating on me was to get angry that she might have screwed up our business deal, too?"

"I think," I say carefully, "that it tells you everything you need to know about that relationship."

He looks at me for a long while. "You've changed."

It's easy to shake my head, to find the words. "Isaac, I've withdrawn from you, from the family, for too long. Of course I've changed."

"Yes," he says, eyes turning wary.

"I'm sorry about that."

The same eyes narrow. "If you're saying this just because you pity me now…"

I laugh, unable to help myself, because it's just what I would have thought in his shoes. The pride running through me is just as strong in his veins, bred into us by parents who saved I love you's for special occasions and told stories about the family legacy for bedtime.

"Anthony," he complains, putting his glass down.

"No, no," I say. "I don't pity you. Sorry."

"Then why are you laughing?"

"Because we're so similar. Christ, Isaac. That's why I've stayed away!"

Confusion is stark on his features. I gesture to the armchair again, raising my glass of scotch. He has a seat, still staring at me.

"Look, two years ago I went to an optician because it was getting harder to read. Instead of being prescribed glasses, he sent me to a doctor. Turned out I'm losing my vision."

He stares at me. "What?"

"I'm losing my eyesight. It's deteriorating rapidly, or so they tell me."

There's no pity in his gaze, and that fortifies me. Isaac's reaction is a benchmark for my parents. If he can take it, so can they.

"You're not serious," he says.

"Serious as death," I reply, smiling wryly. "Wish I wasn't, though."

Isaac looks down into his glass. Turns it around in his hands, once, twice. A memory strikes me, of him doing just that after we got into Grandfather's liquor cabinet. He'd been twelve. Sitting just like that with his contraband in hand, and I'd thought he was the coolest, taking charge and knowing what to do.

"That's why you've stayed away," he says.

I nod. "Couldn't bring myself to tell you until now. Couldn't say it, really. Out loud."

He lifts his gaze to mine. "I hope you take this the right way, Anthony," he says. "But I wish your fiancée had cheated on you instead."

I laugh at that. Here we are, both of our lives in shambles. "Yeah. So do I, to tell you the truth."

———

Isaac comes over for dinner the next day. He's the one who makes the call, showing up thirty minutes later. I open my fridge for his perusal and he shakes his head. "Nothing in here goes together. Did you use a delivery service?"

"Picked it out myself," I say.

"Well, it sucks. Let's order something."

One night won't fix everything between us. I know the things I've said in the past, the anger and irrationality, hanging up on the phone... it won't be undone by sharing what's been going on.

But it's a start.

After he leaves, I take out the trash and wipe down the kitchen counter. Fetch the cane from its hiding place and put it back on the kitchen counter.

Isaac knows. Tristan knows. Only our two remaining business partners and my parents left.

My phone rings, and seeing the name on it, my heart does a double-take. It's been three weeks. Three weeks, and it feels like I'm cutting out my own heart with this self-imposed exile.

I've questioned the necessity of it more than once.

But yesterday, after talking to Ivan about his journey with blindness, I'd been so drained I hadn't made it out of bed for twelve hours.

I answer it. "Hi, baby."

"Hello," she says. One small word. I close my eyes, listening to the warm silence across the line. "How are you doing?"

"Good," I say.

"Can you tell me about what you've been doing?"

I push away from the kitchen counter. Stretch out on my couch instead and imagine she's lying beside me, tucked beneath my arm.

"Anthony?"

"I want to," I admit. "I want to tell you everything. But I'm afraid that if I do, I won't continue."

"Continue making the changes?"

"Yes."

"Why?"

I close my eyes again. It's Summer on the other line. Summer, who's never run from me and my problems. Who laughs and loves freely. "Because it's so fucking hard. As soon as I've... I've done one of these things, I want to get in a cab and go to you. I want to disappear into your apartment. Watch you organize your mismatched mugs on the shelf you have above the sink."

"They're collectibles," she murmurs.

"But if I'm there, Summer, I'll never leave. I know that now. I'll sit on your tiny kitchen chair and ask you to explain the story behind every single one of those mugs because you're irresistible when you light up because of something you're passionate about. I won't walk out the door and fix myself."

"You don't need fixing," she says.

"I do. You showed me that, too."

"I did? Anthony, I like you the way you are."

"I like who I am with you too," I murmur. "But I want to be that man all the time. I'm working toward being him, baby."

She hadn't seen it all. Hadn't seen me snap at my family. At my business partners. At random waiters in restaurants. I hope she never has to.

And I can't risk letting myself snap at her.

There's faint sniffling on the other line. "I'll be here," she promises. "When you're ready."

"It won't be long," I vow. I wouldn't survive this if it was long.

"I miss you," she says. "So much more than I anticipated. Just sleeping at night feels difficult without you in my bed."

"Fuck, baby, I know. Just hearing you mention a bed makes me excited."

Her laugh tightens my chest. I need that sound in my life like

I need air. Like that plastic cane, it shows me the way forward. "I miss that too," she says. "A lot."

"Soon."

"Good, because I'm not the only one who misses you. Ace does too."

"Are you sure about that?"

"Oh yes. He's lying by my side now, and I swear, his ears perk up whenever you say something."

"Hi buddy."

"Yep, his ears perked up."

I laugh, and she joins in, the sound everything to me. Everthing. "Guess what?" she says. "I've decided to do something."

"Oh?"

"Yes. On Saturday, I'm going to an open mic night with Posie. To perform."

"You are?"

"Yeah. It feels like my stomach might give out, though, and it's only Monday."

I push up into sitting. "You've got this. I've heard you sing. Your friends have heard you sing. Summer, you're amazing."

"Mhm. Yeah."

"Do you know how rare it is to sing well? Not a single person in that crowd will be thinking *oh, I could do that better."*

"There might be other performers there."

"Then they'll be thinking how much they want to be up there on stage with you."

"You're great, you know," she says, sighing. "I never used to be like this. I *loved* to perform. I want to find that love again."

"You will," I say. "I have no doubt you will. And Summer?"

"Yes?"

"The people who care about you won't judge, and the people who do? You don't care about them."

"You're right about that."

"Of course I am. Where is it?"

"The open mic night?"

"Yes."

"At a place called Barella, on Saturday." A tentative note of hope creeps into her voice. "I've invited a few friends, but there's still space?"

I want to say the words as badly as she wants to hear them. Promise to be there, to listen, to support. The chance to be there for someone is a responsibility, but it's not heavy. It's liberating. Knowing you're needed and wanted, needing and wanting someone in return.

But I can't do that for her until I know I'm in control of myself. "I'll be there if I can," I tell her. "If I'm ready."

"That's okay. I know you... have to figure things out."

"I am, though. Day by day."

"Good," she murmurs.

My gaze settles on the newspaper I've tossed onto my living room table. I reach for it. "Do you have your copy of the *Times*?"

"Yes," she says. "I stuffed it into my bag from work. Let me get it..."

I open it up in the meantime. Scan the pages. "Open page twelve," I say. "Let me make the world bleak for you."

She laughs again. "You don't make the world bleak. You make it fun."

"Well, I'm happy you can see it that way."

"I can. Oh, there was something I read that made me think of you right away..."

"Large Bird Awareness Week?"

"Very funny," she says, voice light. "No, it was about Bergdorf Goodman. Made me think of the dresses you sent me."

"I remember."

"Anthony, do you really do that a lot with dates? You made it seem so commonplace."

I run a hand over the back of my neck. "I've done it before, yes. But not with many women."

"So you don't have a personal shopper there, ready to whip out the latest styles for your dates on short notice," she says. She's teasing, effortless warmth in her voice.

It softens my own. "Summer, I picked them out myself."

"You… you didn't ask someone to do it for you?"

"No, I went there myself. It should have been the first warning flag, really."

"Warning flag?"

"That I was falling for you," I say. "Instead, I told myself it was a good use of an afternoon, standing there, imagining a woman I'd just met in cocktail dresses."

She laughs. "Oh, Anthony, if only I'd known."

"Perhaps it was better that you didn't. You weren't interested in me at the time."

"I don't know about that," she says. "I was intrigued by you from day one."

"Intrigued, huh?"

"Yes. I just had to figure you out."

"And have you?"

"I'm getting there," she murmurs. "But I think I'll need to spend a lot more time with you in order to do that."

"Then I'd better make sure you never figure me out," I say.

When we hang up, I'm tempted to call it a day. To go to bed with the memory of her words and voice in my ear. To let it soothe me like it has so many times before.

But there's one more thing to do.

I don't let myself consider what I'm doing as I make the call. The woman's voice is surprised on the other side.

"Anthony Winter?" Layla asks.

"Yes, it's me. Hello," I say. "I understand if you're surprised to hear from me."

"I am," she admits. "Not to mention curious. Something tells me you're not calling about our date from two months ago."

"No, I'm actually calling about something you said. Something you… well." I clear my throat. "Do you have the time to take on a new patient?"

Her silence is stunned. But then a professional note bleeds through her voice. "You want to see me as a therapist."

"I do, yes. If you'd be comfortable with that."

"I would," she says. "I have space."

The last thing I do that night surprises even myself. But as I dig out the discarded notepad and find a pen, I sit down by my kitchen table and think of Summer. Of her words and her view on life, on the infectious optimism that colors her world. I stare at the blank piece of paper and let it all wash over me.

And then I write the heading.

Bucket list.

28

SUMMER

My mind is absolutely blank, and beneath my blouse, cold sweat coats my skin. It's a wonder if I'll remember any of the lyrics.

Posie leans against my shoulder. "He's really good," she whispers.

He is, I think, though I haven't paid much attention to the singer on the makeshift stage. He's playing an acoustic guitar, and while his voice sounds like he's had four whiskeys too many, it gives more gravitas to his words. The entire bar is rocking along.

"Your voices would sound great together," Posie murmurs.

I nod and force out a thoughtful *hmm*. On my other side, Brittany is whispering to Ella, and if I had to guess, they're wondering if the singer is single. It's all normal. This is a situation Posie and I put ourselves in often, once. Sometimes on a weekly basis. We couldn't get enough of performing.

The voice of doubt in my head isn't my own. It's Robin's manipulative, derisive comments.

And they need to be drowned out.

Posie must sense my nerves, because the next I know, there's a giant glass of water in front of me. I drain half of it and clear my throat.

We'd spent an evening practicing, the two of us in her apartment like old times. Only, once upon a time I would have been in flip-flops, the couch would've been secondhand, and her guitar case had been covered in band stickers.

We've grown up since then.

Whiskey-Voice finishes to an applause that brings down the house. He looks stunned by the response, but bows his head, half-smiling, and steps off the stage.

This is it.

Nerves feel like a ball in my throat, choking me. I won't get a single sound out.

"This is us," Posie whispers.

My muscles move without conscious thought from me, disconnected, taking me up the stage amidst scattered, encouraging applause. I have to lower the mic from Whiskey-Voice, and focusing on that instead of the crowd is good. So is clearing my throat and looking at Posie. I don't need to sing to all of these people. I just need to sing to her and the tune of her guitar.

But as I scan the crowd, looking for that one face I hope is here, I know they're waiting for more.

They want an introduction.

"Hi," I croak. The silence stretches on and laughs spread, as if I'm doing this on purpose. I crack a smile and the laughs increase. They fortify me. "Come on, guys. I'm not here to do stand-up."

The lights are dimmed, and as the terror inside me locks itself into a tiny ball, memories take over. I've done this before. This is my thing.

"Well, we've got a tough act to follow," I say, looking at Whiskey-Voice. "Thanks for that, by the way."

He pretends to take a bow amidst chuckles. I smile, finding my footing. "But we'll give it our best shot. My name is Summer, and this is Posie."

She gives a little wave.

"What's better than the radio hits of today?" I ask. "The answer? All of them. Played at the same time. Why don't you see how many you can recognize?"

I nod to Posie, and she starts to play, her hand moving over the strings of her guitar. Familiar notes drift out. I open my mouth and close my eyes, and the words come.

They sneak their way past the fear, and they don't sound any worse for it. I sing, watching the reactions of the crowd, until we're one. Me singing, them listening, all of us in the moment together.

They take notice when I shift into another song, picking out the chorus of a dancehall hit. A sharp chord change and we shift again, drifting effortlessly into a popular ballad.

Laughs ring out when we include two sentences from a well-known rap song. The harmonies from that drift into the chorus of the summer's hottest hit, and I sing, my heel tapping along to the beat. I'm made up of energy, so much of it, seeing the delight in their eyes and becoming one with the song.

That's when I spot him.

He's in the back, leaning against the wall, arms crossed over his chest. His eyes are on me. I look at his dear face and feel my voice take on a life of its own, the words effortless, and it's him I'm singing to now. He smiles, like he hears it too.

The performance ends sooner than I'm prepared for. The last note rings out and people erupt into applause, some scattered laughs and a high-pitched *bravo!* tossed our way.

Posie and I give identical, theatrical bows. Grin at each other as we step off the stage on giddy legs. She pulls me in for a hug, and I grip her back. "That was so much fun!"

Her nod against my shoulder is vigorous, and she's grinning when she leans back. "They loved it."

They did, it seems. Two guys give us a *great job* on the way back to our seats and the bartender is already there, setting down a complimentary tray of shots for us and our friends.

My friends stand for hugs. I reciprocate, but my eyes are on the tall shadow in the back.

"Summer?" Posie asks. "Do you want your shot?"

"I'll be right back," I say, already moving through the throngs of people. Someone murmurs that I have a great voice, and I beam at them in thanks.

Finally, there's no one between us.

I walk into his arms. He pulls me in for a hug just shy of bone-crushing and I bury my face against his chest, breathing in the familiar scent of him. His hand curves around the nape of my neck, the two of us trying to become one person.

"You were fantastic," Anthony murmurs into my hair. "Absolutely breathtaking."

I fight against the happy tears burning beneath my lids. "You came."

"I couldn't stay away, not when you were singing. And not when I missed you this much."

"I was counting days," I admit.

"I was counting hours." He releases me slowly, but doesn't let me go. His dark eyes are warm with emotion. An open face, even here, amongst all these people. "Thank you."

"For what?"

"For being you, Summer. For waiting on me to figure myself out."

"I would have waited even longer."

His lip curls, and his gaze travels over my face. I know he's trying to memorize it again. He does that a lot, soaking up the details.

"How have you been?" I ask. "Honestly?"

"Honestly," he repeats, "it's been awful. The most difficult thing I've ever done."

I want to hear about it. The places he's gone to, the people he's told. The doctors he's spoken to. But not now, not here, not when he's looking at me with such happiness. Not when my heart feels like it's soaring.

"You're here now," I whisper.

"Yes, and I'm never leaving again. Not as long as you want me."

"Forever," I say.

He reaches into his pocket and pulls out a piece of paper,

pressing it into my hand. "You told me to write a list of my own," he says. "Things I want to do in life."

My eyes swim as I look down at the neatly folded paper, unable to say a single thing.

Anthony's voice softens. "You reminded me of who I used to be, and of who I want to be again in the future. Vision or no vision."

I unfold the paper. In his sharp-edged handwriting is a short list. The first line is already struck.

~~Tell the woman I love how I feel.~~

"I got ahead of myself with crossing the first one off," he murmurs. "Haven't done it quite yet."

I can't breathe as he cups my cheek, running a thumb over my lower lip. "I love you, Summer. For so many reasons. For who you are. For your goodness and sweetness and smiles. For your optimism. But also for your bad days, and your insecurities, and when you lost your temper at that delivery guy one time."

I frown at the memory, and he smiles wider. "Yes, especially that. I love that you find a silver lining everywhere, even when it's infuriating as hell. I love that you don't need me. You want me. There's a difference.

"I can't promise I'll be the man you deserve every day, all the time. One day I won't see anymore, and that terrifies me, Summer. I won't always handle that well. But I'm going to try. I'm going to live this life to the best of my ability. You were the one to tell me I'm not dying, that I need to stop acting like I am. You were right. Because even blind, I'll have two hands to hold you with, and a mouth to kiss you with, and fingers to touch you, and that's enough. It'll always be enough."

My eyes blur, until I can't make out his features. It doesn't stop me from seeking his mouth. "I love you too."

He kisses me with a low, harsh sound in his throat, arms tightening around me. The rest of his list crumples in my hand, and I laugh, kissing him, trying to push back at the same time. He shakes his head and kisses me again, and again.

Public displays of affection weren't his thing, but here we are.

"I have to read the rest of this list," I say.

His hands dig into my hips, his mouth at my ear. "You can read it later tonight," he murmurs, and there's a promise in those words. "For now, do you want to introduce me to your friends?"

"As...?"

"Yes," he says, eyes bright. "As your boyfriend."

I find his hand with my own, and I lead him through the bar, feeling like I'm floating.

29

SUMMER

I hang up the phone with my aunt, my heart pounding. Even during her vacation, she can't stop working. I can't blame her. Not when things are going this well.

"Anthony?" I call.

"Out here!"

I leave my phone on his kitchen counter and pad barefoot out onto the patio. He's lying on a lounge chair by the pool, his reading tablet in hand. Ace is a furry, golden snake beside him on the shaded terrace.

The sun has darkened Anthony's skin to a deep brown tan, and his hair is mussed with salt water and wind. There's a tiny furrow in the center of his brow. I love it. It always appears when he's concentrating, working, or reading.

"How did it go?" he asks.

"Amazing," I say. "Fantastic. Perfect!"

He puts the tablet down. "Okay, now I'm curious."

"She might have asked me to be in charge of training the new people we're hiring ahead of the app launch."

Anthony sits up and motions for me. I step closer, his strong arms catching me around the waist. "Of course you were asked. You're going to be a great instructor."

"You think?"

"Absolutely."

"I think it could be really fun. I could create manuals. Maybe a team-building exercise, too. That's important, right?"

He smiles. "Very."

I run a hand through his salt-roughened hair. "She asked me to say hi to you, by the way. Jerome did too."

The skeptical look on his face makes me laugh. "Okay, I admit, I don't think Jerome actually said that. But Vivienne claims he did, so I rolled with it."

"Hmph," he says, tugging me down onto his lap. I settle a leg on either side of him and the lounge chair squeaks under our combined weight. "You're sure she's okay with us?"

"I'm sure," I say, pressing a teasing kiss to his cheek. "Most definitely."

"She didn't mind at all."

"She didn't mind at all. Didn't she tell you that herself?"

"Yes," he admits. He'd spoken to my aunt about us at the office a few weeks ago. Dressed in a suit. Very professional, because, as he said, he didn't want her to think he was anything but serious in his intentions toward me.

I'd told him he wasn't asking my father for my hand. He'd winked and said *not yet,* and I'd been completely speechless.

"But," Anthony continues, "she might say one thing to me and another thing to you in private."

"Well, as a matter of fact, she has said some things to me in private," I say, locking my arms behind his neck.

"Oh?"

"She said she's glad I've finally found a good man."

Anthony closes his eyes at that. He's still not good at accepting compliments. "Right."

"She did," I insist. "You know, this is the woman who started a matchmaking company out of her Soho apartment in the nineties. She's eccentric, elegant, free-spirited love personified."

"So she really doesn't mind that I seduced her niece right under her nose."

"You seduced me, did you?"

"Oh yes," he says. "Wasn't that obvious from our very first meeting? You were the one who insisted on setting me up with other women."

"Hmm. I don't think you knew you were seducing me either."

"I was always very clear about that," he says, grinning. But the soft caress of his hands on my hips tells me there's partial truth in the words. I kiss him, and he kisses me back, tasting like the sangria I'd made us after lunch. But he's still distracted. It's there in the slow, careful use of his lips.

"What?" I ask.

"Are *you* okay with it, Summer? With me being your boss?"

I smile. "Vivienne is my boss."

He rolls his eyes, and I laugh, pressing my lips to his again. "Yes, I'm okay with it."

"We'd figure something out if you weren't," he says. "You know that."

"Yes," I murmur. "I know that. If you're okay with dating one of your employees?"

"Well, you're not my employee. You're Vivienne's."

"Right. Besides," I say, "you're a very hands-off boss."

Anthony puts his hands on my bare waist, gripping me tight. "Am I?"

I laugh, closing the distance between us. He kisses me slowly and thoroughly, a warmth spreading through my limbs that has nothing to do with the late summer sunshine. Happiness feels like an ever-present drug these days, hits available at all times.

He gives a low groan of contentment and rests his head against my collarbone. I trail my fingers over the breadth of his shoulders, the skin sun-warm beneath my touch. "What were you reading?"

"Mmm. The same book."

"The memoir?"

"Yeah. He's describing his journey with braille now."

"Any good?" I ask. The adjustments he's making, the things

he's learning, isn't a forbidden topic. But it's sometimes a sore one.

"Yes. Though it still seems like a damn nightmare to learn."

I run my nails softly down his back and he sighs with pleasure, gripping me tighter. "You've got time to learn," I say. "It could be years, still. The doctor said you might end up retaining partial sight for decades."

"The doctor says a lot of things," Anthony comments, in a tone that makes it clear what he thinks of Dr. Johnson's cheery remarks. "But," he says, voice stronger, "I'm not focusing on that. Preparing for the future but embracing the present."

"You sound like a fortune cookie," I tease, but my heart swells at the words. It's what I've wanted him to believe all along.

"Maybe that's the next company I should buy."

"Definitely," I agree. "Or an astrology firm?"

"A palm-reading business," he suggests.

"Maybe a life-coaching consultancy?"

"You know, I think I could have a career writing self-help books after I lose my sight."

I laugh, and he joins in, eyes dark and warm on mine. Being here with me fully. In the house he bought as a prison, but if the week we've spent here together is any indication, it's a sentence we'd both suffer gladly.

His hand presses gently into the muscles between my shoulder blades. "Still sore?"

I shake my head. "Much better now."

"Still as much fun?"

"A lot more," I say, "now that you're doing it with me."

Anthony chuckles. "Neither of us is great."

That's certainly true. Windsurfing the second time had hardly been easier than the first, and I doubt it'll ever be something I'm good at, but trying it with Anthony on board had been too good of an opportunity to pass up.

"What about you? Not sore?" I run my hand down his arms and the strong muscle beneath. I've gone weight-lifting with him once, too. It's not something I'm planning on doing again. The word *sore* is a kind description for the ache in my muscles the next day.

Anthony presses a kiss to my temple. "No."

"Of course not. You're the athlete."

He chuckles. "You're the runner."

"Okay, fine. We're both athletic."

"We are. There is one sport, though, that we're particularly good at," he says, eyes glittering. "A team sport."

I grin at him. "Oh, we're Olympic gold medalists."

"They wouldn't even let us compete," he says, nipping at my bottom lip. "It would be unfair to all the other contestants."

"Unsportsmanlike."

His hands slide down and grip my ass. "Very," he agrees. "We can't have that."

"Glad we're agreed," I say. "Now we don't have to train for the next Olympics anymore."

"But training is so much fun!"

I laugh and kiss him again, and this time, the heat that sparks between us settles deep in my stomach. It's never really stopped burning since I met him.

Much as I want to, though, we have some place to be tonight, and I know he's distracting himself from that very thing. So I lean back in his arms and lock my legs around his back.

"So," I say.

He sighs. "So."

"We've done something for my bucket list yesterday. Now we're going to do something that's on yours."

He closes his eyes. "I know. Two of them, actually."

"You're sure you want to do both at the same time? I'm okay if you want to go alone."

His hands tighten on my hips. "No, I want you there."

"Then I'm there," I say. "You know that."

"Yeah. Christ, Summer, there's going to be crying. My mother's going to burst into tears."

I rest my head against his shoulder. "That's not your fault, Anthony. You're not responsible for their reaction."

He gives a low humming sound that makes it clear he disagrees.

"You're not," I say. "You didn't choose this. They'll be sad for you because they love you and don't want to see you suffer, but you're not responsible for the cause of the suffering itself."

"Yeah," he breathes. "You're right."

I know I am. But the one time I'd met his brother, briefly and over drinks a week ago, I'd seen just how deep the need not to disappoint their elders ran in the Winter family. It led one brother to work himself to ruin and commit to marrying a woman he didn't love. It had led Anthony to strike out on his own in an effort to compete, and then to hurt his family rather than admit to being diagnosed with permanent vision loss.

I think of my own parents, and their hope that I'd one day move back home and marry a nice man. Perhaps the dentist's son, as my mom had hinted at a few months ago. But being happy was really their only wish for me.

"If we're not going to be gone too long, we can leave Ace here," I say. "He's fine being on his own for a few hours."

Anthony shakes his head. "Let's bring him. I'm already introducing my parents to my girlfriend and telling them about my eyesight. They can handle an inquisitive golden and some fur on the rugs."

"All right. Ace is coming."

He nods again, a wealth of emotions in his eyes. Beneath it all is a fear I recognize now, remnants of what he'd told me months ago. Once he tells people, it becomes real. It becomes immediate.

"I ran from this for a long time," he murmurs. "Running can be a lifesaver when things get difficult."

I nod. I think it had saved his life for the past two years. "But it's not a long-term strategy."

"No, it's not," he says. "Isaac will be there too. He already knows."

"Right. Didn't your business partners take it well last week, too?"

"Carter told me how sorry he was three separate times. Then he said it would make no difference to the company. Both he and Tristan seem to have caught on to the idea that I can somehow become a blind mastermind behind a computer."

"If anyone could, it would be you."

Anthony snorts. "You think too highly of me."

"Impossible," I say. "What did St. Clair say?"

"He was just silent. The whole time."

"He didn't say a word?" The most aggressive business partner among the four was rarely quiet when he had an opinion to express, and when he did, it seemed it was always in the harshest of terms.

"Not until the end. Then he just shook my hand. Said he was sorry for my loss."

"Your loss?"

"Yes," Anthony says with a shrug. "Weird thing is, I think he actually meant it."

"Huh," I say. I've only met St. Clair twice, but he hadn't struck me as sympathetic. With some people, you can tell there's a human beneath the stressed, overworked facade. With Victor, the coldness in his gaze seemed bone-deep.

"Did it feel good afterwards? Telling them?"

"It felt nauseating," Anthony admits. I don't think he would have just a few weeks ago. "But it's done now. They know."

"They know," I agree.

He shifts me in his lap, holds me with one arm, and looks down at his watch. "We should shower."

There's a heaviness in his voice, despite the resolution. But what he's going to do is necessary. It's also the second thing on the bucket list he'd written, right below telling me he loved me. *Tell the people in my life about my diagnosis.* Beneath that had been one that made my heart warm. *Introduce Summer to my family.*

So we're doing that, and then he'll be free to move on to some of the lighter things on his list.

Our shower is a long, drawn-out affair, sharing it as we do. The tautness in his shoulders abates with the pleasure of our joining, and his mouth is soft and gentle on mine. But it's back in a scowl as we get closer to his parents' summer house in Montauk.

We stand side-by-side on the sidewalk. Him, looking at a house that contains some of his best memories. Me, awed by the three-story building and its shingle-clad facade. Ace is wedged between our legs, the only one amongst us who is calm and collected.

"Well," Anthony says and reaches for my hand. "Let's do this."

EPILOGUE

One year later

"No," I say. "Stay."

The six golden retriever puppies squirming at my heels don't listen. Despite their floppy, oversized ears, they don't listen to commands. Not yet. One day, they'll be some of the best trained dogs, a companion to people who need their guidance.

But right now, they're seven weeks old, and they're a riot.

"You're not allowed out here," I tell them, one hand on the dog gate. "Will you stop trying to sneak past me?"

Their mother gives me a brown-eyed look from her sprawl on the dog bed. She's the picture of tired, maternal pride. *You're on your own*, the look tells me. *I'm just happy they're not playing with my tail anymore.*

I make it out of the dog gate, but I'm not alone. A budding escape artist makes a mad dash for it, wiggles his way out and bounds on too-big puppy paws past my legs.

"Oh, no you don't!" I swoop down, but he rolls sideways out of my reach, the picture of playfulness. His tiny tongue hangs out of his mouth in a way that… okay. I might have parents who've raised infinitely more dogs than they've raised kids, but I'm not immune. When a puppy hits you with that look, you melt.

So I melt.

I scoop him up and he gives a content wriggle, pushing a tiny nose against my palm. I take him with me through the kitchen and out the door to the backyard. My parents are sitting on their usual chairs under the oak tree, their two adult dogs sprawled beneath their chairs.

Anthony is in a third chair, sitting opposite them.

His long legs are stretched out in front of him, evident in his shorts. It had taken me a long time to convince him he could in fact wear shorts with my parents—no formalwear required—and here he is, tan legs on display. His hand is buried in Ace's fur.

A pair of prescription-strength sunglasses cover his eyes. While they do nothing to stop his fading vision, they make reading a bit easier. For all the dour predictions he spouts when he's in a bad mood, he's not blind yet.

The doctor says the vision loss has plateaued at the moment, but we don't know how long it'll last. *First time I'm happy if a plateau lasts forever,* Anthony had said. He's getting along better with Dr. Johnson these days.

My mother breaks into guffaws of laughter at something Anthony says. His lip curls into that half-smile, and beneath the sunglasses, I know his eyes are bemused. My parents love him.

I think he's quietly astonished by them.

This house, with its dogs, scattered books and boisterous game nights, is miles away from the serene quiet at the Winter family's city townhouse or Montauk residence. One time at his parents' house, I'd seen a housekeeper comb the fringes of an oriental rug.

Combing. The fringes. Of a rug.

In my parents' house, you'd be lucky if there are any fringes left or if they've been gnawed off by puppy teeth.

The puppy in my arms lets out a soft yowl and wriggles. All

three dogs at the table lift their heads. Only Ace's tail starts to wag, the others over the antics of the latest litter.

"Everything okay in there?" my mom asks.

"They've torn down the place," I say. "It'll fall any moment."

"Ha-ha," Dad says. He's got his construction shorts on, pockets heavy with gadgets he needs to fix the house. There's always a screw that needs tightening. "You couldn't resist bringing someone out with you?"

I run my fingers over the puppy's soft head, and he snuggles into the crook of my arm. "Have you ever noticed how often I visit when you have a new litter?"

"Summer," Mom says. "Are you implying what I think you're implying?"

I sink down on the chair next to Anthony and give her a wide smile. "Maybe."

She laughs. "That's my girl."

"Good thing you like dogs," Dad tells Anthony. "Would've been difficult to fit in with Summer if you didn't."

Anthony leans over my arm and runs a single finger over the soft fur on the puppy's head. He receives a soft lick in return. "I met Summer and Ace at the same time," he says. "I always knew it was a package deal."

"Two for the price of one," I say.

"Mhm. Both golden."

The puppy in my arms wriggles, legs pushing against my arm. He crawls over to Anthony.

"Abandoned," I say.

Anthony chuckles and watches the puppy settle against him, putting a hand over the dog's back. It's nearly the size of his curled-up body.

"She likes you," Mom says.

"It's a she?" Anthony asks.

"Mom can always tell," I say. "Don't ask me how she does it."

She laughs. "Comes with the territory, I think. Not to mention seeing the puppies so often during their first few weeks. They look the same, but only in the way siblings look the same. There are little quirks that make it easy to pick them apart."

Dad shakes his head. "She's the only one who ever manages, by the way. To me, all goldens look alike until they're adults, and even then, they're similar."

"How do you decide?" Anthony asks, still looking down at the puppy. "Which ones get adopted to loving families, and which ones will be trained by the Foundation?"

Mom's voice is matter-of-fact, even if she glances my way. "Well, guide dogs need to have a particular temperament. Attentive, eager to learn, willing to work, and thriving on praise. After a few weeks with the pups, it's easy to spot the two or three who exhibit those traits the most."

"Hmm," Anthony says, looking up at Mom. "How long do they go through training?"

"Well, we raise them as puppies, and when they're young adults, they enroll in training at the Foundation for half a year."

"Then they're matched with their partners," I say. "They'll go through training together before they graduate."

"They graduate together?" Anthony asks. His thumb moves in slow circles over the puppy's golden fur.

"Yes," Mom says, and this time, her voice is warm. "Clive and I have been there for every graduation the past eight years. Haven't we?"

"We sure have," Dad says. "Eleven of our dogs have become guide dogs." There's obvious pride in their voices, and I know Mom cries every single time she sees the dogs they've raised up on that stage, sitting by the companions they've come to love, and who love them in return.

"Is it something you've considered for the future?" Mom asks Anthony. "If you do, it would be a pleasure to find you a suitable dog in our litters."

I hold my breath, but Anthony only nods. "I've thought about it," he says. "I'm not there yet, in terms of vision loss, but I will do it when I am."

"You will?" I ask.

He nods, turning to look at me. There's only warmth in his eyes. "Yeah. We already have Ace. What's one more dog?"

"I'm happy to hear that," Mom says. She stands and brushes off her jeans. "Anyone want some more lemonade? Clive?"

My dad looks up at her. "Well, I'll… yes. Yes, I do. I'll come with you. Anthony, another beer?"

"I'm good, thank you."

"I'll get one for myself, then." He puts a hand on my mother's back and they walk side by side to the house. Cooper and Hera rise from their sprawl and follow them, tails held low.

"Well," Anthony says by my side. "That was subtle."

I smile. "A guide dog, huh?"

He looks down at the puppy in his lap, extracting one arm to wrap it around my shoulders. "They're nicer than a cane."

"Cuter, at least."

"Softer to pet."

I chuckle. "A bit less well-behaved, but I think you'll survive."

"So do I," he says. His hand curves around my shoulder. "When do you want to go?"

I look down at my watch. It's a little past two. "Soon. In fifteen?"

"Sounds good."

"Do you know when Tristan and Freddie are driving up?" We've rented adjacent cabins in the Catskills for the weekend and I can't wait to breathe the fresh mountain air. Neither can Ace, though he doesn't know it yet. The last time he met Tristan's son, he received more cuddles and playtime than he knew what to do with.

"They've already made it, I think. They wanted to take Joshua hiking this afternoon," Anthony says.

I bump his chest with my shoulder, softly, not to jostle the dozing puppy in his lap. "See? Hiking is a perfectly acceptable activity in the Catskills. No life-risking involved."

"We're not risking our lives by going white-water rafting."

"I can see the headline now. Two of New York's most

successful billionaires lost to the waters as grieving girlfriends watch helplessly from the shoreline. New York State mounts huge rescue effort."

"That headline is too long," Anthony says. "If you were reading it to me from the *Times* I'd say they need to hire a new editor."

"Anthony," I protest.

He laughs, the sound deep and free. "I'll be careful," he says. "Trust me, I don't have a death wish, and Tristan most definitely doesn't. Besides, I have a feeling both you and Freddie will join."

"What? This is your bucket list wish, not mine."

"Yes," he says, grinning, "but you've never been one to back down from a challenge."

I settle against his side. "You know just how to appeal to my pride."

"Just as you know how to appeal to mine." He presses a kiss to my head, his hand sliding down my arm. He lifts it up and I gaze down at the diamond Cartier watch on my wrist. "I'm glad you finally accepted wearing this, by the way."

"You are?"

"Yes. Means you're getting used to outrageously expensive gifts. Besides, I bought it for you."

"You did not buy it for me."

"Yes, I did. It was the one thing you looked at in that brochure."

"When we were saving the rainforest?"

"Yes. Think about it that way," he says. "You wearing that watch is making a real difference in the world."

I laugh, unable to help myself at the dryness in his tone. His lip curls and he looks back down at the watch. "Besides," he says, "one day I'll give you something expensive for this finger, right here. The watch is good practice."

"Anthony…"

"Summer," he says. Turns my head up and presses a single kiss to my lips, one that spreads through my chest and warms my heart. "But don't worry. I'll involve you in the process."

"Involve me in the process?"

"Yes. I think you'd prefer a vintage ring, if I know you as well as I think you do."

"You do know me very well," I murmur, looking down at my bare ring finger. "I'd love to wear your ring."

He's hinted before, but here it is, spoken out loud. My throat feels thick with emotions. And Anthony knows, because he always does, and presses me closer against him.

His lips brush my temple. I look down at the puppy in his lap and wonder how he can make us feel so comfortable, just by being him.

"Summer," he murmurs.

I press a kiss to his jawline. "It's funny. When you bought Opate, I wasn't too happy about it. I knew you were saving us, but I was afraid you'd change things."

"I did change things," he says.

"Yes, but for the better."

He chuckles. "I had to change it for the better. You gave me no choice."

"Mmm."

"For the record," he says, brushing a tendril of my hair back, "I wasn't too happy about it either."

"You made that clear."

"Have I ever told you how I ended up being the Acture partner who ran point on Opate?"

"No. Is there a story here?"

The puppy in his lap yawns, and he looks down, smiling. "There is, actually. We played poker for it."

"You... played poker? The winner got Opate?"

He gives me a look. "No," I say, bumping his shoulder with mine. "Don't you dare tell me it was the loser."

"It was, and I lost. We were at Tristan's and the lighting wasn't very good. I mistook the suits."

"Oh."

"I was bitter," he says. "I'll admit that. But the thing is, I might have lost that game, but I still won in the end. Opate is doing better than ever and here I am, sitting with a future guide dog in my lap, and you beside me. I saved Opate, but you saved me."

I can't tear my eyes away. He's never been more handsome to me than he is right now. "You saved yourself," I murmur. "By embracing the future."

"Embracing the future," he echoes. "For however long we have, and whatever comes our way."

THE STORY CONTINUES

In **Say Yes to the Boss,** Victor St. Clair is forced to take extreme measures to secure his inheritance.

Like marrying his assistant.

But while Cecilia Myers agrees, it's not out of kindness. No, she has no love for her arrogant, surly, and downright cruel boss.

It's a business deal masquerading as a marriage.
Nothing less, and definitely nothing more.

Right?

Find **Say Yes to the Boss** on Amazon!

OTHER BOOKS BY OLIVIA

New York Billionaires Series

Think Outside the Boss
Tristan and Freddie

Saved by the Boss
Anthony and Summer

Say Yes to the Boss
Victor and Cecilia

Seattle Billionaires Series

Billion Dollar Enemy
Cole and Skye

Billion Dollar Beast
Nick and Blair

Billion Dollar Catch
Ethan and Bella

Billion Dollar Fiancé
Liam and Maddie

Brothers of Paradise Series

Rogue
Lily and Hayden

Ice Cold Boss
Faye and Henry

Red Hot Rebel
Ivy and Rhys

Standalones

Arrogant Boss
Julian and Emily

Look But Don't Touch
Grant and Ada

ABOUT OLIVIA

Olivia loves billionaire heroes despite never having met one in person. Taking matters into her own hands, she creates them on the page instead. Stern, charming, cold or brooding, so far she's never met a (fictional) billionaire she didn't like.

Her favorite things include wide-shouldered heroes, late-night conversations, too-expensive wine and romances that lift you up.

Smart and sexy romance—those are her lead themes!

Join her newsletter for updates and bonus content.
www.oliviahayle.com.
Connect with Olivia

Printed in Great Britain
by Amazon